BLOOD
BROTHERS

Diana Rittenhouse mystery 2/5

Kate Merrill

BLOOD BROTHERS

Cover art: Kate Merrill

Merlin-Janus Studio, Inc.
Mooresville, NC

Publishing History
First Edition 2014
Second Edition 2022
Print ISBN 978-0692333457

Published in the United States of America

For
Herbert James Merrill

Prologue...

The moment Diana Rittenhouse turned into the familiar lane, gravel crunching under her tires, her stomach coiled like a frightened snake. The fear was visceral, unexpected, and the sky so very blue.

She gripped the steering wheel to silence the thunder clapping in her chest. When she lifted her eyes to the arching canopy of green leaves, she saw only an endless claustrophobia of dappled shade. Last time she traveled this lane, she was in an ambulance speeding in the opposite direction. Flat on her back, in a blur of pain. A bullet hole burned in her shoulder, while she choked on the memory of water closing over her head.

She took a deep breath to kill the memory, but the loamy odor of damp summer did nothing to erase the horror. It seemed her recovery had taken an eternity, but she was shot only months ago, her wound now fully healed. Her mind, however, was still convalescing.

Diana snorted in disgust. She deserved to be in the Guinness Book of World Records: *most blunders by one woman in any given lifetime.* Her past unraveled like a shredded quilt: bright patches, then darks—marriage, then divorce—children, then an empty nest—professional success, then failure. It seemed her life had trudged along punctuated by short sprints of joy and tragedy. All mortals shared similar peaks and valleys, but most managed to string those extremes out over a decent interval of years.

Had she been delusional, believing she could start fresh in North Carolina? Had the move attracted evil to her doorstep, like flies to carrion? It had certainly initiated a tailspin, propelling her headlong into her forty-fifth year.

Ashes to ashes. Before she got shot, her former car exploded in flames. The bomb was intended for her, but instead injured the special new man in her life. Matthew Troutman was the sweet southern sunshine to her cold northern winter, and he was waiting at the end of this road.

Rounding the next curve, her emotions ran wild and her heart stopped cold. When she left the forest, the blinding noonday sun caused shimmering white heat to rise from Jedidiah Porter's fallow fields, while Lake Norman lay brilliant and blue on all three sides of the triangle bounding the old estate.

She blinked and caught her breath. It all began right here—the murder and the madness. High on a promontory, the ramshackle Porter homestead canted in dark silhouette and the pecan trees swayed listlessly in a benign breeze. A familiar red and white Ford pickup was parked off the dusty clay driveway, under the shade of an ancient willow oak, and a man lounged idly against its fender. He stood with one boot heel hooked back on the running board, while his hand stroked the enormous black head of the dog that brought them together.

Even at that distance, in spite of the bill of a straw fishing cap shadowing his face, Diana felt his warm eyes seek hers. The lure was as strong as trouble itself, but did she want it?

You bet.e

ONE

Lay the past to rest...

The sun burning down on her skin felt cold as she closed the distance between them. Ursie, the Doberman, broke away from Matthew and bounded towards her. The dog's lips were pulled back in a vicious snarl, teeth and fangs glinting white, but by now she knew this was just Ursie's way of smiling. She dropped to her knees and opened her arms as one hundred pounds of dog flesh toppled her onto her backside.

"Hey, girl!" she gasped as Ursie gave her a wet, slobbery kiss. "God, I missed you!"

Matthew's boots sent little puffs of red dust into the air as he trotted to where Diana struggled like a turtle on its back. He coaxed Ursie off, and with one great yank, she was on her feet.

"Hey, lady, I know you missed my dog, but did you miss me?"

He held her at arm's length, his deep brown eyes smiling and his sensuous mouth curved in a grin. His big hands were hot on her bare arms, melting away the chill, replacing it with a blush of intense shyness.

Her mind was a riot of conflicting emotions. During those months of healing, she had avoided Matthew. The intense feelings he awakened were frightening, too much to manage along with the mending of her body.

Matthew, never a man to waste words, watched her in silence. "Well, last time we were together, we stirred up a hornet's nest of trouble, and that's a fact," he said at last.

"That is a fact." She echoed the sentiment as she backed off to a safe distance and brushed the dirt from the rump of her jeans.

He followed her maneuver with laughing eyes. "You look mighty fine, Diana."

Heat rose to her face as beads of perspiration rolled between her breasts and gathered at her waistband. The day promised to be a June scorcher. He'd warned her to *wear old duds, and dress light,* but she was too self-conscious to be seen in shorts. Her long legs were as winter white as the belly of a dead fish, so she'd chosen jeans and a faded denim work shirt, hoping they'd bring out the blue of her eyes beneath an unruly crop of short, prematurely white hair.

"I feel okay," she said, sensing he didn't want to discuss their past troubles any more than she did. "How about you? All back to normal?"

"Normal?" He chuckled. "Not sure about that."

She returned his frank appraisal and liked what she saw. Matthew was a few years older than she, but blessed with the lean, firm physique of a much younger man. By any standard, Diana was a tall woman, yet Matthew towered above her and carried himself square and erect. Only his hands, the rough hands of a working man, the deeply etched laugh lines at his eyes and the corners of his mouth, and the slight thinning of his soft brown hair, hinted at his maturity. She also adored the sunburn line hidden under his cap—tan below, pale above, the badge of a man who lived outdoors.

He shifted self-consciously under her gaze and ruffled Ursie's head. "We best get going. We're here to work, remember? Bobby and Juanita are waiting."

On cue, Ursie broke free and bolted towards the house, but suddenly she yelped and slowed to a limp.

"Is she hurt?" Diana asked in alarm.

"She stepped on a rusty fish hook, and the darn thing got stuck in her paw. Vet cut it out, gave her a tetanus shot and a couple of stitches. She'll survive."

"Why didn't you call me?" She regretted the words as soon they flew from her mouth. After all, Ursie's well-being was none of her business.

He stood stock-still and searched her eyes. "You know how many times I've tried to call you? Where have you been, Diana? I'm not one to converse with an answering machine."

"Sorry." She walked ahead, unable to face him. Her conflicted feelings weren't his problem.

He followed in silence. The sound of his boots rustling through overgrown weeds was the only disturbance in the deeply quiet fields. As they neared the house, Diana's sense of foreboding deepened. The first time she'd climbed this hill, she'd met the fearsome old recluse, Jedidiah Porter. Jed was supposed to be her very first real estate client in North Carolina, but instead, he was murdered, found floating dead at his dock. The events that followed nearly cost Diana her life. She had, in fact, lost her job, when her Broker in Charge proved to be the killer.

Matthew caught up and guided her into the shade of a lone sycamore tree. "Bad memories? I know how you feel. It's hard to be here again." His gesture encompassed the fields, the farm, and the lake. "But it's time to lay the past to rest."

She stared into the shaded grass and spotted a stand of yellow wildflowers. Matthew was right, of course, but she still felt a measure of guilt for the tragedy. Old Jed was killed out of greed for this land, potentially worth millions to the developers she had worked for. In the end, irony of ironies, Jedidiah had willed his land to the state, to be used as a public park.

9

Matthew knelt to pick a daisy. "Way I see it, some good came from all that misery. Jed's son, Bobby, inherited this house. Now he and Juanita have a chance to make a real life together."

Speak of the devil! When Diana glanced down at the farmhouse, she spotted Bobby Porter balanced atop a ladder, scraping loose paint from the sagging eaves. Last year Bobby couldn't hold a job. He drank too much and ran through women like play toys.

"Good point, Matthew."

She waited expectantly for him to give her the daisy he'd picked, but instead, he used the flower to tickle Ursie's nose. The dog sneezed, eased herself up from the grass, and then limped over to lick Diana's hand.

Diana was disappointed, but she'd get over it. Looking back at the house, she saw a woman step out from the dark doorway. The woman shielded her eyes against the sudden light, and then looked in their direction.

"There's Juanita," Diana said. "I'm surprised she's still with him."

"Yeah, she's lasted longer than most." Matthew bent to pick a fistful of blue violets nestled near the tree trunk. He straightened up, then reached out to touch Diana's arm. He pressed the flowers into her hands. "These are for you." He smiled. "They match your eyes."

TWO

Playing house…

"Hey, guys!" Bobby jumped off the ladder, then sauntered over to greet them. "C'mon in. Juanita has a little surprise."

"Hey, buddy!" Matthew shouted back. "Hope it's not one of those little surprises that gets born *nine months later*." He winked at Diana, who hung back while the two old pals pumped hands and clapped one another on the back.

"No, ain't nothin' like that." Bobby blushed, then glanced at Diana. "Juanita wants to tell you herself. She'll have my hide if I spill the beans."

"Skin you alive, more like it!" Juanita Cruz stepped from the doorway, a brilliant white smile igniting her dark face.

Diana had been dreading this reunion because her history with this couple had been less than cordial. She'd first met Bobby during a hostile encounter through a plate glass window at the Iredell County Jail, where he was being held on suspicion of murdering his own father. And once Juanita, spitting threats in both English and Spanish, had attacked Diana with a pair of lethal stylist's scissors, at the salon where Juanita used to work.

But today Bobby slipped his arm around Juanita's waist, and then gestured at the old house, where ladders and a rickety painter's scaffold lean against the wall. "Don't look like much now, but soon it'll be pretty as a pictures in a magazine."

"Good job, Bobby." Matthew squinted at the fresh white paint glistening on the gingerbread trim around the porch. "I knew you were a tolerable gardener, but you're an artist with that paintbrush."

"Artist?" Juanita scoffed. "Look close and you'll see all the drips."

Diana was truly impressed. Jed's bungalow had been given a total facelift, but the biggest transformation involved its two new occupants. Both Bobby and Juanita had shed a few pounds. Their faces were tan and healthy, so it seemed hard work and fresh air agreed with them.

Bobby rocked on his heels, his snaggle-toothed grin full of pride. "I thought y'all came here to work, so cut the jawin' and get on with it. You girls stay on the ground and paint the steps, while Trout and me climb the ladders."

"Are you *loco*?" Juanita's speech patterns were a weird combination of Spanish red pepper and Carolina barbeque. "Mrs. Rittenhouse and I will work inside. It's too damned hot out here in the sun. She can help me paint the kitchen cabinets."

Bobby shrugged, while Matthew glanced at Diana, a hint of regret in his eyes. She too, had hoped to work close alongside Matthew, but she followed Juanita into the cool bungalow. "Please call me *Diana.*"

"Okay, if you call me *Nita.*"

They eyed one another, two humans with absolutely nothing in common. "When did you start calling yourself *Nita*?"

"Ever since I came to the States. But you people keep calling me *Juanita,* like you don't want me to forget where I came from."

Clearly the woman wasn't keen on her roots. Diana watched her open a cabinet and remove two plastic glasses. Juanita wore a scanty red halter that emphasized her ample bosom, and her sleek, raven black hair fell straight to the waistband of her tight black shorts. Red plastic clogs and hoop earrings completed the ensemble.

"When did you move to the States?" She asked as Juanita poured iced tea and tore open a bag of pretzels.

"My family in Mexico is too big. Right after I finished high school, they shipped me and my little sister up to live with our aunt in San Jose."

As Juanita dumped sugar into her tea, Diana estimated her hostess was about thirty years old. Diana's own memories of California dated back to a road trip with her parents. They took her to Disney World as a treat, before she entered kindergarten. Those were the days of hippies and flower power, before Juanita was born.

"Did you live in California long?"

"Too damned long." She sighed as she stirred the sugar.

"Is that where you learned to cut hair?"

Juanita nodded. "It wasn't my idea, though. I was wild in those days. California had rich boys, booze, and drugs—things my little village had lacked." She flashed her jet back eyes. "I got into trouble with drugs, *big time.* The judge gave me a choice: deportation, jail, or trade school. I chose Beauty College."

As Diana listened, Juanita filled in the blanks. She could easily imagine the kaleidoscope of troubles Juanita was capable of attracting, and she wondered which misstep had caused her to move to Mooresville, North Carolina, of all places. "How'd you meet Bobby?"

Juanita choked on a pretzel, gulped some tea, and then rolled her eyes at the ceiling. "Believe it or not, he was working with a Mexican lawn crew I hung with when I first came here. Me and Bobby got drunk together. Pretty soon he was coming round for haircuts. The man has good hair, I'll give him that…"

The way she talked about Bobby, Juanita could easily have been describing her relationship with a stray cat, instead of with a man she'd chosen to live with for two years. "Are things working out for the two of you?" Diana asked.

"You mean all this shit?" Her dismissive gesture included the whole of the cozy little room. "Do I look like the domestic type? Hey, I'm glad Bobby inherited this dump, because it sure beats the ratty trailer where we lived before, but..." She dropped her voice to a whisper. "This is temporary, right? *He* enjoys playing house, but when something better comes along, *I'm* outta here."

Diana wasn't convinced. For a woman who claimed to hate her life, Juanita had certainly added some heart-felt feminine touches to the sorry old place. There were fresh-cut flowers, including Diana's violets, which Juanita had placed in a souvenir mug from Niagara Falls. Lace curtains, still creased from their *Martha Stewart* packaging, fluttered at sparkling clean windows. And along with paint fumes, the scent of cinnamon hung in the air.

If Juanita had reservations, they didn't seem to include this house, which had fallen into her lap like manna from Heaven. She couldn't complain about money, because Jedidiah Porter had willed his son, Bobby, a generous, lifetime-guaranteed salary as groundskeeper of the new state park.

"Bobby's on a roll right now," Juanita continued. "But if he expects me to give up my job, clean his house, and cook his meals like a good little wife and mommy..."

She couldn't understand the attitude. According to Matthew, Juanita still worked at the salon. Bobby would never administer any *white glove tests,* nor would he expect gourmet meals. They weren't married, had no children, so what was with this *mommy* business? Unless Matthew's joke about a surprise coming *nine months later* wasn't a joke, after all?

Impulsively, she reached across the table and took Juanita's hand. "What's wrong, Nita?"

"*Nada,* nothing!" She jerked her hand away.

As Diana tried to understand her companion's misery, she noticed several items which seem out of place: a plate of Oreos with the cream centers licked out, a stack of *Pokémon* cards scattered on the sofa, and an abandoned baseball mitt in the corner.

And then an explosive staccato of barking started out in the yard and traveled to the screen door. Ursie burst in first, nearly bringing the door down as she bounded into the room, her eyes wide with panic. A little boy followed close on her heels, shouting and waving a dart gun in his small brown fist.

Ursie toppled an end table, but it was the boy who tripped on the lamp cord, bringing it down.

"Jesus Christ!" Juanita screamed, catching the child by the seat of his pants.

"*What?*" The kid flopped onto the rug. The dog escaped, still yelping, through the back door.

"What did you do to that animal?" Juanita shrieked and gave the boy's shoulder a rough shove.

"Nothing." He spread his hands, his gorgeous eyes wide and innocent.

Diana caught her breath and stared. The child was beautiful, with silken black hair and skin the color of cocoa. She judged he was eight years old, a little Latin replica of the red-faced woman scolding him, except that his eyes were as blue as Diana's, the color of sky through ice. He reminded her of her son, Robbie.

"Who's *she?*" The kid pointed a stubby finger at Diana.

Juanita yanked him to his feet. "Mind your manners! This is Mrs. Rittenhouse. What do you say...?"

The child wriggled free and studied Diana with open curiosity, quickly replaced with defiance. "Pleased to meet you, ma'am," he drawled sullenly.

"Tell Mrs. Rittenhouse your name," Juanita prompted.

The boy stared at the floor.

"He's Juan McCord." Juanita spit out each syllable. "And he's sorry he's acting like a spoiled little prick."

The child stomped his foot and bolted for the door. Before he escaped, he turned to Diana and pounded his chest. "My name's not *Juan,* lady. It's *Johnny!*"

THREE

A sad story…

Juanita was telling Diana little bits about the boy when Matthew loped into the house and pulled Diana into the backyard. "Time for a break," he announced. "Let's take a hike."

Bobby called from the roof: "Hey, if you see the kid, bring him home for his supper."

"Will do!" Matthew shouted over his shoulder, then turned to Diana. "Whew… if your afternoon was anything like mine, you'll agree these folks have some issues."

"No kidding." She squeezed his arm.

"The boy is Juanita's nephew," Matthew began. "His mother was Juanita's sister, Maria, who got killed in a car wreck. Am I right so far?"

Diana nodded. Juanita had revealed that much, but no more. Whenever Diana broached the subject of the child's parents, Juanita had retreated on the verge of tears. So they'd spent the afternoon mostly in silence, elbow-deep in paint and turpentine, inverted beneath counters with dripping brushes. Under those circumstances, their conversation had been severely limited.

"Bobby wants to keep the boy," Matthew said as they climbed towards the pecan grove. "He loves that kid. Claims he's gonna be a baseball star. Believes the boy's a good luck charm, even better than the house and salary. He's a sign from God that the three of them are supposed to live happily ever after as a family."

Then God better send a miracle, Diana thought as they reached the top of the rise and beheld the scene before them. Instead of the tangled brush forest she remembered, which had fallen away to a rugged, eroding shoreline, she saw acres of freshly seeded lawn. All the large trees—ancient oaks, maples, and sycamores—had been lovingly spared. Jed's decaying old dock was gone, and now curves of new stone rip-rap neatly held back the waves.

"Can you believe it?" she asked.

Matthew scanned the horizon. "They call this progress, but I'm not so sure."

Like most natives, Matthew resented the whirlwind of change that was rapidly blowing away the old culture and a proud way of life. When Duke Power dammed the Catawba River and created Lake Norman, with five hundred miles of pristine shoreline, this part of the Piedmont, with booming Charlotte at its hub, became a magnet. It attracted everyone from young entrepreneurs to retirees from the four corners of the nation. It had lured Diana, hadn't it?

As a real estate broker, she'd been drawn by the hot economy and the wealth it promised. As a human being, she'd reacted quite differently. Day by day, developers raped the lovely forests and farmlands, transforming them to condominiums, golf courses, and shopping malls. She'd lived here only a little over a year, but she wanted the development to slow down. She wanted it to stop.

"Could be worse," she mused aloud. "At least they saved the trees."

"I expect Bobby's responsible for that," Matthew said. "He has his faults, but he loves nature. I'll bet he's been guarding these trees like a mama mockingbird at nesting time."

They wandered into a field, which had once been a stand of tobacco. Here the red earth had been scraped flat. A yellow backhoe was parked at the perimeter, its great claw curled up in repose for the weekend.

She recognized the configuration immediately. "Look, Matthew, they're building a pair of tennis courts!" Suddenly she was nostalgic for her teenage years on the Main Line, near Philadelphia, where she'd spent many happy hours on the clay courts. "The view of the lake is beautiful from here."

"You're right, it could be worse," he conceded. "People will enjoy this park. It's a great place for a little boy to grow up, for that matter."

"But how can they keep Juan?" she asked. "Even if Juanita wanted the boy, which she doesn't, he must have other family. I know Juan's parents were killed in the accident, but what about his grandparents? Don't they want him?"

Matthew sat down on a log, and Diana joined him.

"It's a sad story…" He stared out at the water. "Bobby says Juanita's all torn up about her sister's death. The boy's a constant reminder, and he makes her feel guilty."

"But why?"

"Juan's mother, Maria, was the younger sister. She was steady, but Juanita was wild. Both gals eventually got their citizenship while they were living with their aunt in San Jose, but somehow Juanita lost her way. She got mixed up with a rough crowd and left Maria to fend for herself…

"Juanita introduced Maria to a dude named Randy McCord, the hotshot son of a wealthy cattle rancher. Juanita knew Randy did drugs, but she never expected her sister to get serious. Long story short, the two got married and Juan was born."

"What about Randy's parents, or the Cruz family back in Mexico? Surely they want Juan."

"Nope. The McCords never approved the marriage. They called Maria a *wetback*, disowned Randy, and never recognized the child as one of their own. As for the Cruz family back in Mexico, they want Juan to stay in the States and enjoy the benefits of American citizenship."

It was a sad story. She was thinking about Juan, gazing into a patch of dark green forest when she saw a flash of movement between the pine trees. "What's *that*?" She pointed to the spot.

"Oh, that's the kid playing with Ursie." Matthew laughed. "They've been chasing each other all afternoon. I saw them from up on the roof, dashing in and out of the shadows, but they never came close to the house. I think Juan's scared of me."

"Maybe he's just shy." She feared Juan might have severe psychological problems, and no wonder. He'd lost both his parents, and now he was an orphan nobody wanted. He'd been uprooted and shipped off to a strange place, to live with Bobby and Juanita—not an ideal couple.

Her maternal instincts clicked into high gear "How did Juan end up in North Carolina?"

"Where else could he go?" Matthew said. "Juanita was the boy's last chance to stay in America, and this summer is a trial run. He's eight years old. If Juanita agrees to keep him, he'll start third grade here in Troutman next fall. If not, he goes back to Mexico."

"Just like that?"

"Yeah, just like that."

Matthew took her hand and pulled her to her feet. "C'mon, let's catch that kid. He's cornered poor Ursie in the gully down yonder."

She trailed in silence. The molten sun had dropped lower in the sky, the temperature fell with it. The grass was cool on her ankles, and the soft lapping of waves soothed her frustration. But then, those natural sounds were joined by something far more primal—the sound of human weeping.

Matthew heard it, too. They picked up their pace and ran into a circle of evergreens. They found the child sitting cross-legged in a bed of clover, tears streaming in dirty rivulets down his face. The dog lay beside him, her head buried in the grass, one paw lifted plaintively in the air.

As they came closer, Juan wailed even louder.

"Are you hurt?" Diana slid down beside the stricken boy, who shook his head and pointed at Ursie.

"What is it, son?" Matthew knelt beside them as the boy's eyes widened in fear.

"I shot the dog!" Juan held up his toy dart gun. "I didn't mean to hurt her, *honest!*"

A flush of crimson spread under Matthew's old hat. Knots tightened in his jaw as he wordlessly examined Ursie. "Guns are serious business, young man..." His voice was deep and stern. "They're for hunting, understand? Never point a gun at anyone, or anything, unless you intend to harm it."

Juan's sobs became hiccups. He threw the dart gun away. "It's just a toy, Mister! We were playing a game, that's all."

"No gun is a game, boy, but this time you were lucky..." Matthew lifted Ursie's paw for general inspection. "Is this where you shot her?"

The child nodded.

"Well, then," Matthew continued. "She *is* hurt, but you didn't do it."

Juan rubbed away his tears with the back of his hand. He was obviously relieved, but his amazing blue eyes were round with confusion.

"Ursie stepped on a fish hook a couple of days ago. That's all this is. She was injured long before you laid eyes on her."

To prove the point, Ursie crawled to her feet, then limped over and licked Juan's face.

"See? Ursie's just fine," Diana said.

"What's a *fish hook?*" Juan remained unconvinced, but his tears had stopped.

"C'mon, you know what I'm talking about." Matthew lifted his big hand into the air. He dangled his long fingers and wiggled them. "A *fish hook.* You get a mess of big, juicy worms, work them onto the hook, then toss them overboard…"

Juan was intrigued, yet he inched away from the big man with the funny hand.

Diana saw the problem instantly. The child was scared of Matthew. "Listen, Johnny, this is Mr. Troutman. He's a friend of your Aunt Nita's. Ursie is Mr. Troutman's dog."

"But most folks call me *Trout,* like the fish." Matthew grinned

A bulb lit up behind Juan's eyes and his mouth opened in a crooked smile. "They named you after a *fish?*"

"Reckon so." Matthew laughed. "You ever been fishing, son?"

Juan looked at Diana, unsure how to answer. "You go out in a boat?"

"You can fish from a boat, or a dock, or even off a bridge." Matthew cocked his head towards the lake. "Lots of big fish right out there, catfish long as a baseball bat."

"For real?" Again Juan glanced at her.

Matthew laid two fingers gently under Juan's chin. He tilted the boy's face in his direction. "Look at me, son. I have a boat. Do you want to go fishing with me?"

The child nodded vigorously.

"Then let's do it!" Matthew prodded Juan and Diana to their feet, then herded them towards the house, Ursie in tow. "We'll get permission from your aunt and go fishing next week. How does that sound?"

Juan grabbed Diana's hand and tugged hard. "Can *she* come too?"

Matthew grinned. "She's *city lady*? You think she can handle those messy worms?" He winked at Diana. "Absolutely, Johnny. She's coming, too."

FOUR

The heavens wept...

    Leona Clontz cracked the door of her trailer and peered out into the evening. She wrinkled her nose, sniffing for a breeze, then turned off the wheezing air conditioner. All day the thing had been rattling and bucking in the window, to where she couldn't hear herself think.

    Maybe *not thinking* was a blessing, for lately she'd been dwelling on her little lost boy, *Baby Bird,* her secret name for him. He'd be near eight years old now, but she dared not let the men know where her mind so often dwelled.

    If the men were fixing to eat with her, they'd be home by now. Seeing as it was a Saturday night, they likely gone to the tavern once the last load of lumber was dropped off. Just as well. When they staggered in later, all lit up like Roman candles, she'd already be asleep and done with it.

    Leona pushed off her house slippers, leaving them behind on the metal steps while she scampered through the damp grass to the abandoned single-wide next door. The folks who lived there had moved away the week the Clontz family moved in, so she'd never really known them. But she'd heard tell the man was a local boy living with a Mexican whore. The couple left Sylvan Acres when they won the jackpot, or some such thing.

    Leona paid no mind to gossip. She was not impressed by easy money. Money was Darryl's thing. Nor was she offended by the idea of the whore—sex was Floyd's thing. Truth be told, all she cared

24

about were the pretty flowers left behind. Pity to let all those daylilies, summer phlox, and black-eyed Susans go to waste. No one was watching, so she picked off those blossoms come to full maturity, then scampered barefoot back to her trailer.

Sometimes their silver mobile home, reflecting the clouds and the setting sun, like now, put her in mind of Baby Bird. She saw him as a helpless, tiny thing, like a fledgling fallen from the nest before he knew how to fly.

Or maybe he was more like an airplane dropped from the sky. She'd never actually *seen* the thing they pulled out from her womb after the accident, but she always pictured him bald, except for a blur of blond fuzz, like a duckling. He had big, blue, staring eyes, like hers. But instead of hands and legs, she imagined withered little wings and claws—an unformed thing.

When Baby Bird came to wake her, and she lay crying for him in the night, her young husband, Darryl, would reach across the covers and said *ain't nothin' but a bad dream*, but Leona knew the truth. This time of year, around his birthday, she imagined Bird all grown up like a regular little boy. He reached for her across time itself, and in her heart of hearts, she knew he was out there looking for his mama.

Rock of ages, cleft for me…let me hide myself in thee. Sometimes she sang all by herself, loud and strong. Mother Mattie always claimed Leona's voice was her best feature. Even Darryl and his brothers agreed, so long as she didn't overdo it.

She rinsed out Floyd's empty *Wild Turkey* bottle and arranged the flowers in it, so the lilies hung out just right, then she set it amongst her dolls. The doll collection was her passion and her pride. Now, with the miniature Raggedy Ann she found at the yard sale yesterday, she had sixteen in all. Darryl didn't care one way or the other, but Floyd flew into a rage when he caught her spending good money on dolls.

But some were old and valuable, especially the ones with porcelain hands, feet and faces. Some of her newborns were dressed in homemade lace. Yet once, when she tried to explain how the dolls were *an investment,* Floyd got so mad he bit off one of the porcelain heads and spit it out in the garbage. Now she tucked the new ones away real good, where he can't find them.

Leona slipped into the single bedroom at the back of the trailer and pulled the door shut. She lifted the counterpane, reached under the bed, and found the shoebox where she kept one special doll segregated from all the rest. She cradled it in her arms and crawled under the sheet, holding its little face to her breast, and recalled how she got pregnant.

She was fifteen years old, and Darryl wasn't much more than a boy himself. He took her away from Mother Mattie and her home in the mountains near Boone, and they went to live with the Clontz clan in strange dark hills where the sun never shined.

But before Leona left, Mother Mattie took some egg money from the jar on the icebox, and they went into Boone to see the Apple Lady. The old woman didn't speak English. She hailed from mountains on the other side of the world, and she made little boy dolls dressed like her people back home, with funny leather shorts and real straw hats.

For as long as Leona could remember, the Apple Lady came into Boone on weekends and set up outside Mast General Store. And as soon as Leona was old enough to talk, she started begging for one of them dolls. When Mattie gave her one as a farewell present, Leona cried and vowed that no matter how far Darryl carried her from Mattie and her beloved hills, the doll would be with her always.

At first the doll's face was round and red, like an actual baby. But as time passed and the apple shriveled, like they're supposed to do, the boy doll turned into an old man. The day it happened, Leona was seven months gone with child, and she was laying on a hillside above the coal mine. Her legs were as weak as toothpicks. She was lying there, minding her own business, just watching her doll's head shrivel up, when thunder commenced and the rain began.

Darryl's little sister, the only girl child in a family of eight boys, was toddling down the hill to where the coal cart was perched at the top of the rails. The brothers were real proud of that cart. They had rigged it up just the week before, with electricity and all. The mule was happy, too, on account of his hauling days were finally over.

That day Leona rocked the doll, and the lightning flashed. Rain poured from the sky like some dam burst up in Heaven, and Little Sister climbed into the cart.

After that, it seemed like everything went wrong all at once. All the others were off at church, it being Sunday morning, but Leona was Seventh Day Adventist and didn't hold with the Clontz family religion. Plus, Little Sister always acted up at church, so the two bad seeds had been left behind at home. Alone.

Little Sister pulled the start lever and the cart careened downwards towards the mouth of the mine. Leona started running barefoot through the wet grass, fast as toothpick legs could carry her. Thunder clapped and the heavens wept. Leona grabbed onto the start lever and pulled backwards, and a bolt of lightning hit the metal lever and shot up her arm like hellfire. Pain jangled through her body, burning like damnation. It chattered her teeth and shook her dead.

But God didn't finish the job, like He should have done. Instead, He saw fit to leave her alive, and she woke up in a strange hospital in Wheeling. Little Sister had been saved, the cart had stopped at the brink of the tunnel. Little Sister told how she found Leona lying still as death in the wet grass, her right arm and leg sticking out stiff and smoking like hot dogs on the grill.

Baby Bird was dead.

Back in the real world, Leona lifted her head when she heard the sudden clatter of the Clontz lumber truck pulling into the drive. Someone leaned on the horn, and then the brakes squealed to a stop outside the door. In a rush of panic, she scrambled upright and peeked out the vent above her pillow.

Sure enough, in the glare of the security lamp, she saw Darryl slumped over drunk on the passenger side, while Floyd staggered grinning towards the door. Sweet Jesus, he was coming for her like he done so many times before! She lunged to the foot of the bed and slammed the deadbolt home, just like Darryl showed her. She crawled into a fetal position and pulled the sheet up over her head, and the shrunken apple doll was a lump of bitter coal pressed to her heart.

FIVE

The subject was men...

The wipers on Diana's new white Crown Victoria cleared the sheets of rain, yet she made another wrong turn. The blur of oncoming city traffic was confusing, cars speeding through the night. The other drivers seemed to know precisely where they were going, but she was convinced that every street sign in Charlotte had been deliberately designed to leave visitors spinning in a hopeless maze. Back in Pennsylvania, whenever friends tempted her to enter Philadelphia after dark, she'd hitched a ride with someone less directionally-challenged, so why on earth had she accepted Liz's invitation tonight?

She offered up a prayer of thanks when she arrived at South End Brewery, her final destination. She pulled into the parking lot without mishap and spotted Liz's Honda parked near the restaurant door. As she switched all systems off and sank into the blue leather upholstery, she wondered again, *why did I come?*

Well, her new car, which she'd nicknamed *Queen Vic*, was part of the reason. It was fully loaded with options she'd never have chosen for herself, but Liz had arranged for her to lease it at a time when Diana was incapable of making decisions. It had been a combination *get well* and *get on with it* gesture, one of many reasons she adored Liz.

They had both lost their jobs when Crawford Realty closed, but during the first six months they'd worked together, through horrible misadventures, the young woman had become Diana's dearest friend.

As though summoned by that warm thought, a vision topped by a blaze of red hair appeared in the misty gaslight glow at the brewery entrance. When Liz waved with wild exuberance, Diana scampered through the rain, oblivious to a nagging headache, and embraced the woman.

"Whoa, girlfriend!" Liz extricated herself from the soggy hug. Her jade silk tank top exactly matched her wide eyes. "Love ya back, but we saw each other only ten minutes ago."

True, they'd just attended their Broker's licensing class together, but the harrowing drive had given Diana a fresh appreciation for those she held dear. "Ten minutes on these slippery roads feels like a near-death experience."

"Tell me about it!" Liz captured her arm and guided her into a cavernous room dominated by a gleaming circular bar. "C'mon, I've saved us an awesome table."

A crowd of young singles had gathered to check out the Tuesday night action. As they jostled through groups of hopeful junior executives and computer programmers, Diana was glad Liz was a take-charge kind of gal, because this was definitely not her scene.

Liz wore tight jeans and platform shoes, and as they slid into their chairs, Diana noticed her green eyes sweeping the male prospects. Since her breakup with Danny, a sweet guy Diana really liked, Liz had become a woman on the prowl.

"Told you this place was hot." Liz signaled for a waitress.

"Do they serve anything besides beer?"

Both Liz and the gum-chewing waitress, clearly a freshman at nearby Queen's College, snickered at Diana's question.

"This place is all about *beer*, Diana. They brew it on location. Relax. I'll order for both of us…"

She could almost feel the yeast and sugar attacking her headache, but listened without protest as Liz ordered artichoke chicken pasta and two Carolina Blonds. Diana eased into the atmosphere, swallowed two Tylenol, and determined to be a good sport.

"Lighten up, Diana…" Liz's eyes ceased roving. "After three hours in that stuffy old classroom, we need to chill. Am I right?"

Diana smiled and toasted with her icy brew. After losing their jobs, Liz and she had teamed up. Instead of going back to work for someone else, they'd decided to get their Broker's-In-Charge licenses and start their own company. They enrolled at Central Piedmont Community College, and by August, if they passed the exam, they intended to write their own ticket to success.

"Here's to us, Diana!" Liz returned the toast. "When we open our office, *McCorkle and Rittenhouse,* we'll kick butt!"

"Don't you mean *Rittenhouse and McCorkle*?" Diana winked.

"Whatever. More important, how do you like our new teacher, Miles Lawton? What a *hunk*!"

It never failed. After five minutes of conversation with Liz, the subject was men. "*Hunk*? That man's old enough to be your father."

"So what? Don't you love his British accent? He sounds just like *Sting*."

"Well, he *is* English." Obviously they didn't see eye to eye about Miles Lawton. The man spent a fortune on his wardrobe, laid claim to the wealthiest clients, and said he was only teaching a lowly night school class in order to find talented closers. He always managed to corner Diana in the hallway, offering unsolicited facts about his personal life, stressing that he was divorced and available.

She had to admit he was attractive, but coiled way too tight. He had a wiry, compact build and close-cropped silver hair. His blue eyes were intensely personal behind rimless glasses and peered out from under improbably bushy black eyebrows. His fake upper-crusty British accent was coupled with a high-powered New York attitude. And most disturbing of all—Miles bore an uncanny resemblance to Diana's abusive ex-husband, Robert Rittenhouse.

"I've seen the way he looks at you, Diana," Liz continued. "If you aren't interested, why not shove him my way?"

Diana's cheeks burned. In fact, Miles had made carefully couched advances. He had offered to hire her on a temporary basis, provide her with a few clients. He sensed she was desperate for cash. That approach was far more tempting than simply asking for a date.

"Miles Lawton is not my type," Diana muttered.

"Who is?" Liz grinned wickedly. "Matthew Troutman?"

Suddenly Diana's mind drifted back to last Saturday, a bouquet of wild violets, and the feel of Matthew's warm hands on her cool arms. He had called her this evening just before class, and they'd made a date to take little Juan McCord fishing. Matthew had cleared the adventure with Juanita, and while Diana hated the idea of worms on hooks, she had finally agreed

Liz had known Matthew since she was a little girl. He used to give her free ice cream when she visited his general store, *Trout's Place,* up on River Highway. Indeed, Liz was a huge Matthew fan, so she'd been encouraging their relationship for almost a year.

"Make up your mind, Liz. Miles or Matthew? They can't *both* be right for me."

Liz blinked in confusion, trying to compare a pompous Englishman to an unpretentious country shopkeeper. Suddenly she stopped blinking and stared at the entrance to the restaurant, her glass of beer poised midair. "Don't look now, but Miles just walked through the door, Diana."

Diana spotted the energetic man, briefcase in hand, intense blue eyes flickering behind rimless glasses, surveying the field like a bird of prey. She groaned aloud.

"And watch out," Liz said. "He's heading straight for our table…"

SIX

The wrong date…

The morning after clubbing with Liz, Diana took a shower to wash the stench of cigarette smoke from her hair, but the pulsing water didn't calm her nerves. She dried her short white hair, slathered her body with stress relief moisturizing lotion—as if lavender, chamomile, and yiang-yiang would do any good. Finally, she selected her best silver and turquoise jewelry to accentuate her eyes. She figured she looked okay in her cream silk dress, yet she felt like a teenager on the way to her first prom—with the wrong date.

Later, as she parked her humble Ford amongst the Mercedes, Jaguars, and even a Rolls Royce, at the prestigious Peninsula Club, she realized she'd been out of the dating game way too long. After her divorce, well-meaning friends back in Pennsylvania had tried to hook her up with eligible men, but the results, while not disastrous, were bland at best.

As she strolled up the walkway, through manicured gardens leading to the club, she noticed the heady scent of money. She smelled the golf course and the yacht club, those odors of privilege that once defined her world. Her divorce from Robert had ended all that, but as time passed, an odd thing happened—the trappings of wealth lost their sweet fragrance and began to stink.

That fact buoyed her confidence. She sensed new grace and purpose in her stride, so that even the sight of Miles Lawton waiting at the door failed to put her off. He was groomed to perfection in a white nautical blazer and pleated navy trousers. From his silver hair to the tassels on his loafers, he reeked of money. So much so, that she laughed out loud.

"What's so funny?" He took possession of her arm. "You look lovely tonight, Diana."

She found herself picturing Matthew in a T-shirt and old jeans, sitting alone in his gazebo by the lake, sharing his picnic supper with the fish.

"I have a regular table by the window," Miles explained in his clipped British accent. Waiters parted like the Red Sea as he guided her through the dining room. "Here we are, the best view of the lake and the golf course."

"Are you a member?" She attempted to sound duly impressed.

"But of course..." he answered, as if to say *isn't everyone?* "And if my Charlotte office continues to prosper, I'll open a branch up here and move to Lake Norman."

Miles was off and running, reciting a litany of his real estate coups, while her mind wandered. His monologue continued through the ordering of drinks and ceased only when a tall young man in a tan, custom-tailored suit approached their table. The man was excessively dark and handsome, like a Hollywood Mafia idol. He stood behind Miles' chair and winked at her.

"Is Lawton boring you to death?" the stranger asked.

Miles nearly choked on his martini olive. He tangled with the leg of his chair as he jumped to his feet. "Oh, John, I didn't see you standing there..." He extended his hand. "Jolly glad you could make it. This is Diana Rittenhouse, the lady I was telling you about. Diana, this is our client, John Sorvino."

"I'm not your client *yet*." Sorvino shook Miles' hand.

Diana recognized his accent immediately. "What part of New Jersey are you from?"

John Sorvino's smile was dazzlingly white. "Camden. Miles tells me you're from Philly, right across the river."

As they exchange hometown pleasantries, she noticed that John's hands were smooth and tanned, with polished, manicured nails and a showy diamond ring on his pinky finger. An Italian ghetto kid who'd made good. As dinner progressed, she learned he attended the University of Pennsylvania, and then graduated from Wharton Business School.

"John's credentials are impressive, eh, Diana?" Miles fawned. "And now he's the CEO of Commercial Finance at Bank of America."

She studied their prospective client in silence. Last night at the singles bar, she'd seen young men who were trying to claw their way to a top position like Sorvino's. Charlotte was a banking town, and everyone wanted a piece of the green pie.

"My wife, Brenda, is a Main Line girl, just like you, Diana," Sorvino said. "She studied Interior Design at Moore College of Art."

Diana had never been a *Main Line girl,* nor had she wanted to be one. No doubt Brenda, with her prestigious pedigree, was another prize for Sorvino's trophy case. Miles and Sorvino deserved one another—the pandering toad and the cocky rooster. She hoped they'd live happily ever after.

"You and Brenda will be great friends." Sorvino's dark eyes flicked in her direction. "She gets lonesome for Pennsylvania, you know? She misses the city…."

What did he want from her? Praise? Approval? A playmate for his pampered wife? She sensed Miles had chosen her to be another Main Line trophy for Sorvino, a real estate agent who'd do his bidding and stroke his ego. If either man believed that, he had another think coming.

At the same time, she sensed insecurity in John Sorvino. Like many self-made men, perhaps he'd been too successful, too soon. If she could peel away his mask, perhaps she'd find a real human being underneath.

They finished their meal, and Miles signed the tab. As they exited into the dark summer night, on the way to the Sorvino home, a nasty thought occurred to Diana. She was no better than these men, maybe worse. After all, why she here? She was out of work, her savings dwindling, worrying about the next mortgage payment, and she'd do almost anything to make that worry go away. She was ready to compromise for money. Was she also willing to climb off her sanctimonious high horse?

Absolutely.

SEVEN

The smell of money…

"You've been to our house before, Miles." Sorvino stepped between them in the parking lot. "No need for you to tag along this time."

"But I'm with Diana…" Miles blustered.

"You came in separate cars, and to be honest, I'd like Diana's opinion of the value of our property before she hears your input."

It was the old divide and conquer routine. Diana almost felt sorry as Miles blushed, then spread his hands in resignation. Sorvino's approach was rude beyond belief, but she got the feeling he was a man who stepped on many toes.

In the end, Miles' bottle green Jaguar turned right at the country club exit, heading back to Charlotte, while Sorvino's silver BMW went left, leading Diana deeper into an exclusive neighborhood called The Peninsula.

The neighborhood was a Realtor's dream, with million dollar mansions sprouting like brick mushrooms all along the lake. The homes extended through golf club communities on either side of Jetton Parkway. Soon the crape myrtles marching up this median would burst into glorious raspberry bloom, but all she noticed was the smell of money.

Sorvino curved through a maze of streets with names like *Flying Jib, Mainsail,* and *Yacht Club Lane.* Eventually they pulled into a meticulously landscaped circular driveway at her new client's pseudo-Tudor home. Sorvino helped her from her car, then hesitated

38

momentarily outside the pretentious façade, allowing her to take it all in. "Come meet the family," he said, once he deemed her sufficiently impressed.

The moment they entered the spacious foyer, Diana began taking mental notes, which she then translated to market value. She had run the comps in advance. After pulling up Sorvino's property from the tax records database, she'd compared it to recently sold homes in his neighborhood. In short, she'd done her homework in advance and had a ballpark asking price in mind. Yet there was no substitute for seeing the property in person.

The foyer opened into a soaring, double-vaulted great room. The open floor plan, tastefully appointed with imported tile and bleached hardwood, was exactly as she had anticipated. Gleaming white archways gave way to the dining room and gourmet kitchen to her right, while an enormous fireplace and media room lead to the master suite and a child's playroom on her left. A grand staircase circled upward to a balcony and guest rooms, so that the total effect was airy, elegant, and ideal—for at least two large families.

"Well?" Sorvino crossed his arms, a smooth, half-smile curving in his tan face.

"It's lovely. Priced right, it should move fast."

He clapped her on the shoulder. "Okay, so I'll give you the grand tour, so you can come up with a price we *both* like."

As she followed room to room, she heard New Age music playing in the distance and expected John Sorvino's family to appear. Judging from the abundance of expensive toys: miniature camping gear, a plastic machine gun, and a child-size computer, the couple had at least one kid.

"Is Bank of America transferring you?" she asked.

"No, we're building bigger and better one block from here. I bought a point lot on the lake, where the Main Channel view is breathtaking." Sorvino seemed irritated as he glanced down a hallway. "Where the hell are you, Brenda?" he called out. "The real estate woman is here. I told you she was coming."

Diana hung back as Sorvino stormed down the hall and flung open the door to the master suite. She caught a glimpse of what appeared to be a home office, with papers scattered across a Berber carpet. A slim, darkly tanned woman in a terrycloth bathrobe, head wrapped in a towel, peeked around the corner.

"Sorry, I'm running late. Be out in a jiffy."

The woman's accent stabbed like a dagger from Diana's past. Brenda Sorvino really was a Main Line girl, with an upper crusty voice like Katherine Hepburn strolling across Bryn Mawr campus. She'd grown up with girls like Brenda, envied their cashmere sweaters and expensive loafers. She'd attended their country club parties, but she'd never been one of them. Instead, she had won her scholarship to Bryn Mawr and had long since forgotten the inequities of her youth.

The Sorvinos closed themselves into the master bedroom, their voices raised in muffled anger. Diana sensed trouble in Paradise, so she made herself scarce. She wandered back to the great room, noting how in spite of the expensive furniture, the house had a cold, unlived-in atmosphere. If Brenda attended Moore College of art, why weren't there paintings hanging on the walls? As an avid collector, Diana could hardly breathe without art and sculpture, but she realized she was relatively alone in that passion.

Where were the books, the clutter of human habitation? The sterile perfection made her excessively nervous, but that was not unusual. Many of the fine homes she sold lacked the warmth of personality, especially those belonging to young couples who hadn't yet discovered their own style.

She opened the glass French doors and stepped out onto the patio, where the balmy summer night soothed her with the scent of freshly mown lawns and overripe roses. Odd, but the aroma of roses always reminded her of stale beer. Sinking into an upholstered chair, she lifted her feet and closed her eyes. A humid breeze washed across her skin and crickets sang from the bushes. As she waited for the Sorvinos to finish their argument, her mind drifted through a sea of remembered faces, couples she'd worked with in the past. Some found happiness, others ended in divorce.

As she brooded, the night sounds changed, and she sensed a sudden disturbance, a rustling or scratching noise, like a creature rushing through the shrubs. She sat upright in the chaise and opened her eyes as a flash of something white hurdled through the atmosphere. It landed heavily on her chest, howling in panic and clawing at the silk of her new dress.

Diana screamed and fought the beast. Finally, she tore it loose and flung it away. Then, through her terror, she saw the flicker of a long white tail scurrying into the underbrush at the edge of the flagstones. At the same time, she heard the pounding of small feet and the squeal of skidding sneakers. A child's screams blended with her own as a little boy ended his headlong run not three feet from her chair.

"Did you hurt my cat, lady?" he demanded.

Stunned and disoriented, she stared at the panting, red-faced child. He was truly beautiful, with silken black hair and smooth skin the color of cocoa. He was about eight years old, with ice blue eyes the color of Diana's, and she was certain they had met before. Perhaps he reminded her of her son, Robbie, who used to chase their family cat with a water pistol. But Robbie's cat was black, and this boy's weapon of choice was a spark gun. As he nervously clicked the trigger, little colored sparks crackled in the dark.

Of course! Suddenly she remembered. She'd seen this child only one week ago, at Bobby and Juanita's place.

"Juan, what on earth are you doing here?" she gasped.

The kid glared at her, his eyes wide and suspicious. "My name's not *Juan,* lady. It's *Johnny*!"

EIGHT

Just like twins…

Liz McCorkle tugged a brush through her thick red hair. "Are you saying this kid looks *exactly* like Juan?"

"Just like twins." Diana rummaged through her purse for lipstick. "The only difference is Juan has a tiny scar above his left eyebrow, and he's built a little chunkier."

They were hiding in the women's restroom at Piedmont Community College, waiting for Miles Lawton, who was lurking in the hall outside, to give up and go home.

"I guess it makes sense, in a weird kind of way," Liz said. "One boy's Hispanic, the other's Italian. Both kids have those *dark n' handsome* genes. What does Brenda look like?"

"Tall, blue-eyed blonde. You know the type—preppy and perfect?"

"I gather you and the lady of the house did not hit it off?"

"Not true. We got along just fine, once the confusion died down. We swapped some memories about the old home town, and then got down to business."

"You can't fool me, Diana. What went wrong at the Sorvino's?"

Diana located her lipstick. "Well, Brenda was distracted and upset. She plays the stock market online, and the NASDAQ just took a nosedive. She lost a bundle."

"Big deal." Liz scoffed. "Like those two really *need* the money? How does the kid amuse himself while Mommy's locked in with her computer?"

The idea of an only child, alone in that neighborhood, with no other boys his own age to play with, troubled Diana, too. "He has lots of toys…"

"Yeah, I bet he has enough stuff for an army of kids. Is he a spoiled brat?"

"I can't say. Johnny was quiet. He stayed off by himself and didn't say one word the whole time I was there."

They closed their purses, each making a final inspection in the mirror.

"At least you got the listing," Liz said.

"Yes, mission accomplished." She had convinced John Sorvino to offer the property at just over one million to encourage a fast sale.

"Did Miles ask you out for a victory drink when he found out you'd landed a new client?"

"Yes, he did."

"And you said *no*? What's your problem, Diana?"

"Look, Liz, if you're still interested in Miles, just step into the hallway. If he's still hanging around, ask him out for a drink."

"What if he insists on waiting for you?"

"Tell him I drowned in the sink."

"Okay, I'll give him a wink, but tell me one more thing… Johnny Sorvino's cat tore your new dress. Did his daddy offer to pay for it?"

The hope had crossed her mind, but Diana didn't believe in the tooth fairy, either. "I should have gone fishing," was all she could think to say.

NINE

Pure aggravation...

Floyd Clontz cranked up the engine of the utility van he'd borrowed off a neighbor and drove out of Sylvan Acres. The van was a sorry piece of junk, but still a sight lot better than the Clontz Lumber truck. His and Darryl's old rig wouldn't hang together one more day, let alone haul another load of rough cut all the way from West Virginia.

The morning sun burned the left side of his face as he headed south on Interstate 77 towards Charlotte. It was pure aggravation having to crawl along in the right lane, with all the hotshots with their fancy cell phones passing him like he was a piece of shit. All those assholes would sing a different tune when he was driving his new eighteen- wheeler. Then he'd be their worst nightmare, a ton of hot steel blocking the passing lane. He had a vision of his load letting loose, mashing those jerks in their matchbox cars under an avalanche of logs.

The vision made him smile as he checked his reflection in the rearview mirror. Floyd's long hair, the color of dull coal, was fresh washed and pulled back neat in a ponytail, like a county/western idol, and his eyes were chips of polished anthracite. His face was shaved smooth as a baby's bottom, but a red scar traveled across his mouth and into his lean, cleft chin, shattering any illusion of innocence.

He wished his idiot neighbor's van was air-conditioned, because at this rate, he'd be sweating like a pig before he got to the bank. Already the shirt Leona ironed for him was hanging on his back like a wet dishrag. Floyd punched on the radio and tuned to his favorite gospel channel, but nothing come out but a crackling static even the Lord Almighty couldn't fathom.

The static caused a familiar pain to throb behind his left eye, and his hands commenced to shaking on the wheel. He squeezed his eyes to drive away the pain, but it kept on twisting like the worm in the Tequila. When he reached under the seat, he felt the smooth leather case for his Beretta Minx .22. The little semiautomatic pistol was his comfort and joy, and as a rule, he kept it close—like the solid gold crucifix on the chain against his heart and the plastic Saint Christopher with magnets in its feet attached to the dashboard. Saint Chris would always keep him safe, so Floyd had set it up in the borrowed van.

Today he couldn't keep his gun as close as he'd like. Floyd figured Bank of America would have high security, maybe even pass him through a metal detector, or some such thing. But hell, he wasn't fixing to rob a bank, only to borrow a little of their money.

He tucked the Beretta case farther back under the seat and pulled out his flask of Wild Turkey. He took a long swallow, and the heat burned up through his gut like embalming fluid. After that, Floyd put the whiskey away. No banker lent money to a drunk, so he'd best fly straight.

To his way of thinking, Friday was the perfect day for this mission. By the end of the week, the ill effects of Floyd's Saturday binge had worn off, leaving his brain sharp as a bar room razor. Darryl and Leona both argued how Friday was bad on account of the banker would be itching to get a head start on his weekend. They said the banker wouldn't pay attention to Floyd's application. But they were too dumb to know that Friday was the ideal time for the scam. A man already asleep in his inner tube, didn't feel the shark nibbling at his toes.

The Lord helps those who help themselves.

Floyd lifted his eyes to where the Charlotte skyline jutted off the plain like a gang of robots with steel erections. The towering bank buildings were pumped on money—they had a hard-on for the sky. The image excited him. He rubbed himself and thought about Leona. The last time he caught her alone was when Darryl was off doing the lumber run. Floyd couldn't go because he'd bunged up his leg and could hardly lift himself off the bed.

When Leona came in with his supper, like a little nurse, he surprised her real good. He caught her wrists and wrestled her under him. He tied her hands to the bed with his belt and plugged her mouth with the sheet. The harder she cried and struggled, the faster he came. He had her twice before the urge left him, and then he turned her loose.

He told the bitch he'd kill her if she told Darryl. Besides, who would believe Floyd, with his injured leg and all, could take a strong girl like Leona? Still, something must have slipped out, because Darryl went and put a lock inside the bedroom door. The harlot had planted the seed of doubt, and things hadn't been the same between him and his nephew again.

Thou shalt not covet thy neighbor's wife.

But Leona wasn't a neighbor. She was family, and families share n' share alike. Besides, the girl was a gimp. She walked twisted on the right side ever since her stupid accident, couldn't cook worth a plugged nickel, so the only thing she was good for was sex and keeping the company books.

And the books came in handy from time to time. Leona couldn't cook, but she helped Floyd cook the books. Delighted by his play on words, he howled like a wolf as he careened off the highway at the Uptown exit and steered towards the tallest buildings.

Last week, when him and Darryl went to Enterprise Truck to buy the rig, the salesman laughed like they were hayseeds fresh off the farm. That was half right, because Darryl sure enough looked the part. His nephew was a good boy, but he was big as an ox and twice as dumb. Plus, he suffered from hoof n' mouth disease. Boy couldn't open his mouth without sticking his foot in it, and the only words that ever come out were the gospel truth, even when the truth wasn't convenient.

Thou shalt not be false to any man.

Honesty was fine and dandy, unless you're talking to a loan officer, who held your future in his hands. Today Floyd decided it was best to leave Darryl at home with his little wife. What Leona didn't know wouldn't hurt her, and Floyd wasn't about to explain how all her bottom lines got erased, or how come the profit margins swelled to where Clontz Lumber looked like a Fortune 500 company.

He patted his briefcase and pulled into the Bank of America parking garage, but then a uniformed guard, with a gun holstered on his belt, blocked the entrance. Floyd mopped the sweat off his face as the guard stomped up to the van.

"Move on, Buddy," the ape growled. "You'll have to park down the block and use the overhead walkway to enter the bank."

Floyd glared as the rent-a-cop peeked into the back of his van. "How come I can't park here?"

"You deaf, pal?" The guard waved him away.

Floyd backed up and slowly moved down the road. He was fucking pissed by the time he circled twice and entered a garage well down the street.

"That'll be fifteen dollars, sir…" The voice belonged to a pimply- faced kid behind a glass wall.

Floyd frowned at the rates posted on the booth. "Says right here it's three dollars for the first hour, and a buck fifty for every hour after. I ain't gonna be but an hour."

The parking attendant pushed his glasses up the bridge of his bumpy nose. "Yeah, but we collect up front. Some deadbeats pull in and stay all day unless we do it this way."

"Well, I ain't no deadbeat!" Floyd shoved three dollar bills at the kid. "Take it, or leave it."

The kid grinned, flashing a mouthful of braces. He crossed his arms and shook his head. "Sorry, sir, no exceptions. Fifteen bucks, or take a hike."

The twisting pain flared up behind Floyd's eye as he eased his van right up against the yellow entrance gate. The money he'd already left on the shelf outside the booth fluttered off and drifted along the pavement.

"Shit, look what you done!" He snarled at the boy. "Move your ass outta there and pick up that money!"

"Get it yourself, Mister." The kid laughed.

Floyd reached under the seat and fingered the Beretta case. He has a vision: the kid's brains scattered like spaghetti around the booth, teeth and silver braces clinging to the ceiling. At the same time, the kid lifted the panic phone.

"I'm calling security…"

Floyd gulped, swallowed his anger, and lifted two fingers in the peace symbol. His fingers trembled as he removed a ten and all the change from his wallet. In the end, after counting out his last penny, he had to climb out of the van and chase down the three bills like a moron.

"That wasn't so hard, was it?" The kid smirked as he lowered the phone receiver and finger-walked Floyd's bills under the bullet-proof glass separating the kid from sudden death.

Floyd's head pounded and his teeth ached like he'd been chewing on tin foil. When the yellow gate finally lifted, he peeled out, leaving the kid in a tunnel of burning rubber and a fart of exhaust. By the time he spiraled up six flights to find a parking space, his pain had receded and his nerves were calm. He knotted a tie around his neck, smoothed back his hair, and put on the linen jacket he'd bought at the thrift shop.

And if ye lend to whom ye hope to receive, what thank have ye? For sinners also lend to sinners to receive as much again.

TEN

A hog at slaughter...

Floyd strutted through the plate glass door of the Bank of America office and was greeted by a bitch who was black as sin.

"You don't have an appointment, Mr. Clontz." She frowned when he introduced himself. "But I'll be happy to process your application, if you're willing to wait."

No way would he work with the colored woman. "I want someone else to help me."

She lifted her glasses, gave him an uppity glare of disapproval. "Suit yourself. Please take a seat over there."

Ignoring her attitude, he pushed through a swinging gate to where a heavy young white man slumped behind his desk. Floyd helped himself to a chair. When the man ignored him, Floyd reached out and tapped his shoulder.

"This is your lucky day, son. I come here for a loan."

The hands on the wall clock moved slow and jerky as Floyd explained how him and Darryl needed a tractor trailer to move the rough cut. They had already picked one out—make, model, and preferred color. He told the kid how they intended to build the crib themselves, made custom to haul logs from the forest.

"Fill this out, please..." The clerk shoved an application form across the desk.

"Already done one." Floyd opened his case, with the same papers already filled in. "They give me this application at the truck lot last week."

The boy's fat cheeks above his tightly knotted tie put Floyd in mind of a trussed up sow. Little beads of sweat broke out on the fatty's forehead and his pudgy hands trembled as he fingered Floyd's papers.

The clerk said, "Peterbuilt offers its own financing. Why didn't you and your nephew apply at the dealership?"

A tick of anger flared at the base of Floyd's skull. "Me and Darryl prefer to do business with an actual bank."

The kid cleared his throat. "I appreciate that, sir, but according to this application, Clontz Lumber makes a great deal of money. Are you sure you need a loan? Where's your profit/loss statement?"

"I'm way ahead of you, brother." Floyd lifted the bogus tax return and cash flow statement from his briefcase, then propped his boots up on an empty chair and stretched out his legs. After the knife fight, his short stint in jail had yielded a college education in bunko techniques. His crib mate had taught him every angle, including how to pick up extra copies of IRS forms at the local library. Then Floyd simply filled in a high income and made Xerox copies. Worked every time.

"Impressive numbers, Mr. Clontz. Is this your social security number?"

Floyd nodded as the kid passed him a release form.

"Mind if we run a credit check now?"

"You can run it up, down, and sideways, boy. But make it quick. I'm a busy man."

The kid waddled into an inner office and handed the papers to a tall man, most likely his boss. The boss wore a suit worth a year's groceries. He walked to the glass wall and frowned at Floyd through insolent black eyes set in a tanned face. Floyd hated him instantly. He cocked his little finger at the bastard and wiggled it in a lazy greeting.

The fatty finally returned and raised his eyebrows. "You said your name was Floyd. According to the credit report, this social security number belongs to a man named *Edward* Clontz. Why is that?"

Floyd sighed and swung his feet down to the floor. He rolled his elbows onto the desk and glared at the kid. "I go by my *middle* name, asshole."

Again, it worked every time. Floyd's brother, Eddie, was a successful insurance salesman in Wheeling. Eddie had perfect credit, and Floyd knew his social security number by heart.

"Yes, but the report says you live in West Virginia. On your application, you claim you live in Mooresville…?"

"Give me a break, pal. I used to live in Wheeling, but now I live here." Floyd yanked out more phony documents and waved them under the pig's nose. "These here are letters of recommendation. Three different lumber mill owners say I'm a hard worker. I'm out on the road every day, busting my balls to earn good money."

"Okay, I'll show these to my manager…" The kid shuffled back towards the inner sanctum.

Floyd watched the kid sit at the boss's big desk. On the desk was a framed picture of the hotshot's perfect family—pretty little blond wife and a dark-haired son who looked to be about eight years old. No doubt that boy was spoiled rotten. Bored, Floyd stuffed a wad of gum in his mouth, then tossed the balled wrapper at the colored girl, who had ventured into his space to drink from the water fountain. "How's tricks, baby?" He leered as she stomped away in her ugly, sensible shoes.

Floyd had stolen blank letterhead stationery from all the mills on his route. Then he forced Leona to type in the testimonials, so him and Darryl came off looking like the best carriers on the road.

"Sorry, Mr. Clontz…" When the kid returned, he was sweating like a hog at slaughter. "Mr. Sorvino is not convinced. He says these letters look like they were all typed on the same old-fashioned typewriter."

Floyd spat his gum into the waste can and pulled his army knife from his pocket. He flicked out the blade and started cleaning the dirt out from under his fingernails. Next he spun around in his chair, so the colored girl could see the knife, too.

"I'm sorry, but Mr. Sorvino says we can't give you the loan." The pig's voice was a high squeal, his eyes riveted on the sharp blade.

"Tell your retard boss to haul his ass out here!" Floyd stopped spinning and climbed to his feet.

But Sorvino had already slipped into the room. "What's the problem, Clontz?" The man towered above Floyd. He opened his hand, palm up. "Give me the knife."

Floyd considered his options as the fat clerk ran off to huddle with the colored girl. Floyd had one last ace in the hole. He had stolen the deed to Leona's property in the mountains, and he was willing to sell the farm out from under her as collateral. He could lie, claim Leona was his wife, not Darryl's, if it came right down to it.

Or, he could slice off Sorvino's fingers right there and then, but the boss man's eyes were cold and hard. In spite of his expensive suit, Floyd saw that Sorvino was a street fighter. He'd met punks like him before, in dark alleys and in the Joint, not a dude you'd want to lie to. Floyd's gut contracted like the tail under a whipped dog as he folded his knife and dropped it in his pocket

From the corner of his eye, Floyd saw the colored girl reach under her desk. "Should I call Security, Mr. Sorvino?" she squeaked.

"That won't be necessary." Sorvino smiled. "Mr. Clontz is leaving."

In the temple Jesus found the money- changers at their business. And making a whip of cords, He drove them all out of the

Temple. And He poured out the coins of the money-changers and overturned their tables.

Floyd's face burned with shame and hatred. The belly of the parking lot was hot as the fires of Hades. He cranked down the van windows and breathed the foul stench of exhaust and urine. Sinking low into the cracked upholstery, he drank from the flask. The searing liquid sent a shiver of righteous purpose down his spine. Prison had taught him patience, and he had all day to wait. Lord knew, he'd already paid fifteen bucks for the privilege. That bastard, Sorvino, would emerge eventually, and Floyd had a clear view of the only elevator leading to the Bank of America hallway.

Vengeance is mine, sayeth the Lord.

Floyd removed his Beretta Minx from its case. He inserted a magazine, and then tucked it out of view under his jacket lying on the seat. When Sorvino came out, he'd be on his tail. An accident at highway speeds was risky and inaccurate, so Floyd decided to bide his time and follow the bastard home.

ELEVEN

A noble proposal...

Diana balanced a tray of coffee cups, while Mama maneuvered her walker to a table near the rose garden. They had left the residents of Shady Oaks behind in their air-conditioned dining room and gone looking for fresh air.

"If we had one lick of sense, we'd be drinking iced tea like the others," Mama grumbled.

"Yes, but it's hard to leave the old Yankee habits behind. We can't function without our caffeine fix."

"Speak for yourself, Diana. First of all, *I'm* not a Yankee. Second, I now prefer iced tea. I'm only drinking this coffee to keep you company."

Diana chuckled as they settled at a table. It was the story of her life. Her mother, Vivian Whitaker, was stubborn as the tick in a dog's armpit—Mama's metaphor, not hers. When Diana said *yes,* Mama said *no.* Yet somehow, since Mama had moved back home to her native North Carolina, the tension between them had eased considerably. Now they truly enjoyed their Friday night dinners together.

Ordinarily Mama resisted change and had trouble accepting happiness. During her long marriage to Diana's father, Will Whitaker, a handsome Northerner who carried Viv away to the land of ice and snow, Mama came close to that elusive emotion. When Will died a few years ago, Mama's world crumbled. She began a rapid, downhill slide that climaxed when she accidentally burned down the family home.

"Spring was way too short this year," Mama complained. "The dogwoods lost their blossoms in the blink of an eye, don't you know?"

"Yes, but winter is short, too, and we can't complain about that."

Mama snorted a grunt of automatic dissent, but Diana knew she was secretly ecstatic about her new living arrangements. When Diana had been in personal turmoil over her decision to move south, Shady Oaks had presented itself like the answer to a prayer. The assisted living facility was brand new, so she had reserved one of the first rooms for Mama. It was an added bonus that even the food at Shady Oaks was down-home spectacular.

"Must you carry that cell phone everywhere?" Mama pouted. "It's not like you're a brain surgeon, Diana. Everyone stared when it rang and you jumped up and left the table."

"Sorry, Mama, I should have waited to return that call."

"This Brenda Sorvino may be a good client, but she has no right to disturb your dinner. You said she's an interior designer, so how come she needs *you* to help pick out furniture?"

Diana sighed. This mess was all her fault. Her second big mistake was telling Mama about Brenda's plans for an elaborate Open House, featuring Diana as hostess. Her first big mistake was agreeing to help select furniture to "stage" the Open House, because now she'd have to cancel her fishing trip with Matthew and Juan. She already felt guilty because she never told Matthew about her so-called date with Miles Lawton, and now she had to break a date with Matthew.

They sat in silence as the sun began its slow descent behind a border of spruce trees. Mama didn't understand that when Diana became a Realtor, she gave up her right to personal privacy. She was always at her clients' beck and call, and Brenda Sorvino was more demanding than most.

"Won't that little Mexican boy be terribly disappointed if you don't go fishing with them?" Mama demanded.

Part of Diana's first mistake was confiding the details of Juan's sad story. Mama's heart wept for the boy, just as it recoiled at the image of the privileged, spoiled, Johnny Sorvino.

As their coffee grew cold and the sun fully set, Diana listened to the tinkle of Mama's spoon in her cup. It began as a slow, thoughtful stirring, then escalated like a demented clapper in a porcelain bell.

"I have an idea…" Mama suddenly exclaimed. "Use your blasted phone to call Matthew right now!"

Diana braced herself. "Why?"

"You said Juan's a lonely little guy, and Johnny's a solitary rich kid, right?" Mama's face was pink with excitement. "They're the same age, and they're both need some fun…"

"Are you suggesting that Johnny go along on the fishing trip?" She was beginning to get Mama's drift.

"Why not? It's perfect, Diana. You and Brenda will be free of the boy, and each kid will get an adventure and a new friend."

"What will Matthew get?"

Viv laughed and winked. "If he's half the man you say, Matthew will *get over it*."

58

TWELVE

A drowning man's raft...

Matthew sat on the back stoop with Juan McCord. His large hands and Juan's little brown ones were digging through the bait box, sorting the worms and night crawlers, and then transferring them to the cooler. The boy talked a mile a minute, but Matthew's mind was elsewhere, his ears tuned for the first sound of tires on gravel.

Not much traffic on Matthew's peninsula. He and Lynn had bought their point lot back when Duke Power built the dam and filled up the lake, before the cost of waterfront went sky-high, before the summer people and wealthy folk from Charlotte began eating up the shoreline like blood crazed sharks, so that Matthew remained one of the last holdouts. In spite of powerful pressure from developers, he'd refused to sell. He clung to his scrub forest and to the rustic cottage he and Lynn built together. Every front foot of his prime shoreline was like a drowning man's raft.

Before Lynn died, five years ago, her bridge ladies came around once a month. Before Ginny took off, soon after her mother passed, his daughter's teenage pals swam from the dock, exercised the water skis, and filled the house with laughter. Since then, the place had been mighty quiet, and Matthew liked it that way. Except for the occasional lost tourist who turned around at his dead end street, no one invaded his privacy. Again, he desired no visitors—except maybe one.

Ursie heard her first. The dog's ears pricked and she took off running up the road at the same time Matthew spotted the cloud of dust lifting behind Diana's car.

"Here they come!" Juan piped up nervously.

As Matthew climbed stiffly to his feet, Juan grabbed his hand and hid behind his legs. The boy made it plain he resented a strange kid butting in. He disliked the change in plans, and so did Matthew.

They watched in silence as Diana, sensibly clad in a tan pantsuit and sandals, helped a blond woman in a fancy dress and high heels extract a reluctant little passenger from the back seat.

Finally the kid climbed out, shook off both women, and scuffed his expensive Nikes through the dirt as he approached. "I'm Johnny," he muttered.

"Me too." Juan eyed the new kid.

Further introductions took a back seat as the adults watched the strange tableau play out. The boys stared at one another, each a mirror image of the other. The two Johnnys were virtually identical: same age, height, complexion, and hair. Twin sets of round blue eyes locked together in a ballet of disbelief as each child confronted his twin head-on. Their clothes were similar, though Johnny Sorvino wore designer sneaks and an official Atlanta Braves T-shirt, while Juan's battered Keds, ripped shorts, and knock-off Lakers tee were strictly Wal-Mart.

As he watched the pair, Matthew recalled a story from his childhood: Dickens' *The Prince and the Pauper.* Now the boys from the old book had come to life in his own backyard.

Finally, Ursie broke the magic spell. Having been distracted by a squirrel, she now galloped towards the visitors, fangs bared and ferocious in her unique smile of greeting. Johnny screamed, ran for his mother, and then clung like a baby behind her skirt.

Juan hooted with derisive laughter. "She won't hurt you!" To emphasize his supremacy, Juan flung himself to the ground and tussled with the beast.

"Don't worry, Brenda." Diana giggled "The dog's a pussycat. Johnny will love her."

"Yeah, Mom, let me go!" Johnny pulled loose, and soon both boys were roughhousing with Ursie, pushing and playing with one another. Without asking permission, they ran off in the direction of the lake.

Diana introduced Matthew to Brenda Sorvino.

"The resemblance between those boys is uncanny," he told Johnny's mother.

"I don't see it." Brenda frowned.

Clearly Mrs. Sorvino did not appreciate her son being compared to a ragtag Mexican boy. Her eyes appraised Matthew as she weighed whether or not it was safe to leave Johnny in his care.

But Matthew saw only Diana. She smiled at him while Brenda jabbered on and on about their upcoming shopping trip to Hickory. Diana's soft white hair caught the morning light and laugh lines creased the corner of her expressive mouth. The scent of jasmine, her favorite perfume, distracted him so badly that all he could think about was his hands, filthy with worm dirt. He jammed them into his pockets to keep from reaching out and touching her face.

"I've changed my mind," Brenda announced. "Johnny should come along with us."

A shadow of irritation clouded Diana's eyes. Matthew had failed the chaperone test. He squared his shoulders and tried to reassure the woman. "Johnny will be safe with me, ma'am. We'll wear life jackets and stick close to the shore, I promise. Please let him stay."

Fortunately Matthew's unique blend of treacle and molasses charm won the day, and Diana's grateful smile was a fine reward. But as they drove off, Matthew suffered an acute tug of regret. He had visualized this day quite differently. Diana, Juan, and he should have been together in the boat, like a real family. Then later, alone in the gazebo, with Juan off playing in the yard, he and Diana might have… Matthew pulled back from the image with an ache in his chest as her car rounded the bend, and she was gone from his little world.

THIRTEEN

The great equalizer...

Matthew had to admit their launch had been rocky, because the kids fought about everything from *who gets which life vest,* to *who carries the worms,* to *why can't Ursie come?* They nearly toppled Matthew's rowboat over *who gets to drive the outboard?* In the end, with Juan in the stern, Johnny in the bow, and Matthew in the center like a hulking referee, no one got to drive. Instead, Matthew rowed and Ursie howled mournfully from the end of the dock as the little hull disappeared across the lake.

"Once we have our house on the lake, my dad will buy a motorboat *six times bigger* than this one," Johnny bragged.

"So what? My dad owns a ranch *ten times bigger* than this lake," Juan countered.

Matthew was alarmed to hear Juan lie as the one-upmanship escalated.

"Big deal. My dad's the boss at the biggest bank in Charlotte."

"My dad's a cowboy!" Juan snapped.

Matthew took a heavy pull on the oars, then allowed the boat to glide. His feet were planted against the bulkhead, on either side of Juan's, and he gave the boy a long, hard stare.

"Oh yeah?" Johnny challenged. "There's no ranch or cowboys round here. Where *is* your daddy?"

Matthew warned Juan with his eyes, but decided not to interfere. Juan knew full well his parents were dead, but this was not Matthew's truth to tell.

"My dad's in California." Juan averted his eyes.

"Pipe down, kids," Matthew interceded. "Keep yappin', and you'll scare the fish away."

"Can the fish hear us?" the boys asked in unison.

"Loud and clear," he said, and they both shut up.

They dropped anchor in a shallow, reedy cove—a secret hole where Matthew had caught many a striped bass and crappie. Of course, he'd prefer different bait, a different season, and a different time of day. Because now, at high noon, in the heat of June, they hadn't a hope in Hades of catching anything bigger than a minnow or small bream.

Some men relaxed chasing golf balls, but Matthew would just as soon save the green fees and dangle worms, and he'd never met a boy who didn't share that philosophy. On the other hand, his parenting experience had been with a girl, his little Ginny, who could poke a hook through a minnow's eye or wait out a strike good as any boy. These sorry lads today had already fed most of their bait to the bilge in the bottom of the boat.

"Pass me your line, Johnny," Matthew told the Sorvino boy. "I'll show you how it's done…"

With that, two sets of hooks flopped through the air and attached themselves to Matthew, who instantly saw the problem. "Look, we can't have *two* Johnny's aboard." He lifted an eyebrow. "How 'bout we call one of you *Juan*?"

"*My* name *is* Juan!"

"*Whaan?*" Johnny giggled. "What kinda stupid name is that?"

"It's an Indian name!" Juan's blue eyes flashed.

"Honest?" Johnny looked to Matthew for confirmation, but Matthew shrugged. Then Johnny peeked at Juan. "Cool," he said with grudging respect.

One small victory. Now Juan was Juan, and Johnny was Johnny, but Matthew was determined to have a talk with his little friend from south of the border. The child had a problem with the truth, a problem Matthew had shared at Juan's age. Maybe Juan could avoid the consequences, if he stopped lying before it was too late.

The afternoon spread out like pancake batter on a griddle hot lake. They stripped off their shirts and washed their hands overboard before eating peanut butter sandwiches. They went swimming in the shallows, and Matthew taught the boys how to pee in the bushes when nature called. By the time they rowed out for another round, Johnny and Juan had become best friends. Matthew decided that fishing was the great equalizer—rich or poor, everyone was united by the mutual lack of good fortune.

"Are there any fish in this dumb lake?" Johnny complained.

"Bet not." Juan pouted.

"Bet so…." Matthew said as the bobbers on both boys' lines suddenly ducked under the surface. "Tug up a little on your poles, boys. Looks like someone's finally hungry down there."

Ignoring his instructions, the kids jumped to their feet and began jerking their poles and reeling like there was no tomorrow.

"Get me the net!" Johnny screamed.

"No, get *me* the net!" Juan shrieked.

Matthew pulled them both down to the seats. "We can land these fish by hand." He wrapped a rag around each line and lifted two tiny bream into the boat. "Too bad these little fellers are too small to keep. You'll have to throw them back, boys."

"No!" They rebelled as one.

"Yep, it's the law." Matthew was firm. "They aren't big enough to eat yet. Pass over your lines, and I'll take 'em off the hooks."

"No!"

Matthew fingered his jaw until a compromise presented itself. "Okay, kids, I have an idea. We'll keep fishing as we head home."

The boys watched in silence as Matthew rapidly removed their bobbers, clipped more weight on their lines, and then reset the hooks in the little bream. Then he tossed Juan's line off the port side, Johnny's off the starboard.

Matthew switched places with Juan, yanked the starter cord on his Johnson motor, and set out at trolling speed. "Hang onto those poles," he warned. "You might just hook onto something big enough to pull you out of the boat."

"For real?" Juan gasped.

"You best believe it, son." Matthew knew snagging a striper on a bream was a long shot, but stranger things had happened.

For once the boys were quiet as they watched the threads of silver dragging behind in the waves. At the same time, Matthew eyed the storm cloud that had been gathering on the horizon all afternoon. First it was yellow, then it was black as an angry bruise. Summer gales blew up like magic on Lake Norman, and racing home against rain and heavy winds could be a challenge. On a positive note, bass got mean and hungry right before a storm, and these poor boys deserved some success. He drove slow, hugging the edge of the drop-off where the shallows met the deep. If the granddaddy stripers were inclined to rise off the bottom for a quick dinner, now was the time.

The strikes came just as the first gust of rain poured from the sky. Suddenly each boy's rod bent like it had been hooked on a log. They screamed with excitement and hung on for dear life.

"Stay calm and keep your thumbs on the line… but if your fish starts to run with it, let the line out easy!" Matthew was anything but calm. When the boys stood up, he bellowed, "Sit your butts down, or I'll strap you in your seats!" They dropped without an argument.

66

"I can't do it alone!" Johnny wailed.

"Take my pole, Trout!" Juan pleaded.

Matthew shook his head. "Nope. I know you can do it. Just ease it out, then reel it in whenever the line goes slack."

They nodded, two sets of blue eyes glazed by panic and joy.

"There's a storm coming..." Matthew chuckled. "So you'll have to land those monsters yourselves. I'll head for the dock, and once we get there, you're home free."

The boys' knuckles were white as they gripped their rods. Clumps of soggy black hair draped their foreheads, while identical grimaces of concentration animated their faces. Matthew focused on the growling thunder and the lightning flashing ever closer. He picked up the pace, his heart swelling with pride as the kids hung on like old men against the sea. He realized he was putting the boys in some danger, yet giving them the adventure of a lifetime. Ultimately, he believed the rewards outweighed the risks.

When they finally bumped against the dock, and he was able to tie up to the mooring posts, only then did Matthew scramble for the net. First they brought Johnny's, then Juan's catch aboard. Both were whoppers to take your breath away. Each fish weighed upwards of three pounds and had delivered enough pulling power to tire a grown man.

"Lordy, boys!" Matthew whooped. "How'd you do it? They should put your pictures in the paper."

The fish flopped, the boys leaped and pushed one another in sheer ecstasy, and a thunderclap shook the dock. Amid the chaos, Matthew spotted Diana's white Crown Victoria parked in the carport and saw two women jumping and waving their arms from the shelter of the porch.

"Uh, oh...looks like we have company," he groaned aloud.

The boys noticed Diana and Brenda at the same moment and scrambled out of the boat.

"Hi, Mom!" Johnny screamed. "Wait till you see the fish I caught. It's awesome!"

"Yeah, me too!" Juan stretched his arms wide to show the length of his catch.

"You two go on up to the house and be sure to tell them you're okay," Matthew urged, but the boys didn't move. "Don't worry, I won't throw your fish back. I'll bring 'em soon as I tie down the boat."

Reassured, the boys took off running, spinning their arms like pinwheels. As Mrs. Sorvino watched them approach, Matthew could tell from her body language that he had a lot of explaining to do.

He always hated the next part. If he had his druthers, he'd throw every fish back into the lake to live out its life in peace. Not this time. He lifted his hammer from the tackle box, swung high, and dealt each bass a swift deathblow right between the eyes. Though their tails still thrashed and their little fins fluttered, the proud creatures had passed on to a better world, their demise quick and painless.

In the distance, Matthew felt Brenda's eyes burning with disapproval. He sighed and passed a chain through the fishes' gills. He prayed that facing her wrath would be quick and painless for him, too.

FOURTEEN

Blood brothers…

Juan McCord was so excited he could hardly breathe. When Miss Diana dropped him off at Johnny Sorvino's house, he couldn't believe Johnny's mama would really let them play together. After she'd screamed at Trout that day they went fishing, he figured he'd never see Johnny again. Maybe Miss Diana told Johnny's mother how they had to give Johnny his fish, and that's why she let him come.

Aunt Nita and Uncle Bobby had already helped eat Juan's fish, but Johnny's bass was packed on ice in a cooler in Miss Diana's trunk. Plus Trout had sent along a recipe so Johnny's mama would know how to cook it. They'd stopped at Trout's Place on the way, and Juan saw Trout kiss Miss Diana when they thought he wasn't looking. But now Miss Diana was sad. Trout had asked her to go on a picnic, but she'd said no, because she had to work for Mrs. Sorvino. Grownups were really stupid.

As they walked towards Johnny's house, Juan was suddenly shy. The place wasn't like a normal house, it was a mansion, like where movie stars lived. Juan's mama and daddy once took him to Hollywood on a bus. They saw pink and gold castles, and the driver told about all the famous people who lived inside.

"How many families live here?" he asked Miss Diana.

She laughed. "Only Johnny's family. It's big, isn't it?"

"*Awesome!*"

They rang the doorbell, and Mrs. Sorvino took them into a big hall. She didn't hug him or say hello. Instead, she called upstairs for Johnny.

"I'll be back around four," she told Miss Diana. "That drive-by couple said they were coming to see the house after lunch. Maybe you'll sell it to them, and we can skip the damned Open House."

Then she left.

Johnny trotted down the stairs while Miss Diana carried the cooler to the kitchen.

"Who else lives here?" Juan asked as Johnny took him to the playroom.

"Just me, my mom, and my dad. Who else did you think?"

Juan felt ashamed. Kids on TV lived in places like this, but that was only pretend. "My grandpa and grandma in California have a house big as a motel!"

"Like a *ranch*?"

"Yeah. Cowboys live there, too." He'd seen the photos in Daddy's album: cows, red hills, and a big gate with *McC* for McCord hung above it. The big white house was off in the distance. When Juan was a baby, Daddy took him there, but now he couldn't remember much about it.

Johnny showed him all his toys, but then got bored. "Hey, you wanna play outside?"

Juan wanted to stay inside with all the cool stuff, but he had a secret of his own to show. "Yeah, okay."

"Where do you two think you're going?" Miss Diana blocked the front door.

"We're allowed to go out," Johnny whined. "Didn't Mom tell you?"

"Yes, she did. I'll give you a lunch bag to take along."

70

They trailed her to the kitchen. Johnny grumbled and rolled his eyes, but Juan had already decided he loved Miss Diana. She was so pretty and funny, and she smelled real good. Plus, she didn't talk too much, like Aunt Nita.

She opened the refrigerator and lifted out a glass pan loaded with slabs of gooey white meat.

"Ooh, gross!" Johnny made a face and stuck out his tongue.

"What's wrong with you, man?" Finally Juan had one up on Johnny. "That's the fish you caught, stupid. Trout sent it."

An enormous grin spread across Johnny's face. "You sure it's *my* fish?"

"Absolutely." Miss Diana smiled. "Your mama will fry it up for your supper."

"*No way*! Mom can't cook stuff like that."

"Sure she can," Miss Diana said. "But in the meantime, here's something special for your lunch…"

She had little sandwiches with all the crusts cut off, some fancy cookies from a high shelf, and two cans of Mountain Dew. She put everything into a plastic bag, like Juan's mama used to do. Aunt Nita never made him lunch. She cut people's hair and never came home at noon, so Bobby and he always ate whatever dumb stuff they could find.

"Be careful, and don't wander too far. Your Aunt Nita will come to pick you up pretty soon," Miss Diana said.

Juan nodded, then followed Johnny outside. Why couldn't he live with Miss Diana instead? Aunt Nita didn't love him. She wanted to send him away. He heard her talking late at night, when they thought he was asleep. Maybe he could live with Johnny, or with Trout?

They took turns riding Johnny's bike past big houses with shiny new cars in the driveways. The sun sparkled off chrome bumpers and hurt his eyes. They stopped where the shiny lake rolled around the land and the wooden bones of a new building rose into the blue sky. The building was empty and quiet, like when Mommy took him to the museum where a dinosaur lived.

Johnny dropped his bike and ran inside. "This is my new home," he said. "My room's right here on the lake."

"Who's building it?"

"Daddy says the lazy bums never work a full day."

They wandered through pretend rooms in hushed silence, where open rafters cast hard patterns on the cracked red earth. They sat cross-legged in Johnny's room and ate their lunch, while Juan told him about Porter Park, and how he lived on the lake, too. He decided to save his big surprise for later, but showed Johnny the two pictures hidden in his other pocket.

Johnny cheered when he saw the one of Juan posing with his fish. "Who's that man standing beside you?"

"Uncle Bobby, but he's not my *real* uncle."

Then Johnny's eyes bugged at the picture of Aunt Nita in her tight halter and short shorts. He pressed his finger against her breasts. "She's *sexy,* like those ladies on MTV."

Juan blushed. He wasn't quite sure what *sexy* meant, but he knew it was good. "She's my *real* aunt."

"Cool."

After lunch they raced to the lake, kicked off their shoes, and went wading. Soon, off came their shirts. Juan left his photos on the shore so they'd stay dry, and then the boys dove in. They played man and shark, taking turns pulling the other under and biting his leg. Finally, exhausted and happy, they crawled onto the grass and flopped in the shade of an old willow tree. Juan decided the time has come.

"Hey, Johnny, check this out…" He pulled apart the Velcro pocket in his shorts and brought out the knife. The sun sparkled on its red enamel casing and gleamed on each blade as Juan plucked them out one by one.

"Radical!" Johnny followed each movement with his eyes. "Where'd you get it?"

"It's Daddy's Swiss army knife. He gave it to me before..." Tears pressed behind Juan's eyes.

Johnny turned pale and stared. "Before he *died*, right?"

Juan nodded and looked away.

"Your mom died, too. Miss Diana told my parents, but Mom said I shouldn't talk about it..."

Juan picked up his shirt and wiped his eyes. The sky, water, and blazing sun spun in dizzy circles. He couldn't catch his breath.

Johnny's chest heaved as tears also spilled from his eyes. "I'm real sorry, Juan. Are you scared?"

Juan glanced at his friend and saw a reflection of his own terror. "I'm not scared," he lied, jabbing the blade of his knife in the dirt.

"Can I see it?"

Juan hesitated, but then handed the knife to Johnny. "When Daddy gave me this knife, he told me never be afraid, *not ever*. Long as I have this knife, the Indian spirits will protect me."

"Honest?" Johnny's tone was heavy with respect. "What else did he say about the Indians?"

The boys crawled deeper into the shade as Juan whispered, "He told me the legend of the blood brothers..."

With heads close together, Johnny listened in silence as the tale unfolded. Juan knew every word by heart... the story of the Braves in battle, of honor and death, and of the ancient pact between warriors who were kindred spirits.

"And so they cut each other, pressed the wounds together, and their blood flowed as one. From that moment on, they were brothers, bound and responsible to one another till death."

The knife in Johnny's hand assumed a life of its own. "Will you be *my* blood brother, Juan?"

Hair pricked the back of Juan's neck. He wanted to be Johnny's brother more than anything in the world, but his daddy had said *never use the knife on another human being*.

"C'mon, give me your finger, chicken!" Johnny pleaded. "Please?"

Juan squeezed his eyes, and then looked at the sky. In the distance he saw Johnny's mama and Aunt Nita coming for them, but he extended his hand, gripped his wrist, and held out his finger. He hardly felt the sharp blade pierce his flesh, so when he looked, the bead of red was a complete surprise.

"Good, now cut me..." Johnny passed the knife. "Hurry up, before Mom sees us."

Juan held his breath and did it. Then Johnny had a red bead, too. "Okay, now press them together and squeeze real hard..."

They locked fingers and pressed, chanting the blood brother's oath, making it up as they went along. The grownups started to run, and Juan knew there'd be hell to pay. But the sky was blue, his heart was pounding with joy, and he'd never been so happy.

FIFTEEN

Nothing for free…

Leona Clontz helped her husband set up their wares at a pull-off on River Highway, across from the convenience store where Darryl liked to buy his favorite chewing tobacco off a pretty high school girl who'd caught his eye. Leona paid no mind to her husband's harmless flirtations. Lord knew, she hadn't been tending to his male needs of late, not like she used to.

Darryl stood up in the bed of the rig. "Come 'round to the back, Leona, so I can pass the stuff down to you."

She limped over and dropped the tailgate. Darryl was stripped to the waist, sweating like a prize bull at the county fair. At twenty-three he was still a fine specimen, and just looking at him made her proud.

They didn't need no permit to sell off their truck here. Others did it all the time and never got in trouble, so why not? Maybe it was a waste of time, though, because all they had to sell was a couple of rough wood rockers and some reindeer.

"Line 'em up under that tree," Darryl said. "And I'll put the sign out near the road."

She dragged two rockers into the shade. God knew they need the money. They hadn't seen hide nor hair of Floyd all week, not since he took off half-cocked for the bank to get a truck loan last Friday. Darryl said *no news* is *good news,* but far as she was concerned, any news about Uncle Floyd was all bad.

Darryl had been sound asleep last Friday night when she heard Floyd drive into the trailer park. Floyd never came inside, though, and next morning he was gone. They found the van he'd borrowed off a neighbor trashed and smelling like a brewery, so they figured Floyd took off again with his drinking buddies.

She prayed to high heaven that Floyd had drove himself off a high cliff to nowhere, so she'd never see his ugly face again. But that wouldn't help Darryl, who was nervous and broke. Darryl couldn't take on lumber jobs alone. Couldn't take no job at all unless they got a new rig, and that wouldn't happen in this lifetime.

Darryl jumped off the truck and flopped into the rocker beside her. "Hey, darlin', you reckon the weekend crowd will buy?"

She smiled at how his blond hair fell across his wide brown eyes. His eyes were his best feature. He looked like a frightened deer. Next she looked out to where the little herd of wooden reindeer waited to be sold. Darryl created each one with love, by hand, like a real artist. He made them from barky scraps trimmed off the logs, and each one had a short, sawed-off body with four stick legs. Darryl carved little round heads, sanded them smooth, and then attached them with stick necks. He drilled holes in the heads for twig antlers, holes in the butt for a tail, and two half-holes for the eyes. It was Leona's job to glue plastic eyes into the sockets. Each eye had a black pupil inside that rolled around when you twisted the deer's head from side to side—google eyes.

"Reindeer are more a Christmas item," she answered slowly. "Can't rightly expect folks to buy 'em in the heat of summer."

Darryl frowned. "Don't be thinkin' that way. Up in Boone tourists bought 'em fast as I could make 'em, no matter the season."

His mention of Boone made her think back on the best time of her life, when Darryl and her got loose of the Clontz clan and returned home to Mother Mattie. Darryl's kin had chucked Leona out

76

when she lost the baby. She was sixteen and Darryl was eighteen, but their love was so strong he left his own folk to live with hers.

Those were the quiet days. Even Mother Mattie, who was stingy with praise, bragged on Leona's young husband who worked magic with the wood. When Mattie gathered up her eggs and vegetables and took them to sell in town, she told all her rich customers to come round and buy Darryl's creations. They earned enough to make ends meet and live in peace till Floyd showed up.

Floyd had arrived like a bad penny, with money in his pocket and mean tricks up his sleeve. Claimed the money come from his honorable discharge from the army, but she knew better now. Floyd told her the real truth later, when he got her alone and hurt her so bad. Today she couldn't hardly think on that truth, it scared her so bad.

"Leona, did we make a mistake, leaving the mountains?" Darryl read her mind.

Her heart soared with hope. He'd never asked such a thing before. "We was better off in Boone. Can we go back real soon?"

But Darryl shook his head and took out his knife. He picked up a stick and commenced to whittle. "We ain't heard from Floyd yet. I figure we should wait a spell."

Her heart dropped like a lump of coal to the bottom of an empty bin. When it come to his uncle Floyd, Darryl would wait till the last can of hash was cooked and the last egg fried.

"We don't need Floyd," she told him.

He looked up from his carving, a cold shadow darkening his warm eyes. "I figure we should wait for Floyd."

Leona shrunk up inside and held her tongue. She looked out to the highway, where evening was coming on. The road was jammed with expensive cars dragging big boats, but nobody stopped to buy. She watched as a tall man come out from the store across the street and weaved through the traffic to reach them.

"Howdy, folks." He smiled. "I've been watching you all day. Business is slow, right? I thought you might enjoy a bite to eat and something to wet your whistle…" He held out a brown paper bag.

"We don't take charity, Mister," Darryl said through slit eyes. "If we want to eat, we'll cross the street and pay, like everyone else."

Leona smelled the pungent aroma of barbeque through the bag, and her stomach clenched with hunger. "We'll trade you, Mister. See anything you want?"

The stranger folded his arms and leaned against the truck. "Matter of fact, I've had my eye on those reindeer. Do I get a discount if I buy two?"

"They cost twenty-five each," Darryl said. "But I'll let a pair go for forty."

"You got yourself a deal…" The man took two twenties from his pocket and handed them to Darryl. He gave the food to Leona.

Before she could thank him proper, he tucked two reindeer under his arms and jogged back across the street. "What a nice man!" She dug into the bag and screwed the cap off a bottle of Cheerwine soda. "Who is he?"

"That's Mr. Trout, the boss man. I've seen him at the store lots of times. If he's so nice, how come he didn't buy a rocker, too?"

Leona stuck out her tongue at her grumpy husband, but she knew he was only fooling as he wrapped his mouth around a barbeque sandwich. Still, he should work on his attitude. Both him and Floyd thought rich folks owed them something for nothing. The family could get along just fine without handouts, but Floyd had warped Darryl's mind. He thought Floyd's word was gospel and clung to his uncle's wrong-headed notions like a drowning man to a lifeboat. Leona firmly believed that when Darryl was a baby, Floyd cast an evil spell on the child, and even as a man, Darryl couldn't shake the poison.

She finished her meal, wiped her lips with the napkin, then watched cars turning on their headlights as darkness fell. After a time, Darryl showed her the tiny carving he'd done. It was a blue heron, like the one they once seen on the lake. The workmanship was truly beautiful—delicate and real, with all the feathers in place.

But then a shiny white vehicle swerved off the road, throwing gravel. It scared them so bad, Darryl's knife slipped and he chopped off the heron's head.

"Shit! Look what that asshole made me do!" he howled.

She lifted her arm to shield her eyes from the blinding light as the car stopped just shy of their display. A sick taste rose in the back of her throat, and she wanted to run even before the man slammed the door and staggered into the headlights. He wobbled on his feet and pointed a bony finger at them.

Bring forth the best robe and put it on me; put a ring on my hand and shoes on my feet: and bring me the fatted calf...

"Jesus, Floyd, where you been?" Darryl embraced him.

I once was lost, but now I'm found...was blind, but now I see.

Leona retreated into the shadows, but there was no place to hide. She knew Floyd was drunk by the way he was quoting the Bible. He always bragged on how he'd memorized the Good Book in prison. He fancied himself a preacher.

"What's wrong, missy? Ain't you glad to see me?" Floyd said to her.

His breath stank of whiskey. His coal black hair had pulled loose from his ponytail, and he was still wearing the same shirt she'd ironed for him last week. His beady eyes were rimmed with red, and black stubble hid the scar across his lips.

"Wow, man, where'd you get this car?" Darryl stroked the waxed hood.

Ask and ye shall be given.

"Yeah right," Leona snarled. "You stole it, Floyd. Did you *kill* somebody for it?"

A little pulse in Floyd's forehead started to throb, like it always done just before he hit her. His fingers twitched, but she knew he wouldn't do nothing hurtful with Darryl standing near.

Floyd chuckled and licked his lips. "Tell you what, missy. I come real *close* to killing somebody. I drew a bead right between his eyes, but then God reached down and stayed my hand..."

"Did you have the shakes, Uncle Floyd?" Darryl teased.

"No such thing. God told me to bide my time and reap my reward at a later date."

Bullshit. Darryl thought Floyd's talk was a game, but Leona knew better. She knew he'd once shot a man, but kept her mouth buttoned. One wrong word, and the Lord Himself couldn't save her from Floyd's wrath.

"What are you two staring at?" Floyd hissed. "Pack up your junk and follow me. We got work to do."

"Where are we going, Floyd?" Darryl's mouth fell open. "I hope it ain't too far, because our old truck ain't running so good. I doubt it'll make it past the edge of town."

"That old truck ain't goin' past the edge of town. Remember that gully out past the dump, the one with all them scrub pines down at the bottom? You drive it that far, then we'll push it over the edge."

Leona snatched her husband's hand and hung on tight. "What about Darryl's chairs and reindeer?"

Ashes to ashes, dust to dust... May they rest in peace.

Even Darryl understood this wasn't a game. He squeezed her fingers and swallowed his loss as he pictured all his wooden creations cast to oblivion. Sweat broke out on his forehead, but he watched like a beat hound while Floyd took the license tag off their old truck.

He shoved the tag into Leona's hand. "Make yourself useful, girl. Drop this in the dumpster across the street, you hear?"

She did as she was told and limped over, dodging traffic. When she looked back over her shoulder, Floyd was waving his arms like a madman, while Darryl just stood there, nodding and hanging his head. His arms dangled useless at his sides, and she knew her husband was scared shitless.

By the time they'd loaded up and were alone in the cab of their doomed truck, fear had turned Darryl to stone.

"What's he up to?" Leona demanded. "Do we get a new truck, or not?"

"Reckon not," Darryl muttered. "He didn't get the loan."

"Then why ditch the old rig? Even if we drop it in the dump, somebody's gonna find it."

"Don't matter. By that time, it'll be too late."

"Too late for what?"

Darryl shrugged. His eyes were glued to Floyd's taillights as they followed him through the night. His fear chilled her heart like ice water. "Take me home to the trailer right now!" she begged.

"Sorry, darling, we ain't goin' back to that ratty old trailer ever again."

SIXTEEN

A circus finale…

Sunday was so hot that Tom dug a cat-sized pit under the hydrangea bushes on the shady side of the Sorvino's patio. He raked the earth and kicked it onto the tiles with his hind legs. This minor mishap sent Brenda, who was already nervous about the Open House, right over the edge, so Diana decided it was time for her to leave.

"Believe me, Brenda, it is better if the owner's not around. Then potential buyers can relax and speak their minds."

"But you need help with all this food," Brenda fretted. "What if you run out?"

"Don't worry, I can handle it. Just take the boys to the Peninsula Club, so they won't be underfoot."

"But they won't go. They claim they want to spy on all the people who come. Frankly, I think they mind *you* better than they mind *me*."

Diana was tired of arguing. Truth was, Juan and Johnny were double trouble, a united front of resistance to all adult authority. They behaved no better for her than for Brenda, but clearly Brenda didn't want them tagging along. "Okay, you win. They can stay, but they'll have to play outside."

"No problem, but don't let them leave the yard." Brenda agreed.

"We'll go swimming down at the lake!" Johnny materialized from out of nowhere, with Juan close behind.

"No way, young man." Brenda frowned. "You can take your toys to the patio, but that's as far as you go."

"Aw, mom…" Johnny whined.

"And as for you, Juan McCord—no knives allowed. *Comprende?*"

Juan blushed and stared at his sneakers. "Aunt Nita took my knife away. She's keeping it safe until I'm older."

Good call, Juanita. Diana had never expected to see Juan and Johnny together again after the pocketknife incident last week. Brenda Sorvino had shaken Juan until his teeth rattled and accused him of cutting her son. Juanita Cruz had screamed at Brenda and hit her with her purse. By the time Diana intervened, both boys were crying their lungs out. In the end, Johnny confessed that the blood brothers ceremony had been his idea. Brenda apologized, which she seldom did, and Juan declared that his aunt's attack on his behalf was *awesome.*

"Okay, we'll stay in the yard…" Johnny conceded. "But only if Miss Diana makes us another picnic lunch."

"It's a deal." Diana smiled.

Most Open Houses were so boring that even a suspenseful mystery novel couldn't keep Diana awake, but today was a major exception to the rule. So many people showed up, she couldn't keep accurate count as the guests staggered into the air conditioning, all vaguely dazed and disoriented.

Because it was a high-end listing, the Sorvino property attracted more window shoppers than serious buyers, but Diana was determined to sort out the viable clients. She tried to approach each visitor and had placed a guest registry in the foyer to collect names and email addresses. If push came to shove, she'd contact the potential buyers later.

She steered folks towards the food and urged them to help themselves to wine or iced tea, feeling more like a glorified waitress than a real estate professional. Plus today she was also a babysitter. Glancing into the yard, she saw the boys dangling bits of lunchmeat from a string, trying to catch a *cat*fish. Tom had the good sense to stay buried under the hydrangea.

What's the secret ingredient in your chicken salad?" The plump wife of a local pediatrician tapped her arm.

"Curry?" Diana answered hopefully.

"Yes, *now* I can taste it." The woman smiled.

Diana tuned out the wife's culinary observations and focused instead on her husband. The good doctor was an eminently qualified buyer. He was as skinny as the wife was fat, but instead of being a jolly couple, like Jack Sprat and his wife, these two were the consumers from hell. While the wife found fault with the gourmet kitchen (not enough hip room between the island and the stove), the husband complained that the enormous closets in the master bedroom were too small (not enough room for my clothes). Fact was, these folks would never make up their minds.

By late afternoon, the Open House had become a circus. Diana performed like an acrobat, balancing her time between passing out brochures and business cards to answering tax and utility questions. One of the visitors, a shy country girl who wandered in from the street, required no sales pitch. Clearly this girl, with her faded print dress and plastic purse, had come to bask in the glow of wealth, if only for a moment.

Diana had cautioned Brenda to hide her jewelry and other valuables, yet she kept a watchful eye on the young woman. She hated to *profile* the girl, but she did seem excessively nervous as she tugged at her dirty blond hair. Plus, she refused to make eye contact or even speak to Diana.

Diana followed quietly as the girl limped into the kitchen and discovered the food. She looked to see if anyone was watching, and then devoured a chicken salad croissant in two bites. Either the poor thing was extremely hungry, or the chicken salad was special indeed. The girl checked again, then stuffed a napkin filled with croissants into her plastic purse. Diana wondered if she was homeless, and her heart went out to the child.

Not wanting to embarrass her, Diana moved into the hallway and glanced out at the road. She saw Juan crawling out of a pup tent the boys had erected in the front yard, and then he dashed around the corner of the house, apparently hot on Johnny's heels. The street was parked tight with expensive cars. Remembering the poor girl in the kitchen, Diana expected to see an old pickup truck or other modest vehicle amongst them, but the only car out of the ordinary was a glistening white sedan parked down the block. It was remarkable only because it was occupied by a bored husband who'd rather wait in the oppressive heat than look at real estate with his wife.

Just then, a bottle-green Jaguar turned into the lane, followed by a caravan of luxury vehicles including a Rolls Royce and a Range Rover. Diana groaned, because Miles Lawton had threatened to bring his retinue of out-of-state clients to her Open House, but she'd pushed that unpleasant possibility to the back of her mind.

"Cheerio, Diana!" Miles winked as he led a group of well-dressed prospects up the walk. "I hope you haven't already closed a deal on this fine property, because this lot is ready to sign on the dotted line."

She opened the door wide and welcomed them. At the same time, she distanced herself from Miles. She got busy passing out more business cards, and somehow in the confusion, she missed the country girl's departure and that of *Dr. Consumer.* Just as well. By four, she was exhausted, yet happy, because she had avoided Miles' advances

85

and assembled a decent list of viable prospects. The last guests were leaving when Brenda bustled up the sidewalk.

"Whoa, you had quite a turnout!" she gasped.

She pulled Brenda inside the house and closed the door. "We call it a *feeding frenzy.*"

Brenda trailed her into the kitchen, barely able to conceal her excitement as Diana poured two glasses of chilled white wine. "So, did we sell the house?"

Diana enjoyed a long, welcome swallow, savoring the sharp flavor on her tongue. "Not yet, but we will."

"With all those people, didn't anyone bite?"

As Brenda fished for details, Diana heard the front door slam and prayed it was not a latecomer to the Open House. Instead, John Sorvino burst into the kitchen. His face was deathly pale under disheveled black hair, and his eyes were strangely unfocused.

"Where the hell is Johnny?" he demanded, tripping over a barstool as he rushed at Brenda.

"What's wrong with you?" Brenda shrieked as her husband lurched forward, grabbing her arm to break his fall. "Have you been drinking, John?"

Diana put down her glass and helped to steady the man. "Are you ill?"

Sorvino jerked free. "Are you deaf? Where's Johnny?"

Brenda's eyes were wide with panic as she looked to Diana for support.

"Calm down, he's out in the yard," she reassured them. "He's playing with Juan. I saw him in the tent a little while ago."

Sorvino took a deep breath and stared at his wife. He yanked his collar loose. "Go get him Brenda. Do it now!"

Brenda was too startled to argue. She scuttled through the French doors to the patio as her husband poured himself a stiff scotch.

"What's the problem?" Diana asked. Sorvino was either drunk or sick, but there was no excuse for his rude behavior. Normally in a situation like this, she'd make a fast departure, but at the moment, she actually feared for Brenda's safety."

"You were supposed to be watching my son!" Sorvino downed another scotch.

The tiny pulse in her left temple started to twitch, a sure sign she was about to lose her temper. The wall phone at her shoulder nearly scared her out of her skin when it began ringing in the charged atmosphere.

Sorvino froze. He made no move to answer, so she picked it up and listened to the man at the other end. In the meantime, Sorvino sank into a chair. Diana was sure he was about to faint.

"Who is it?" Sorvino demanded in a hoarse whisper.

She cupped her hand over the mouthpiece. "It's a pediatrician who visited today. I think he wants to buy your house."

"Hang up the damned phone!"

"But he's making an offer..."

"Just do it!" Sorvino flew to his feet and wrenched the phone from her hand. He slammed it into the cradle before she could object.

At the same moment, another phone rang, a faraway, muffled sound that hit Sorvino like a slap to the face. He located his briefcase, pulled out a cell phone, and then ran from the room to take the call.

Before Diana could compose herself, Brenda returned. Her hands were spread open, empty, and her eyes brimmed with tears. "God, Diana, I can't find the boys! I looked everywhere. They sure as hell didn't stay in the yard like they promised. I swear, I'll kill them both when they come home!"

As the women stared at one another, helpless to alter the situation, a knot of dread tightened in Diana's stomach. In the hyper stillness, the sailboat clock on the wall ticked off the minutes. A lone fly landed on the scraps of chicken salad, and Diana didn't know whether to laugh, or cry. She feared she might throw up.

When John Sorvino returned to the kitchen, he dragged his feet like a sleepwalker. He melted against the counter to support himself, and when he looked up, his eyes were filled with terror. "They took Johnny…" He choked. "The kidnappers got my son!"

'What's he talking about?" Brenda's voice was shrill and tremulous as she stared at Diana.

"A man called my cell as I was driving home from the Club. He made me listen, and I heard Johnny cry…"

Brenda rocked on her feet, keening like a dying kitten.

"That was him again," Sorvino explained. "Now he wants money…" Suddenly he broke into sobs. The violence shook his body and he couldn't continue.

Sometimes truth hides. Sometimes it's direct as a knife to the heart. Diana knew Sorvino's words were true, and when the bile surged up in her throat, she ran to the sink and hung her head over the edge… just in time.

No one heard the door open.

No one saw the small figure walk quietly into the kitchen. He looked around, shy and confused by the scene before him.

"What's wrong?" Johnny spoke at last.

His parents made sounds of joy and tearful relief. They embraced one another, then reunited with their son.

Diana slowly lifted her head. "Where's *Juan*?"

SEVENTEEN

The sacrificial lamb...

Only Johnny heard her question. He pulled free of his parent's embrace and they locked eyes.

"I told you not to leave the yard!" Brenda scolded.

"We were worried sick, son." Sorvino rocked back and forth on his heels, his voice gruff with emotion.

"What's the big deal?" Johnny kept watching Diana. "I took a ride on the Blackwell's pontoon boat."

"Did Juan go, too?" Diana asked as another wave of nausea washed through her.

"No, ma'am." Juan blushed. "Juan stayed in the yard."

"So Juan was a *good* boy," Brenda said. "What's *your* excuse, young man?" She captured Johnny and swatted his bottom.

"Where's Juan now?" Diana unsteadily approached the trio.

"In the tent?" Johnny shrugged. "We were playing cowboys and Indians."

"I'll get him..." Sorvino stomped out the front door.

Diana heard Sorvino calling Juan's name, his voice advancing, then receding like the last echo of hope.

"I'll go help Daddy..." Johnny struggled to escape, but his mother dragged him back by the seat of his pants.

"Not so fast. You get a time out in your room, young man!" She hooked the child under his armpits, and with the strength born of maternal fury, she lifted and carried him, his shoes bumping on each step.

Johnny's blue eyes were saucers as he glanced back at Diana. "You'll find Juan, right?" he whimpered.

"Yes, I will. I *promise,*" she told the child.

Why on earth had she promised such a thing? As soon as they reached the top step, Diana fled down the hall seeking sanctuary in the bathroom. She washed her face and rinsed the bitter taste from her mouth, but the horror wouldn't go away. When she lifted her head, the woman staring back from the mirror had guilt etched around her eyes and her lips were stiff with shame.

When she returned to the hall, she found Brenda sitting on the bottom step, her head buried in her hands. Lilting cartoon music drifted down from Johnny's room, the comic sound seemed maniacal in a world gone insane.

"This isn't happening," Brenda moaned.

But when John came through the door, his sagging shoulders said it all. "I looked everywhere. Asked the neighbors, but no one's seen him. Even walked down to our building site—nothing."

"Call the police," Diana told him.

"No! The kidnapper said he'd kill Johnny if I called the cops."

"But they don't have *Johnny*…" The tension retreated from Brenda's face.

"They probably think they grabbed the right kid." Sorvino's expression echoed his wife's as his fear faded to cold composure.

Diana witnessed the couple's transformation with alarm. "Look, the kidnappers will soon know the truth, because Juan will tell them. At least he knows who the hell he is."

Sorvino's eyes narrowed. "So, the bad guy figures he's made a mistake and lets the kid go?"

"Or, he figures he has nothing to lose by killing him!" Diana was frantic. Now that these selfish parents were off the hook, they seemed willing to make Juan the sacrificial lamb. "For God's sake, call the police!"

Brenda sighed and massaged the bridge of her nose. "Diana's right, John. Call the damned police."

Sorvino's expression, void of all human emotion, prompted Diana to recall her first impression of the man: a kid from the tough ghettos of Camden, a heartless scrapper who respected the bloody code of the streets, a guy who wouldn't hesitate to greet violence with violence.

Finally, Sorvino squared his shoulders and managed a smile. "You win. We can't handle this alone, so I'll call 911."

Diana turned her back and stared out at the patio. These long summer nights never get fully dark until ten—five hour to go. She couldn't bear to think of Juan alone out there, confused and scared, in the company of strangers. She prayed with all her heart that he'd be home safe before sunset.

Sorvino dropped his phone in his pocket. "Okay, the cops will be here in ten minutes…"

Diana excused herself and wandered into the Sorvino's master bedroom, closing the door. She perched on the edge of the bed, took out her own phone and made the hardest call of her life. Understandably, Juanita Cruz did not take the news well.

She concentrated on breathing—in, then out—as Juanita screamed, cried, and then lapsed into Spanish. All the verbal abuse in the world couldn't ease the guilt that all but paralyzed Diana's vocal chords. In the end, she conveyed the basic facts without imparting too much detail.

She was listening to Juanita's tirade when a white Crown Victoria, exactly like Diana's *Queen Vic,* parked in the driveway outside the room. The police logo on the door was the Cornelius town seal, depicting a sailboat floating through a peaceful sunset. The incongruity was jarring, as was the enormous young officer who stepped from the vehicle. He tucked his white shirt into crisp navy trousers, then hiked up the heavy holster supporting his weapon.

"The police are here," Diana muttered into the line.

As Juanita tearfully ended the conversation, saying that she and Bobby were on the way, Diana followed the cop's gaze to a second story window, where the last rays of sun glanced golden on the glass. She caught her breath to see the ghostly face of little Juan McCord pressed against the pane. In that moment, she was seized by a terrifying premonition: a vision of death. In the next moment, the officer lifted his cap and waved at the apparition, and it waved back. Of course, the ghost was Johnny.

EIGHTEEN

The wrong kid...

"He took the *wrong kid*?" Officer Andy Monroe's round, boyish face was incredulous under a close-cropped fuzz of blond hair. "Jeez, what a fuckup!"

They were all seated around the kitchen table: Brenda and John together at one end, Monroe at the head, and Diana on the side. As the officer asked the same questions over and over, she began to lose confidence. The young cop took copious notes, but couldn't learn how to spell *Juan*. So far, he'd established that John Sorvino was a banker, Brenda a homemaker, and Diana a Realtor. These facts were hardly front-page news.

Clearly Monroe was in over his head. He said he couldn't cordon off a crime scene, since no one knew exactly where the abduction had taken place. The challenge of physical evidence had him completely stumped.

"What about fingerprints?" He scratched his duck-like head. "Can you give me a list of names? Whose prints should we reasonably expect to find in this house?"

Everyone groaned as Diana explained yet again about the Open House. "So that list includes you, me, the family, and about fifty others—and that's just today."

As Brenda refilled everyone's glass with iced tea, Officer Monroe put in another call for a detective or shift commander.

"We've never had a kidnapping before," he admitted. "Least not since I've been here."

Diana figured Monroe had been on the force about five minutes, so she was extremely grateful that more experienced help was on the way. To be fair, the case was bizarre, even in terms of big city crime. In all her years in Philadelphia, she'd never read about a kidnapping involving mistaken identity, and she was an avid news hound. Indeed, no one around the table could believe what had happened.

Neither could Chief Jay Keener, who had been summoned away from a dinner party. The moment Keener entered the house, some of the weight shifted off Diana's shoulders, for clearly the Cornelius Chief of Police was a take-charge kind of guy.

Monroe sprang to his feet. "Wasn't expecting you, Chief. I thought they'd send Joey."

"I hope you approve." Keener smiled. "Joey and the others are on the way."

Keener wasted no time. A small, intense man in his mid-forties, his clipped manner and brisk movements conveyed urgency, so that even the sullen Sorvino rose to shake his hand. The chief was impeccably dressed in dark trousers, navy blazer, and a conservative tie. He pulled a small black leather wallet from his breast pocket and quickly flashed his badge.

"I was a Special Investigator in Charlotte for twelve years, but last month they transferred me home to Cornelius."

"You're a local boy?" Sorvino asked. "I thought I recognized your name. Your father is my insurance agent. His name is Jay, too, am I right?"

Keener offered a terse smile of confirmation, but no comment. He excused himself and took Monroe aside. After a brief consultation, the rookie left the room.

"Andy Monroe and two others will canvass the neighborhood. They'll knock on every door. Maybe someone saw something out of the ordinary," Keener said.

Brenda's tan forehead wrinkled in a frown. "Should we bother our neighbors at dinnertime?"

"Absolutely." Keener frowned. "Sunday night most folks are home preparing for the upcoming week. In that respect, we're very lucky."

Brenda started to protest, but Keener silenced her with one firm glance.

And in spite of the panic pressing under Diana's breastbone, she was fascinated by the whole procedure. She noticed how Keener's small dark eyes darted restlessly in her direction. His face was sharp-featured, clean-shaven, and his high, narrow forehead was made more prominent due to premature baldness. Absurdly, his name, *Jay,* made her think of the bird, and she hoped he would pursue Juan's abductor with aggressive, jay-like tenacity.

"What's on your mind, Mrs. Rittenhouse?"

Keener caught her staring, throwing her off balance. "I was just thinking about the guest register," she stammered.

"I saw it in the hall. What about it?"

"Well, as far as I know, everyone who visited today signed the register. Can't you call those people? Maybe someone saw something suspicious."

"We'll definitely contact them, Mrs. Rittenhouse…" Kenner grinned. "But in the meantime, *you* are our most stable witness. You were here all day."

"Do I look *stable,* Chief?" Her hand trembled as she lifted her glass of iced tea.

"You're our best shot." Keener laughed.

John Sorvino cleared his throat. "Listen, Keener, don't hassle the folks who signed the guest book. After all, those people are potential buyers of this house. Invading their privacy will put them off."

"*You* listen, Mr. Sorvino, this kidnapping puts *me* off, and we will contact each and every one of your guests. This type of abduction, with no obvious physical or trace evidence, is the hardest to solve. Unless we clear it up in two days, the trail gets cold and our chance to recover the boy is greatly reduced. So get with the program."

At that moment, Diana spotted the silhouettes of Bobby and Juanita through the frosted glass front door. Her chest constricted with fresh guilt, and she braced herself for the next chapter.

NINETEEN

About the money…

The interview with Bobby and Juanita was a nightmare. Juanita, crazed by grief and anger, attacked Brenda, Diana, and even God Himself, saying they were all to blame for Juan's abduction. But it was Bobby, hanging in the background like a broken puppet, who broke Diana's heart.

Any contact with the police was hell for Bobby. His relationship with the law had been a disaster, and when Keener heard the name *Bobby Porter*, Diana was certain the chief remembered the case. Last year Bobby was accused of murdering his own father, Jedidiah Porter, and even though he'd been acquitted, the scandal still lingered.

"Bobby Porter, you say?" The chief's eyebrows lifted in his white forehead, but much to his credit, he did not mention Bobby's past trouble. Instead, he laid a gentle hand on his shoulder. "I know this is difficult, but I need to speak with you and Ms. Cruz privately." He turned to Brenda. "Can we use the living room?"

"No problem." Brenda shrugged.

Brenda and Diana hovered over the sink rinsing dirty dishes from the Open House. John Sorvino quickly retreated into the back yard to punish plastic golf balls. Diana was transferring plates to the dishwasher when Keener summoned her to the inner sanctum.

She followed reluctantly to where Bobby and Juanita were seated side by side on the loveseat, stiffly holding hands like worried teenagers. Juanita was uncharacteristically subdued, while Bobby was almost comatose. Whatever Keener had told them so far must have been sobering.

"May I call you *Diana*?" The chief asked.

"Yes, of course." Like a child called to the principal's office, she accepted the chair Keener indicated.

The chief remained standing. "Diana, will you come down to the station and give us a full statement?"

"Yes, of course." Now she sounded like her pet parrot.

"But first we have a more immediate problem..." Keener glanced at Bobby and Juanita, who looked away in shame. "You two aren't married, and you're not Juan's parents. Is that correct?"

"So what if we're not married?" Juanita snapped to life. "Juan's parents are dead. His mama was my sister."

"Being his aunt doesn't automatically make you his legal guardians. You told me Juan's paternal grandparents live in California. By law, they'd be considered Juan's closest blood relatives, so they must be consulted in this investigation."

"Bull! Those snobs think they're too good for the likes of us. They refused to see Juan when he was born, and they haven't seen him since. Me and Bobby are Juan's only real family."

Diana squirmed in her seat. Why had he dragged her into this? The situation was highly personal and definitely not her business. But it was fascinating and surprising to hear Juanita fighting for custody of Juan, when before she'd desperately wanted to get rid of the boy.

"What do *you* think, Diana?" Keener asked.

She sat up straighter. Did he want a character reference? "Well, I've seen Bobby and Juanita at home with Juan. In my opinion, they make a great family. These two are like his parents."

Keener faced the couple. "You're willing to take full responsibility?"

"Yes, sir!" They spoke in unison.

"We love the boy," Bobby added softly.

"I'm sure you do, but still, the grandparents must be notified. Who knows, maybe they'll be able to help with the next problem…?" He paused and suddenly excused himself, leaving the three of them hanging in a vacuum.

He returned immediately with the Sorvinos in tow. Without ceremony, he waved John and Brenda into their seats. "Okay, folks, let's talk turkey. How will we pay the ransom money?"

Sorvino flushed crimson. "Why should *I* contribute one red cent when they took the wrong boy?"

"Did anyone ask for your help?" Keener barked. "So far, the kidnapper's only motive seems to be money, unless…" He took a long hard look at John. "Do you have enemies, Mr. Sorvino? Was this kidnapping personal?"

John's laugh was bitter. "You kidding? I'm a banker, for Christ sake. I say *no* to people every day of my life, and most of those people hate my guts. But that doesn't mean they'd do something like this."

"Maybe not, but we'll explore that angle later." Keener closed his eyes and pinched the bridge of his nose. "Right now our only concern is the child's safety."

"You figure the bastards will turn him loose if we give them the money?" Bobby asked. "How much do they want?"

"A half million," Sorvino answered soberly.

"Mother Mary!" Juanita shrieked. "Who has that much money?"

"*He* does." Bobby cocked his head at Sorvino. "Even little Juan, who don't know nothin', told me how much you were asking for this house."

"You're onto something, Bobby," Keener said. "With the Open House and all the high-profile advertising, every criminal in three counties smells money."

Brenda's face darkened under her tan. "That's ridiculous. Just because John's a banker, everyone assumes we're filthy rich."

Juanita's eyes scanned the expensive surroundings. "If the shoe fits…"

Both Sorvinos glared at Juanita.

"You're not suggesting that *we* should pay these assholes?" Sorvino fumed. "I thought cops never gave in to blackmail, never bargained with terrorists and all that crap."

"In fact, the experts usually recommend paying the kidnappers," Keener explained. "Statistics show that Juan would have a much better chance of survival if the demands are met."

Sorvino crossed his arms and averted his eyes. Brenda did the same.

Diana saw no help coming from them, and whatever respect she'd once had for her two selfish clients crumbled on the spot. "What if the kidnappers *think* we intend to pay them?"

"Yeah, can we string 'em along?" Bobby asked.

"Too risky, "Keener said. "When it comes down to an exchange and the kidnappers realize they've been tricked, Juan's in real trouble."

The group fell silent as the implications sank in. Diana calculated that even if she put every last penny into a pot with whatever Bobby and Juanita could scrape together, they still couldn't raise enough to interest a petty thief.

Juanita screwed up her courage and faced the Sorvinos. "Brenda, John, would you be willing to *loan* us the money?"

Bobby leaned forward. "Please, Mr. Sorvino. I don't have much, but I own my house outright and have a steady job. If you'd lend us the ransom, as God is my witness, I'd pay you back with interest."

Bobby's appeal hung in the air, but Diana knew by the way Brenda stared at her lap, by the way Sorvino rose from his chair shaking his head, that the plea was hopeless. Sorvino was an investment banker, and Bobby was a bad bet.

"Look, I'm sorry…" Sorvino gestured to Brenda. "Can we go now…?"

Keener cast a sympathetic look in Bobby's direction, and then climbed to his feet. He walked to the window, where night had fallen. "Before you go, Mr. Sorvino, I'll explain how you can help. The kidnapper will call back, so we'll arrange for a wiretap on your ground lines and a trace on your cell phone."

Brenda joined her husband at the door, poised to escape. She sighed in exasperation, but Keener's suggestion was obviously not open to negotiation.

"Do what you need to do." Sorvino said as they left.

"Nice guy…" Keener mumbled under his breath, then turned to them. "Look, folks, time is short, and we have a lot to do. I want to extend an arm of the investigation to your house, Bobby. We should consider a number of options, including a public appeal. Do you understand?"

Bobby and Juanita nodded, but the couple seemed paralyzed by fear.

"Tomorrow morning, Special Agent Miller of the Charlotte FBI will arrive at your place. Is that okay?"

"Can Diana come, too?" Juanita asked.

"Good idea." Keener winked at Diana. "I'll interview her tonight at the station house, but the Feds will want to question her, too. Agent Miller can interview her at your place. How does that sound, Diana?"

"Sure, why not?" Her mind was short-circuiting from conflicting emotions. All of a sudden she was Juanita's best friend. What was that about? Especially since she was responsible for losing Juan in the first place. Diana was sick, weary, and hardly fit for a grueling at Jay Keener's police station. The entire day was a blur of grief and guilt, but when she glanced at the dark sky and thought about Juan, how could she say no?

"Thanks, Diana," Keener said before herding them briskly into the hall. "But one more thing—what does young Juan look like?"

Diana sensed a shuffling in the shadows at the bottom of the stairs. She had no idea how long Johnny had been standing there, or how much he'd heard, but obviously he was in distress. When he stepped boldly forward, his face a study in tearful defiance, the adults were transfixed as he beat his chest with one small fist.

"That's easy," Johnny said. "Juan looks just like *me*."

TWENTY

Redneck territory…

Special Agent Beaufort Miller scowled at the directions Jay Keener had given him. Bo had entered them into his GPS, but the route was leading him deeper and deeper into the boonies, away from civilization.

Shortly after dawn he'd had coffee with the Cornelius police, and the strong brew was now eating a hole in his stomach. Those guys had a suicidal addiction to caffeine, but other than that, they were an efficient team of cops, especially Keener. Back when Jay was detective in Charlotte, he and Bo had worked several cases together, and Bo had a healthy respect for the man.

Even so, this abduction case, the astounding stupidity of kidnappers snatching the wrong kid, presented some nasty challenges for Cornelius. The town had a small department with limited resources, but fortunately Keener did not suffer from territorial machismo. He had the good sense to call the FBI immediately, meaning Bo, whose specialty was missing persons.

Bo checked the route again. Taking another leap of faith, he turned left onto a dirt lane called Porter Farm Road. He drove into a valley where trees closed in on both sides, and as his tires pounded from rut to rut, he hoped his old shocks would withstand the punishment. His car climbed up to where the forest parted and the early morning sun burned through the fog. The day promised to be another scorcher, but Bo didn't mind. He loved hot weather.

At the top of the rise, he saw a patch of shimmering lake dead ahead, and the sight caused a powerful tug of homesickness. These rolling hills were nothing like his beloved low country, and Lake Norman was fresh, not salt, yet it seems any body of water pulled his emotional trigger. Bo could almost smell the brackish tideland and feel the coastal sun on his face.

Daydreaming, he nearly missed his turnoff—a gravel path cutting into the forest on his right. As soon as he made the turn, Bo found himself following a slow-moving backhoe. The truck's big wheels kicked up a cloud of dust, but Bo rolled up his windows and recalled what Keener had told him: *The land is being developed as a state park, slated to open on the Fourth of July...*

It was the same story all over North Carolina, including in his hometown of Beaufort. Everything was changing as wealthy outsiders took over the land and the sea. The kids he grew up with, all sons of fishermen, were leaving the area as expensive yachts and pleasure craft drove out the fishing industry. Some called it progress.

Bo glanced at a crew of workmen lounging against their equipment. They were smoking and drinking coffee, struggling to overcome the ill effects of the weekend, dealing with Monday morning. At that rate, Bo doubted the state park would ever open on schedule, but at least these guys were creating something good, preserving a few natural acres for everyone to enjoy.

He smiled and waved at the men, who followed his progress with openly curious stares. Bo suppressed his irritation. It wasn't like he was driving a marked car or wearing the standard issue jacket with FBI emblazoned across his back. No, for this mission, he was deliberately anonymous in loafers, summer slacks, and a lightweight cotton jacket. Yet somehow, no matter how regular he looked, as long as he was out here in redneck territory, folks always took a second look.

Was it his imagination? He had few friends, but the handful who knew him well said he was paranoid and urged him to brush the chip off his shoulder. He knew they were right, so he parked in the shade of an ancient willow tree and adjusted his attitude.

As he walked towards the trio waiting on the front porch, a man and two women, he knew he'd need no introductions. Thanks to Jay Keener, he was already familiar with the players in this drama. They had pulled in-depth background on everyone involved, from credit checks to criminal records. Bo even knew the date when Juanita Cruz received her citizenship papers.

So while he had a clear idea of the personalities he was about to encounter, these people didn't know Beaufort Miller. He braced himself, zipped up his jacket to conceal his shoulder holster, and then willed his long legs to carry him forward. The moment he climbed onto the porch, he sensed three distinctly different reactions. He also realized that these strangers' initial impressions went no deeper than his skin. He quickly introduced himself and showed his badge.

"It's a pleasure to meet you." The tall woman with striking blue eyes extended her hand.

He flashed a brilliant smile and shook her hand. The profile of Diana Rittenhouse had prepared him for an urbane northerner with close friends and associates in both flavors—vanilla and chocolate. Keener had liked this woman and her generous nature, which came through loud and clear.

The Mexican woman, on the other hand, had done a double-take when she first laid eyes on Bo, but recovered quickly and now seemed to regard him with wry amusement.

"Hi, I'm Juanita." Her dark eyes sized him up from beneath heavy eyelids as she folded her bare arms under an ample bosom. "We figured you'd show up sometime."

Bo knew Juanita has suffered her share of hard knocks, a kindred spirit of sorts. America's underdogs came in all colors, so he hoped she'd give him a fair shake.

Only Bobby Porter held back. He shifted uncomfortably in the shadow of the overhang, his odd, watery blue eyes unable to meet Bo's.

"Let's move this conversation inside," Bo suggested, nodding towards the group of curious workers drifting in their direction.

They trailed into the bungalow, ladies first, with Bobby bringing up the rear. Bo had to duck under the eaves in order to enter the cozy living room.

"You *sure* you're from the FBI?" Bobby asked the inevitable question.

"That's what they keep telling me back at the office." Bo held his temper in check.

"Sure you ain't *Magic Johnson*?" Bobby smiled shyly, exposing a row of crooked teeth.

Bo laughed in relief. Bobby's perceived prejudice was just another figment of his imagination. "Funny you should ask. Folks make that mistake all the time. Matter of fact, I played a little basketball in college, but my feet got in the way."

"How'd you get a name like Beaufort?" Bobby asked.

"Guess my parents lacked imagination, so they named me after the town where I was born. It's on the North Carolina coast, above Wilmington."

"Do they call you Beau?" Diana wondered.

"Yes, ma'am, only I spell it *Bo*, so people don't confuse me with those folks from the *other* Carolina who call their town *Byooofort*."

"I guess I have a lot to learn." Diana smiled.

They continued to question him about how he got hooked up with the Bureau, so he explained about his stint in the Marines, the training program at Quantico, and finally how he'd landed in Charlotte. When he completed his resume, an uneasy silence descended like poisonous smog. They could no longer ignore the unhappy reason for his visit.

He and Diana settled into easy chairs on either side of an old stone fireplace, while Bobby and Juanita sat stiffly on the sofa. No one sampled the iced tea Juanita provided as Bo explained the progress the authorities had made so far.

"The neighbors saw nothing?" Diana was disappointed.

"I'm afraid not, at least nothing useful. They saw cars and people coming to the Open House, but nothing out of the ordinary."

"What about the Blackwells, the neighbors who took Johnny out on their pontoon boat?"

"They spoke to Juan. He declined their invitation and stayed in the yard. When the Blackwells left with Johnny around three, they saw no one suspicious in the vicinity." Bo watched Diana very closely. Keener had kept her at the station until well after midnight. She had been tired, upset, and unable to remember. "What was happening inside at that time, Diana?"

She answered slowly. "I was very busy. I looked out the window and saw the boys playing in the tent."

"*Both* boys?"

She stretched for a memory. "No, just Juan. He was running around the corner of the house, like he was chasing somebody..." She closed her eyes. "I also saw a man across the street."

"A man?"

Before Diana could answer, a phone rang from the bedroom. Its shrill intrusion startled them all, but Bobby and Juanita seemed frightened by the sound. Bo had seen it before, agonized parents afraid that any news was bad news.

Finally Bobby climbed shakily to his feet. "I'll get it…"

Bo knew better than to proceed until the phone call was resolved, so he tried to ease the tension by sampling some of the tea. Diana and Juanita did the same until Bobby returned.

"It's for you, Juanita." Bobby looked sick.

The couple left together, closing the bedroom door behind them. Bo was distressed. The team had not yet placed a trace on the Porter's line. He turned again to Diana: "Tell me about the man you saw…"

"He was sitting in a white Chevy Malibu… I think."

Bo's heart rate quickened. Diana had not offered this information last night, but today she was rested and not so prone to second-guess herself. When witnesses responded quickly, their instinct was usually correct and the information accurate. "Can you describe him?"

"His face was in the shadows, but he was young."

"Dark hair?"

"No, he was blond, or light brown."

Bo moved to the edge of his seat as Diana extracted details from her subconscious. The man was young, with blond hair. Unfortunately, that description matched a large percentage of Charlotte's population, while white Chevy Malibus were standard issue in most rental car fleets.

"Was anyone with the man?" Bo drove the point home.

Diana blinked in surprise. "How should I know?" She paused. "But I think he came with the country girl. That's why I noticed."

Bo was fascinated as Diana spun a yarn about a poor young girl with a limp and long, dirty blond hair. The girl had worn a print dress and carried a plastic purse. She'd stole chicken salad croissants off the hors d'oeuvres tray.

"She seemed out of place, don't you see?" Diana continued. "I was afraid she'd steal Brenda's jewelry, but then I felt guilty for profiling the poor thing."

"Why did the girl steal the food?" Bo pressed. "Was she creating a deliberate distraction, diverting your attention so you wouldn't see what was happening out in the yard?"

"No way."

"Stay with me, Diana…" He leaned forward, twisting his long dark fingers together. "Why did you think the man in the car came with the country girl?"

"I don't know. When I looked outside, I expected to see a pickup truck, or something…." A strange light ignited behind Diana's lovely blue eyes. "The girl came in alone, but I knew she hadn't driven herself to that neighborhood. She couldn't have."

"She couldn't drive a car?"

"I can't explain it, but I feel she wouldn't have had the courage to come on her own, and the man was the only one waiting. They were together. I'm sure of it."

TWENTY-ONE

It's not fair…

After answering Bo's questions about the country girl, Diana sat bolt upright in her chair. This FBI man had a knack for getting at the truth, like he'd been pulling her teeth without the benefit of Novocain, but why hadn't she made those connections last night?

Before she could explore the idea, Bobby and Juanita returned from receiving their mysterious phone call. Bobby was drained of all color, while Juanita was as red as her halter-top, her eyes spilling with tears.

"A*ssholes*!" Juanita strangled a remote receiver in her fist. "They called my sister Maria a *whore,* and when I told them what has happened to Juan, they called me something even worse!" She shook the phone at Bo. "You people are all alike. Chief Keener forced me call those bastards, and what the hell good did it do?"

Bo seemed confused.

Bobby placed a calming hand on Juanita's arm, but she slapped it away. He turned to Bo. "We left a message for Juan's grandparents last night, the McCords out in California. They just now got 'round to calling back, more's the pity."

Diana moved close to Juanita, longing to comfort her. "What on earth did they say?"

"They didn't *say* anything, they *screamed*! Juan's grandmother blames *me* for the abduction, can you believe it? Like she gives a shit? To them, Juan's always been a stray cat. If they had their way, they would've tied him in a bag and drowned him at birth."

"Will they help with the ransom money?" Bo seemed stunned by Juanita's account of the grandparents.

"I asked, but Mr. McCord just laughed and hung up on me."

How could people reject their own grandson? Diana's heart went out to Juanita. She watched as Bo shook his head and gazed sadly at his feet. Finally, Bobby eased the phone from Juanita's hand and gently urged her to sit on the sofa. His kindness induced a fresh flood of tears:

"It's not fair!" Juanita pinned Bo with stricken eyes. "*You* know what I'm talking about, Mister FBI man. You know your place, I know mine, and even though folks pretend we're all equal, we know different."

Bo wiped a large, dark hand across his face. "Public servants like myself are supposed to grant all citizens equal protection under the law. Fact is, we have rich white justice and something less for black, red, and yellow. We have a sworn duty to investigate all crimes equally, but certain groups may get better service."

"Amen, brother!" Bobby nodded vigorously. "And it ain't just about color. I'm a white man, but I'm dirt poor. We don't get no favors neither."

Diana looked at each in turn. Being advantaged by almost any definition, should she feel guilty? In her experience, life was seldom fair, but did they need to worry about that now? "Look, maybe everything you say is true, but I don't see how worrying about it helps us."

"You're right, Diana, but it doesn't hurt to be realistic." Bo said. "I got into this game to equalize the odds, and as long as I'm on Juan's case, the investigation will be first class."

Bo's eyes lingered on an abandoned baseball mitt in the corner. His passion was possibly colored by his own agenda, but she was confident that Juan was in good hands. She continued to watch as Bo shucked off his jacket. Everyone gasped to see the gun holstered under his left arm.

"Hey, man…" Bobby inched closer for a better look. "What is that thing?"

"Glock semi-automatic."

Diana was unimpressed. Weapons left her cold, as did men who brandished them as an extension of their masculinity. This was Bo's job, however, and it was reassuring to know that Juan was being protected by some actual firepower.

"So the grandparents are out of the picture?" Bo changed the subject. "Maybe that's a blessing, because now we can proceed with you two as the sole responsible guardians. Is that okay?"

Bobby nodded solemnly.

"Yeah, that's good." Juanita dried her eyes.

Again Diana was moved by the woman's apparent change of heart. Only two weeks ago Juanita had been ready to ship Juan off to the family in Mexico. Odd how tragedy sometimes brought folks together. Bobby took Juanita's hand as Bo told them about the potential lead from Diana's Open House:

"So we'll work with Chief Keener on this one. He'll run the Chevy Malibu through the Charlotte database and look for matches in the area. Then we can narrow down the hits to Malibus owned by young couples."

"Must be hundreds like that out there," Bobby moaned.

"Yes, it's a long shot."

"But they don't *own* the car!" Diana interrupted, surprising herself. "Intuition tells me it was a rental."

Bo lifted his eyebrows and smiled. "I agree. My office will handle that end. We'll contact every agency and nail these guys."

"What else are you doing?" Juanita demanded.

"As we speak, the Cornelius police are interviewing everyone who signed in at the Open House. We also tapped the Sorvino's phones."

"Have the kidnappers called back?" Diana held her breath.

"I'm afraid not." Bo picked at an imaginary fleck on his knee. "By now they must know they grabbed the wrong boy. How they'll react is anyone's guess."

No one in their small, unhappy band cared to speculate. The guilt, which had never left Diana's chest these past hours, intensified as she tried not to imagine the worst scenario.

"We're also investigating any enemies John Sorvino may have made in the banking industry. Possibly snatching Johnny was an act of revenge."

Bobby snorted. "You start listing that man's enemies, the names will fill a phone book. You can write my name at the top of that list."

Diana agreed that Sorvino's behavior since the abduction had endeared him to no one. Even Johnny, who'd overheard his father refusing to help with the ransom, now refused to speak to him. Last night she'd felt almost sorry for Brenda as she tried to calm the boy's tantrum.

"We work closely with the National Center for Exploited Children in Washington, DC," Bo proceeded in a strong, positive voice. "As soon as we get a handle on these kidnappers, we'll plug them into VICAP, the most sophisticated criminal profiling system in the world."

It all sounded good in theory, but no one seemed convinced. As Bo rambled on about the powerful capabilities of the FBI, their three long faces attested to the sorry fact that the authorities had little, or nothing, to go on.

"Why don't you put his picture on a milk carton?" Juanita asked snidely.

Bo frowned. "Actually, those milk carton people do a lot of good. They're put out by The Missing Children Information Clearing House, and we have a branch here in North Carolina. We will file Juan's information with them."

"But it's a last resort, right?" Juanita asked. "Let's do something now. Let's go on TV and let people know what's happened. Someone out there has seen Juan."

"Can we offer a reward?" Bobby asked. "We ain't got much, but maybe we can come up with a couple of thousand...?"

Bo shifted his long body in his chair and looked to the ceiling for an answer. "It's a good idea, but it's risky. The kidnappers have demanded that there be no police intervention. A public appeal is like spitting in their faces. Once we go on TV, they'll be on the run. They may even panic and hurt the boy."

As Diana listened, her mind reeled with indecision. If either of her children's lives were on the line, what would she do? She watched as Bobby opened Juanita's hand. Wordlessly, he stroked it inside, then out.

At last Juanita lifted her face. "I say we either shit, or get off the pot."

Her words broke the tension. Diana said, "I agree, Juanita."

Bo jumped to his feet and clapped his hands. "Okay, I'll call the major networks and set you up on the evening news. Let's do it!"

TWENTY-TWO

Johnson's Hideaway...

Leona shuddered when thunder rattled the plate glass window and lightning flashed behind the drawn drapes. She pulled the limp boy closer in her arms as they lay together on the bed. Ever since the accident, she couldn't tolerate a storm. If she'd had her druthers, she'd drag the child under the bed, but the broken springs hung down to the floor. So she began singing again, soft and low, so as not to rile the men in the next room. She rocked the boy to push back her fear.

The room stank of cigarette smoke and cat box. The combination of odors made her sick to her stomach, and she couldn't rightly remember when she'd last ate. The past two days were dizzy and unreal, like a bad dream where you never woke up.

After taking the boy, they'd driven the back roads till it got good and dark. Darryl and Floyd sat up front, with her in the back seat and Johnny knocked out in her lap. Floyd swore the nasty stuff he poured on a rag and pressed to the kid's face wouldn't hurt him none. Each time the boy came 'round, Floyd made her press the rag to his nose till he passed out again. But she was worried about giving the kid too much, so when he threw up on her skirt, she used the dry end of the rag and only pretended to give him more.

When they come to Johnson's Hideaway, she laid low while Floyd checked in. They backed the rental car clean up to the motel door and snuck her in behind Darryl, and then Floyd carried Johnny under an overcoat with an armload of clothes. Once they were inside, the men locked her and Johnny in the bedroom and made her close the curtains.

Now they were prisoners, but she didn't mind. At least she had a lock on the inside of the door, so that when Darryl went out for supplies an hour ago, she put the bolt between herself and Floyd. By the time Darryl come back, the burgers and fries he brought were cold and greasy. The boy was too sleepy to eat anyway. Darryl handed her a sack from the drugstore.

"Now, Leona, you give him two of these pills every four hours, you hear?"

"What are they?" She held the little pink and white box up to the bed light. It said Benadryl. "Will they hurt him?"

"Nope. Talked to the man behind the counter myself. It's the stuff you take for a bee sting. It'll make him sleepy, that's all."

"What's this?" She pulled out a box of ladies' hair color and some scissors.

Darryl smiled and ruffled the sleeping boy's hair. "He'll look cute as a blond, don't you reckon?"

Leona had never done hair before. Should she put on the bleach, or do the cutting first? Before she could ask, Darryl left, locking them in the room again.

After that, she lost track of time. Life was a blur of waking, then sleeping. With the drapes closed, a body couldn't tell night from day. When the boy peed his pants, she helped him use the toilet and gave him the pills. He was so little and frail, like a bird.

Like Baby Bird. Leona figured she was losing her mind, but once the idea took hold, she couldn't let it go. She'd always known Bird was out there somewhere looking for his mama, and now he'd come home.

Bird threw up during the night, so she washed his little face and skipped the next pills. When he woke up sniffling and crying for his real mommy, she held him close and told him that she was his new mommy. She helped him suck warm milkshake through a straw and fed him little chunks of the biscuit Darryl left in the room for their breakfast.

The child even ate like a bird, looking up at her through the wide blue eyes of an infant. When he cried, she sang her special lullaby and cuddled him close in their tight little nest.

But the next time she woke up, Darryl was standing over the bed.

"Me and Floyd's going out," he said. "I see you ain't fixed that boy's hair yet. Floyd'll be pissed if it ain't done when we get back."

"Where you goin'?" The sudden flood of light hurt her eyes as she reared up on her elbows and stared at her husband.

"Stinks like shit in here." He wouldn't look her in the eye.

"I asked you a question, Darryl. Where you goin'?"

He sighed and flopped down on the bed beside her and Bird. "Can't see no harm in telling you, darlin'. Me and Floyd's looking for a different car. We'll take the Chevy back and find something new."

"We ain't got no money for a car."

"We ain't planning to buy a frigging Cadillac. Anything will do, so long as nobody asks questions."

"Like Mr. Johnson don't ask questions?" She'd heard Floyd talk about this motel, Johnson's Hideaway, in the past. He'd bragged how he brought his girlfriends here when he got the urge, how Mr. Johnson didn't tell tales out of school. Point was, she'd never imagined she'd set foot in this fleabag herself.

Darryl reached across her body and squeezed her breast. "Can't say I enjoy sleeping out there on the sofa. Come this weekend, we'll be living in style. I promise, Leona."

She pulled away and inched closer to the boy. "This weekend? You set up a meeting? Are we getting the money?"

He swung his boots off the counterpane and sat on the edge of the bed. "Floyd's still draggin' his tail. Won't make another call till after the TV news. So far, the kid's parents haven't gone to the police, but Floyd figures if they break that promise, we'll hear about it on the evening news." Darryl lit a cigarette and moved to the door. "A storm's coming…" He eyed her cautiously. "Now I know you hate thunder and lightning, but I need to lock this door. Be a brave girl, Leona, and you 'll be all right."

But she wasn't all right. The thunder come again and again. The bed lights blinked off, then come on again. After that, the alarm clock on the table flashed the same time again and again, and the song she was singing died in her throat.

She hugged Bird so tight he made a little chirping sound and tried to pull away. She buried her face in his hair, but it still smelled funny, like the peroxide from the bottle. Doing his hair had wrung the strength clean out of her. When she propped him over the sink, his head dangling like a broken doll's, she'd somehow managed to snip away his bangs and cut off the hair around his little ears. The bleaching was the hard part, but now he looked real cute. Lying there on the pillow, he was her own true Baby Bird, with fuzz the color of the duck down she remembered from all her dreams.

When the men come back, they dropped another box of chicken into the bedroom and forget to lock the door after. She was still too queasy to eat, and Bird was dead to the world, so she listened through the door to Gospel music blaring from Floyd's radio. The music was a sure sign Floyd was hitting the bottle real hard, so she decided to stay put where she was safe.

When the thunder stopped, she figured it was safe to visit the bathroom and answer a call of nature. On the way, she eased back the drape and saw the evening sun breaking through the clouds behind the neon motel sign. The cracked pavement in the wet parking lot glistened real pretty, almost like a rainbow.

As she watched, one eye to the crack in the drapes, she recognized the sound of Darryl's boots crossing the concrete. He walked to where a rusted old blue station wagon was parked. The car sagged on one side. It had no hubcaps and a web of masking tape held together a crack in the side window. Darryl was right: it was no frigging Cadillac.

Her husband bent onto one knee and changed the clunker's license plate, a game she'd seen Floyd play many times. His collection of tags was a family joke. They'd stop at junkyards, garage sales—anyplace Floyd was likely to find an old tag. This particular one for the old blue wagon was from Tennessee. Its letters and numbers were rusted so bad God Himself couldn't read them.

Suddenly Darryl turned back towards the motel and stared at her window. Leona let the drape drop real fast and scampered into the bathroom. When she came out, something was different. She heard silence. Floyd had turned his radio off. Seconds later, the TV came on.

The evening news.

Time for Bird's pills. Since she hadn't decided whether or not to give him the next dose, she figured she'd put her ear to the door and listen a spell. She heard some familiar music, but when the voices came on, they were so muffled she couldn't hear a thing.

"Son of a fuckin' bitch!" Floyd's voice roared through the door loud and clear.

"Jesus Christ!" So did Darryl's.

Leona twisted the doorknob open a crack. She saw a pretty dark-haired woman and a scrawny man on the TV screen. They were crying and holding up a photo of little Johnny, but they were calling

119

the child by a different name. Leona reckoned these two were Bird's parents, but they didn't look rich at all, and they weren't the folks she'd seen in the framed pictures at the Open House. All the same, they were pleading with the television audience to help find their boy.

"Shit, I don't believe it!" Her husband turned up the volume.

Leona's mouth went dry and her throat ached. Something had gone real wrong. She quietly closed the door and pushed the deadbolt home. She hated locking herself in when every instinct told her to cut and run, but she had the boy to consider.

Whatever bad news was coming out of the TV, it would soon come back at her. She'd best get gone. But where? She crawled across the floor and searched under the drapes for a latch, but the window was solid glass. She remembered a small vent in the bathroom. It was just big enough to pass Bird through, but if she did that, he'd just drop into the weeds and lie there.

The violence beyond the door got louder. Floyd started hollering religious curses and somebody toppled a chair. Next a hideous crash silenced the TV, and she whimpered in fear. Leona gathered the limp child into her arms and carried him towards the bathroom, hoping to put yet another lock between themselves and danger. But before she reached the door, the shattering of wood dropped her to her knees.

Darryl fell shoulder-first into the room. He staggered to his feet, a stunned expression on his face. But it was the sight of Floyd that stopped her cold. His devil eyes were bleeding with insanity.

"Step aside, bitch!" he slurred, a broken whiskey bottle in his hand. "I aim to kill that boy!"

TWENTY-THREE

The specter of inhumanity…

Beaufort Miller leaned over the drinking fountain.

"Hey, Beaufort, rumor has it the old man pulled the plug on you." Special Agent Carla Williams sneaked up from behind and pounded Bo on the back, nearly ramming his teeth against the spigot.

He stood upright, wiping water off his chin with the back of his hand. "Say what?"

"C'mon, Bo, you sound too *ethnic* to field the incoming leads. Grim Reaper's doing the job himself."

"You're right, soul *sistah*, but I don't see you answering the phones, either."

She flashed a brilliant smile. It was a long- standing joke at the Agency that Bo and his female African American counterpart liked to dish slang to put certain white clients off. The notion was good for a laugh, or two at best.

Carla's intelligent eyes sparked behind her glasses. Everyone at Headquarters had tried to hook them up, but Bo kept resisting. Her neat little figure was enough to make a strong man weep, but she possessed double Bo's brainpower. If he weren't such an idiot, he'd make peace with his own inadequacies and marry her tomorrow.

Carla trailed him down the hall to his office. "But is it true?" She pressed. "Did Max really take you off the hotline?"

Carla was in charge of Public Relations. She answered concerned citizen's questions about the FBI and closely monitored the branch's publicity. Last night she had directed Bobby and

Juanita's television appeal, but it was Supervisory Special Agent Maxfield Grim, the humorless veteran known as *SSA Grim Reaper*, who directed them all.

Bo paused at his door. "Yeah, but Max was right this time. Most folks calling in want to talk to the parents, and let's face it, I don't sound anything like Bobby or Juanita."

"And Max *does?*"

"Maybe a distant uncle?" Bo laughed. "But really, I'm okay with it," he lied. If he had his way, he'd field each and every response to the TV appeal, but it was out of his hands. Carla didn't seem to buy it. She knew how much the Juan McCord case meant to him, but she had the good grace to let it go.

"Okay, so what happen if the kidnappers call and ask to speak to the parents?" she asked.

"No problem. We're patched into the Porter house, so Max can silently switch the call without missing a beat."

She squeezed his arm as he grappled with his disappointment. She lingered, probably hoping for an invitation into his office, but he wasn't in the mood and suffered only a small pang of regret when she left. And then he barricaded himself inside. He sank into his chair overlooking a busy Charlotte intersection and waited for the two aspirins he'd swallowed at the drinking fountain to work their magic. No such luck. The broadcast had put him and everyone associated with the case through an emotional wringer.

He shucked off his jacket and stowed his weapon in a desk drawer. Loosening his tie, Bo switched on the little portable fan on his file cabinet and tried to focus. His second-story corner office was considered prime, a reward for surviving six years in the agency, but in summer it felt more like a punishment. Sunshine streamed through the windows, heating the place like a pizza oven, and those windows were sealed tighter than the lips of the CIA.

The location of the thermostat regulating the building was also guarded like a government secret, so that all agents were forced to conform to some national ideal temperature standard devised by a sadist who worked elsewhere.

Screw it. He leaned forward on his elbows and listened to the muffled rattle of jackhammers drifting up from the street. The concrete roadway out front had been torn up forever, with swarms of hard-hats climbing in and out of the subterranean pits like ants in a web of yellow construction tape. Either the city of Charlotte had a major problem with their water and sewer lines, or this was a giant conspiracy and the guys working below were really radical Muslim terrorists planting dirty bombs under the FBI building.

Bo sighed, closed his eyes and tilted his face at the fan. At thirty-six, maybe he was too old for all this? He had no friends and his social life was a disaster. The women he dated were initially attracted to the romance and danger of his career, but when he told the last girl about his special training for CASKU, she had to ask: *Yeah? What does that stand for?* When he explained: *Child Abuse and Serial Killer Unit,* she nearly choked on her wine.

Even if a woman could deal with the more gruesome aspects of his job, it was just a matter of time until she discovered his true nature. Dealing with the dark side, the unspeakable horror of the criminal mind, fed Bo's dark side, too. It was perversely alluring, a drug injected against his will, but addictive all the same.

His boss, Grim Reaper, had OD'd long ago. The man could retire, and yet he hung on. By now Max was numb to the specter of inhumanity that had caused three divorces and had finally become his bride.

Did Bo really want that for himself? He rubbed his eyes, then opened them wide. This kid, Juan McCord, was getting to him big time. Bo hadn't suffered the old nightmare for weeks, but last night the three-year-old girl came again. Her naked body was mutilated beyond recognition, and then abandoned in a warehouse. She had been his case, but Bo had come too late to save her.

It could happen again. He broke into a sweat, but he pushed the panic aside and picked up his phone. By now Keener's vehicle search should be complete. The chief himself answered…

"We have close to one thousand white Malibus in our area. One third are owned by young couples matching the description Diana Rittenhouse gave us, but short of a door-to-door search, and then a line up long enough to fill the Panther's stadium, I don't see how we can narrow this thing down. Sorry, Bo."

"What about the interviews from the Open House?"

"Nothing. No one remembers seeing either of the kids or the country girl. End of story."

Bo shared Jay Keener's frustration. "Did you check the stolen vehicles report?"

"Yeah, but we hit the wall. All white Malibus are present and accounted for."

They agreed to stay in touch, but as Keener hung up, Bo sensed the chief had exhausted his options. He dialed the central switchboard. "Can you connect me with Henry?"

The operator giggled. "Sure, Bo, but if you wait ten seconds, you'll see him yourself. He just galloped past with his tail on fire, and he's heading for your office."

Bo's heart thudded with hope. The horse metaphor for SA Henry Morse was right on target. The senior programmer should have been put out to pasture long ago, but the guy was a genius. The original nerd, Henry was building computers in the playpen before anyone else in America could even spell the word.

He burst into Bo's office, his long, equine face leading. "You were right, Beaufort!" Henry slapped a printout down on the desk.

"The white Chevy Malibu was a rental, and the dumb fuck leased it from Rent-A-Wreck in Huntersville, only a few miles from the abduction site."

"Good work, Henry." Bo snatched the report. "It says the guy rented the vehicle last Friday, then turned it in yesterday afternoon. The timing fits."

"And check out the mileage…" Henry grinned through long yellow teeth. "Asshole put less than two hundred miles on the car in a five-day period, so this wasn't your average traveling salesman. He's local. You'd think the moron would spring for some gas and run it out, just to put us off track."

Bo frowned at Henry. So far he'd called the kidnapper a dumb fuck, an asshole, and a moron. Although Bo wanted to embrace those theories, in his experience, criminals were seldom as clueless as they seemed.

"That means the kid is still in the neighborhood!" Henry was on a roll.

Bo shook his head. "Or maybe the kidnappers pulled the Chevy into a private garage, transferred the kid into a van, and then drove him to Alaska? Anyone could have returned the rental."

"Nope, the same jerk who rented it, also turned it in. It's all in my report."

Bo was losing patience. Henry was not authorized to conduct interviews with car rental agents or anyone else. He was a designated search engine, nothing more. Only experienced field agents, skilled in interrogation methods, were permitted direct access to witnesses. Too often a witness's memory was as fleeting as quicksilver, and the wrong questions could distort it altogether.

"Can you give me a verbal briefing?" Bo snapped.

"The man who rented the car is Horace Waddell, comes from a big family in these parts. The rental clerk said the creep was medium

125

height with a small, wiry build. He was thirty-some years old, and get this—pale with a scar across his mouth, long black hair in a ponytail, and dark, beady, mean-looking eyes."

"Jesus, Henry, the clerk actually *said* that?"

"Yes, sir, word for word."

"Maybe your witness has been watching too many gangster movies. Besides, the man Mrs. Rittenhouse described driving the car was big and blond. What about that?"

"The agent said there was another loser outside waiting to drive for Horace, maybe a blond guy."

"Did the agent check Mr. Waddell's driver's license?"

"Yep. The photo ID was a match."

"Can you get me a copy of the photo?"

"Sure, the agent has it on a disc. He promised to e-mail it within the hour."

Bo's anger faded. Maybe Henry was onto something, after all. "Naturally, you arranged to impound the car?"

"Sorry, Beaufort..." Henry backed towards the door. "I insisted, of course, but it was too late. The Malibu had been leased again. It's out on the road."

"Damn! Then reel it back in, Henry!" Bo saw a treasure trove of fingerprints obliterated for all time, but if they were lucky, a company called Rent-A-Wreck might not give their vehicles a meticulous wipe-down between customers. "Plug Horace Waddell into VICAP and the SBI computers in Raleigh. If this lead is for real, I want to know everything about him."

"Like what he ate for breakfast, sir?" Henry teased. "And I suppose you want this yesterday?"

Bo gave Henry a look of cross-eyed incredulity as his headache returned with a vengeance.

TWENTY-FOUR

Both made mistakes...

Matthew followed Diana along a mulched path through the forest. She was carrying the red and white checked tablecloth Juanita had supplied down at the house, while he carried the fast food chicken they'd bought on the drive to the Porter farm. Soon Bobby and Juanita would join them for the picnic, and Matthew hoped everyone's mood would improve in the meantime.

He noticed the defeated slope of Diana's shoulders. That special jauntiness was missing from her stride. Maybe Bobby's notion to get together wasn't such a hot idea after all. But Bobby was worried about Juanita, and Matthew wanted to cheer Diana up, so the men came up with this idea as a potential distraction from the gloom that had descended upon them all.

Matthew had taped last night's TV news broadcast and watched it time and again. Juanita and Bobby did a great job, but something about the description of the suspects bothered him. The news anchor offered Diana's account of the girl with a limp and the big blond guy driving, and that image triggered a memory in Matthew's brain. It was as elusive as a birdsong. He couldn't pin it down, so he might as well let it go.

"I hope Bobby and Juanita are hungry," he called to Diana's back. "We bought enough chicken to feed our troops in Iraq. Bobby said the two of them haven't been eating lately."

"I'm not surprised," Diana mumbled.

What could he say? Diana had agreed to this outing, but by the dismal look on her face when he'd picked her up her condo, you'd think he was dragging her to her own execution. She still blamed herself for Juan's abduction. Apparently both Diana's mother and her partner, Liz, also believed Diana should have watched the boys more closely. That was nonsense, of course, and Matthew would happily strangle both women for adding to Diana's misplaced guilt, but again, what could he do about it?

Diana has also missed two real estate classes, and he knew how important the classes were to her future career. It seemed like she was retreating from life, and he would not let that happen.

"Hey, did you see all those guys guarding the gate as we entered the park? Maybe *they*'re hungry." He joked.

"Those were FBI men," she grumbled. "After the TV broadcast, folks will recognize Bobby and Juanita. The kidnappers could find out where they live and try to hurt them."

"Relax, Diana, the bad guys won't come anywhere near this place. But well-intentioned citizens might make a nuisance of themselves trying to help. With a little luck, the FBI men will turn *them* away. Bobby and Juanita don't need a gang of do-gooder curiosity-seekers pounding down the door."

"Maybe they don't need us, either."

Maybe she was right. Only last week Bobby had been outside laughing and laboring with the workmen creating Porter Park. He'd been nagging the men about their laziness, barking orders and cracking jokes. Tonight they'd found the couple locked in the dark silence of their house.

"I think Bobby and Juanita just want to be alone." Diana spread the tablecloth across a brand new picnic table. The table was located on a grassy hilltop overlooking the lake.

Sure they wanted to be alone, Matthew reflected bitterly. Just like he'd wanted to be alone when Lynn died. After losing his wife, he'd built walls around himself. They were so high that even his daughter, Ginny, could not climb over.

I get it," he said. "But sometimes it's not good to be alone." Diana slid onto a wooden bench, then stared unseeing at the sun hovering low above the water. "You have children, don't you, Diana?"

They hadn't really discussed the subject, and that was Matthew's fault. Some selfish part of him didn't want to know the intimate details of Diana's life with another man, so the past hung between them. She pinned him with troubled blue eyes, and he realized the topic was difficult for her, too.

"My son, Robbie, is the oldest. He's in college, and his father wants him to go on to law school at Penn. Mandy, my baby, lives in Florida..." Her words trailed off.

So, she had two grown children. The fact started a churning sensation in the pit of his stomach. "Didn't Mandy go to college?" was all he could think to say.

Diana sighed. "When I divorced my husband, both children were devastated. I think Robbie understood, but Mandy was always Daddy's girl. She couldn't come to terms with it, and she ended up rebelling against both of us. She refused to go to college, although she'd always dreamed about attending art school, and then she ran off to Florida when my ex remarried. He didn't even try to stop her, and she won't return my phone calls...even now."

He was stunned. He ached to hold her, but he couldn't seem to reach out. "What about your son? Are the two of you close?"

She shrugged. "We used to be, but Robbie doesn't share his feelings anymore. Robert, my ex, expects him to excel in law school and then enter the family firm when he passes the Bar Exam. Thing is, Robbie always wanted to be a teacher, not a lawyer, but he doesn't have the guts to stand up to his dad—not yet."

Matthew's emotions raged in unexpected directions. "This business of being a parent…it's tough, isn't it?"

Her eyebrows arched in surprise. "Are *you* a father, Matthew?"

This moment of truth had come, so he met it head on. "I have one daughter. Ginny is maybe a little older than your Robbie, but I haven't seen her in almost five years."

"My God, where is she?"

Matthew averted his face. He couldn't bear to see his own failure reflected in Diana's eyes. "She was in Texas last I heard. She called to say she'd eloped with some guy who worked on an oilrig in the Gulf. That was three years ago."

Diana blinked. "Maybe you're a grandfather, Matthew."

He hung his head. "Who knows?" What could he say in his own defense? "It was my fault, Diana, I drove her away. We didn't fight—nothing like that—but I wasn't there for her, you know? I disappeared when my wife died."

"Haven't you tried to find her?"

How could he begin to explain? He had traveled throughout Texas, with no success. He'd hired a string of investigators, who also failed. The last private dick had followed the case for six months, then come up empty. He had spoken the words Matthew now repeated to Diana:

"Ginny doesn't want to be found."

She reached across the table and took his hand. Her fingers were cold, but her grip was strong. "We *both* made mistakes," she said softly.

The scent of pine needles mingled with the humid fishy smell rising off the lake. Footsteps broke the silence as Bobby trudged up the hill with Juanita clinging to his arm. This was supposed to be a picnic, but they were walking like mourners on their way to a funeral. They, too, had lost a child, but for them, perhaps, it was not too late. Diana's fingernails bit into Matthew's hand as she realized the tragic parallel of their situations. Matthew prayed silently to any force willing to listen: *Let there be an end to it, and bring Juan home safely.*

TWENTY-FIVE

Death on the line…

Bobby Porter slumped on the bench, his elbows propped on the picnic table as he stared at the chicken bones piling up on Juanita's plate. At least she was eating, so the company had done her good. Bobby never knew what to expect when trouble came Juanita's way. Where most folks got all quiet and depressed, she usually carried on like a cat in heat. In the past three days, she'd washed every dish in the house when they weren't even dirty and twice changed the sheets when they weren't even slept in. He knew enough to stand clear until she ran down, but he didn't see that happening anytime soon.

"The cops and the Feds have nothing," Juanita said as she pushed her plate away in disgust.

They had been talking about the rental car lead. Bobby trusted cops about as far as he could throw them, yet Juanita had taken a fancy to the black FBI guy. She actually believed Bo might help them, and she prayed to the Lord night and day. But Bobby's faith was shaken. Hadn't this same Lord sent Juan to them in the first place? The Lord suckered Bobby into believing the boy was a gift that would bring them together as a family. Then that same Lord took him away.

The Lord helps those that help themselves, so Bobby had located his daddy's shotgun tucked away at the back of a closet. It hadn't been fired since Jed killed some geese a few years back, so Bobby snuck it into the barn and cleaned it real good. He oiled it and filled it with shot, and he knew damn well the old man's antique

132

Winchester was a better weapon against the kidnappers than any cop's snarl of red tape.

"What about the reward?" Diana's voice interrupted Bobby's lust for revenge. "You mentioned it on TV, so the kidnappers must be curious."

Juanita wiped chicken grease from her mouth with a crumpled napkin. "Me and Bobby came up with ten thousand. It's not a fortune, but it's all we've got."

Bobby looked at his old pal, Trout. "I reckon that's not enough to make 'em take notice."

"As I recall, you didn't say how much you had available on TV," Trout pointed out. "Maybe they think you have a whole lot more?"

"So why don't they call?" Juanita asked. The Feds had given her a cell phone and told her to carry it everywhere. It had the number they'd announced on TV. She shook the phone angrily at the air.

Trout turned to Bobby. "Where'd you get ten thousand dollars?"

Not that it was any of his damn business, but hell, Trout was like family. "I sold my landscaping equipment, truck and all," Bobby lied. In truth, he had stolen it a lifetime ago.

Bobby gazed out at the lake. The spot where he'd found his daddy floating drowned at the dock was gone now, replaced by a fiberglass pier for the new park. Not long ago, Bobby had taken Juan down to the old fish-cleaning table under the willow tree. Together they'd scaled and gutted Juan's bass, just like father and son. He'd never told Juan how Bobby's own daddy used to cut off the fish heads and nail them to the tree trunk, how season after season, the sight of those wide, beady eyes rotting from their sockets and the grinning, toothless jaws, used to scare the shit out of Bobby. How they haunted his dreams even now.

When Juanita's cell phone rang, he near jumped out of his skin. She lifted it to her ear, her eyes frozen with terror, but all he saw was those fish heads, so he knew that Death was on the line.

"It's for you, Bobby," Juanita choked. "It's the FBI, with one of the kidnapper's wanting to talk. It's for real. He won't talk to anyone but you."

The three faces at the table gaped at him, then shimmered away like the lake had swallowed them up. Bobby steadied his wrist to keep his hand from shaking, and once the phone was in his hand, he turned his back on them all.

He listened, and it was the Devil, sure enough. The man sounded exactly like Jed come back from the dead. The voice was rough and country like his daddy's, and when Bobby told him about the reward they'd got together so far, the man got mad as hellfire.

"But it's all we got," Bobby whimpered. "'How can we be sure you really got our boy?"

The kidnapper swore Juan was alive, but he wouldn't let Bobby talk to him. He said he could prove he had Juan and described the tiny scar above Juan's left eyebrow. Bobby saw it sharp as a knife to his heart. Every night when he tucked Juan into bed, he touched that little scar. "How much money do you want?"

The man claimed Juan was worth at least a tenth what he asked for the rich kid, which was five times what Bobby was offering. The Devil wanted fifty thousand by Saturday, so Bobby knew the game was up. He felt like a helpless child again, back in his parents' kitchen. As the Devil spoke, Bobby saw Jed beating on his mama, while little Bobby clamped onto his daddy's leg with his teeth. That night Jed had dragged him into the yard and hit his head with a shovel. And Bobby had crawled off to the neighbor's barn like a dying dog.

Next the Devil quoted from the Bible:

Give me John the Baptist's head on a platter. And the king was sorry, but he commanded it be given…

Bobby's stomach lurched.

"You listening?" The Devil laughed. "Unless you come up with the money, the kid's head will arrive special-delivered in a whiskey box. I'll send it right to your door."

TWENTY-SIX

We call him the preacher...

Bo didn't hear the soft footsteps in the hall, so when the door at his back flew open and hit the wall, he automatically ducked behind his desk and went for the gun in his drawer.

"Hey, don't shoot!" Carla giggled nervously as she slipped into his office. She held up two white paper bags as protection. "I come bearing gifts..."

Bo sheepishly replaced his weapon and shut the drawer. "Sorry, I didn't hear you coming. My nerves are shot."

"Yeah, so they say..." She smiled and lowered the bags to his desk.

"Who says?" The rich odor of Chinese food filled his nostrils.

"Grim Reaper says you're climbing the walls. Chill, man. Don't let this Juan McCord thing get you all bent out of shape."

Bo leaned back and massaged the tension between his eyes. His boss was trying to deal him out, and it just wasn't fair. "I don't get it. I'm the one who knows the family, I'm the one connecting all the dots."

"Maybe that's why Grim thinks you should step back and let the crisis agents step in. Maybe he doesn't want to risk you on the front lines."

"Or maybe he's so busy chasing the rat, he don't see the wolf nipping at his ass?"

"What's that supposed to mean?" Carla flopped into the chair opposite, pushed off her shoes, and lifted two shapely feet onto his lap.

Bo laughed. All the other agents left long ago to get a jump on the weekend, but Carla had stayed behind. He captured her brown toes with his darker hand and squeezed them one by one. "Is this a mercy mission, Carla?"

"I saw the light under your door and figured you needed feeding. I am in charge of Public Relations, you know."

"What kind of *relations* we talkin' here?"

Carla pulled her feet off his lap and scooted her chair back a few paces. "Strictly business, Beaufort. Employee morale is part of the job." She lifted a chilled bottle of rice wine from her oversized bag along with two paper cups from the drinking fountain.

"I like the way you do business, ma'am. Does this mean we're off duty?"

Carla pleaded the First as she heaped General Tso's chicken onto paper plates at the uncluttered end of his desk. "They say Henry Morse drew a blank on the driver's license. Too bad."

"The license was fraudulent," Bo grumbled. "This unknown subject knows how to work the system."

"You think the UNSUB's a pro?"

"Apparently he searched the local County Recorder's office and found a death certificate for a male child born the same year he was. He ordered a copy of the dead child's birth certificate, likely by mail, and then assumed his identity. He used the birth certificate to obtain a legal driver's license, then he was home free."

They ate in silence and drank more wine. The food was Bo's favorite, yet he couldn't appreciate the flavor, and nothing sat easy in his empty stomach.

"If the kidnapper isn't Horace Wadell, then who the hell is he?" Carla wondered aloud.

"I'd bet the farm he has a prison record, but all we have is his photo on the driver's license." Bo couldn't get the image out of his mind. The creep had a scar, ponytail, and evil eyes, just like the rental agent had described. If Bo asked one of the Bureau artists to render a portrait of a classic psychopath, this guy's face would emerge.

"What about fingerprints?" Carla asked.

"No such luck. The rental car was leased out after the crime. When they pulled it back in, all the trace evidence had been smudged beyond recognition."

"Tough break."

"Our profilers peg this as an impulse crime, but creating a fake license requires weeks of planning. I think the kidnapper has a whole portfolio of bogus identities he uses at will. It's a way of life for some cons. Maybe Juan's abduction was supposed to be his big payoff after a life of petty crime."

Carla put down her fork and studied him through solemn eyes. "I didn't hear the tape of the kidnapper's phone message, but I know you've listened countless times. Word is, the abductor is one sick dude."

Bo didn't want to talk about it. Reviewing the kidnapper's first call to Bobby had brought Bo's bloody nightmare back with a vengeance. The grisly, insane talk of sending the boy's severed head in a box sounded all too real, and when the asshole started quoting the Bible, Bo's gut told him the man really was capable of such an atrocity. "We call him *the preacher.*"

"Yeah, all the agents are calling him that now," Carla said. "I don't want him behind the pulpit at *my* church, though."

"Amen, sister."

The preacher's call had scared Bobby Porter so badly he couldn't remember half the conversation. Thank God they had it all on tape. Bo poured more wine, acutely aware that Carla was watching his every move. "The kidnapper demanded fifty thousand and wants the cash delivered in twenties. I can't believe the family actually raised that much money, with some help from their friends."

"Very *good* friends," Carla amended.

Everyone at the office had heard how a man named Matthew Troutman wrote a check for twenty-five thousand, no questions asked. Diana Rittenhouse went groveling to her mama and raised an additional fifteen grand. Add this money to Bobby and Juanita's life savings, and they'd come up with the ransom.

The FBI's stance on ransom payments was ambiguous. While they hated to bargain with criminals, the child's safety was always the number one priority. "Those people made an amazing grassroots effort to raise the cash." Bo smiled. "Hope it works…"

"How come they're not showing the preacher's face on TV?" Carla asked.

His stomach lurched. "The kidnapper was furious when he saw Bobby and Juanita's appeal on television. Said he'd kill the boy if anything else appeared in the media, so we intend to honor his wishes. But we do have an APB out to the police and sheriffs in five counties. They have strict orders to maintain a sharp watch, but keep their hands off. The cops have been discreet so far, but if they spot the preacher, I'm afraid they'll go ballistic and take matters into their own hands."

"God, I hope not." Carla knew better than most that public relations between federal and local authorities were often a tug o' war. Each group was territorial, and everyone was a cowboy. With a child's life at stake, however, brainless heroics were not an option.

"So tell me, Beaufort..." she continued. "How's the drop going down?"

He shot her a stern look. He wasn't inclined to share the details of a stakeout with anyone, especially when the element of surprise was critical and the risks so high. But this was Carla, after all. They'd worked together for six long years, not as intimately as he might have liked, but he knew she was close-mouthed and reliable. Even her personal life remained a mystery, because he'd never had the guts to probe her secrets.

"The preacher laid it out for us," he confided. "He made all the rules and he's calling the shots. It's set up for tomorrow afternoon in Concord. Bobby is supposed to take the cash to a convenience store directly across from the Charlotte Motor Speedway."

"Is there a race scheduled tomorrow?"

"No, but they're having speed trials. Some NASCAR superstars are running, so the place will be a zoo."

"Sounds like the preacher's looking for comfort in a crowd."

"Yeah, *he* should blend right in," Bo said bitterly. "I hope *we* will."

"What's the plan?"

"Bobby's supposed to come alone, unarmed, of course. The kidnapper knows he'll be driving his beat-up '94 Ford pickup and calculated that the drive from Troutman to Concord should take one hour. If Bobby doesn't arrive at two o'clock sharp, the deal is off."

"Good luck." Carla snorted. "What if there's a traffic snarl on Interstate 77? If there's an accident, God Himself would be late."

"That's why we're planning an early start for Mr. Porter, and *I* have the dubious honor of booting him out the door on time. After that, I'm out of it."

"What happens when Bobby gets to the convenience store in Charlotte?"

Bo sighed. Obviously she didn't understand how much he hated being cut out of the action. "Bobby was told to bring the cash in a red gym bag. When the preacher comes out of the store, he'll open a pack of Winston cigarettes and light up, so Bobby will know who he is. Then Bobby turns the red bag over to the man, they shake hands, and Bobby climbs back into his truck to wait."

"How very civilized." Carla smirked. "When does Bobby get the kid?"

"When they shake hands, the preacher will pass Bobby a sealed envelope containing the address of a motel where Juan's being held. Then Bobby is supposed to wait forty minutes before leaving to collect him."

"While the kidnapper makes a leisurely getaway, right?" Her cheeks flushed with anger. "That's bullshit, Bo. What kind of a deal is that?"

"It's the only deal we've got. Grim thinks he has it covered. He left with a crisis team an hour ago, and they'll work all night setting up a sting. Plainclothesmen will be stationed across at the Speedway, in both adjacent lots, and inside the convenience store…"

"Jesus, Bo, what will our guys be doing inside? Cutting salami or working the cash register?"

A hot rush of embarrassment crept up his neck. "Matter of fact, as we speak our guys are taking a crash course in deli management. We'll even have an agent pumping gas."

Carla giggled. "You're well out of it, Bo."

Not true. He beat down his disappointment and glared at her. How could he expect her to understand? She wasn't the one in need of redemption. Tomorrow's confrontation could have been his one perfect chance to make up for past mistakes. Again he saw the three-year-old victim, her mutilated body abandoned in the old warehouse, and fought the horror rising in his throat.

141

Carla reached out to him. She took his hand and lifted his fingers to her lips. Her kiss was soft as a butterfly's wing. "Let it go, Bo," she whispered. With her free hand, she touched the hot contours of his face. "Let Grim handle it."

"Something doesn't feel right," he told her. "God help us all…"

"That sounded like a prayer. I never took you for a religious man."

Had she thought of him as a *man* at all? A powerful sense of longing, of time lost, invaded his spirit. Impulsively, he captured the small hand touching his face and flattened it against his chest, so she could feel his beating heart.

"When this is all over, will you go out with me, Carla?"

This time, it was a prayer.

TWENTY-SEVEN

Not a team player...

Bo arrived at the Porter's house too early. Because it was Saturday, only a handful of laborers were at work erecting an impressive stone monument at the entrance to the park. He spotted the agent assigned to guard Juanita today. Disguised as a workman, the FBI man was leaning against his car smoking a cigarette. When the man lifted his hand in a listless greeting, Bo realized the sentry was bored out of his mind.

Bo wasn't bored, he was wired. After parting with Carla last night, he'd called Max Grim at the stakeout in Charlotte and begged for a role in the ransom drop. Finally Max had tired of his whining and assigned him a job as Bobby's tail. His part would be one step removed from the real action, but it beat twiddling his thumbs.

As he entered the Porter's small house, the couple's nervous energy charged the space like electric current coursing through a fish tank. The door swung open even before he knocked, and as Bobby and Juanita bounced around the living room, Bo got the jitters, too.

He saw two untouched plates of food on the table. "Hey, why don't you folks sit down and finish your breakfast? We have plenty of time."

"The eggs are cold..." Juanita paced the kitchen. "So I'll fix us some lunch." She scurried from the refrigerator to the counter, each time trading one plastic container for another in helpless indecision. The special phone the agents had given her, a hotline connecting with the FBI, never left her hand.

"She's strung tighter than a drum," Bobby confided in a whisper. "She ain't finished one thing she started all day."

"How are you holding up, Bobby?"

"Fair to middlin', but I'm ready. Here, I'll show you…"

The bright red streaks staining Bobby's normally pale neck and face implied that Bobby wasn't good at all. He watched the agitated man drag an enormous red bag out from under the table.

"The money's all here, Beaufort—fifty thousand, like he said." Bobby unzipped the bag and brought out fat wads of banded twenties, each pack worth one thousand dollars. "I went to K-Mart and had me some trouble finding a bag big enough to hold it all. You wanna count it?"

"No thanks, Bobby, I trust you. But what the hell were you doing at K-Mart? We assigned an agent to buy that bag."

"Yeah, and I told that agent to take a hike. I won't be a prisoner in my own house."

Bo exhaled in exasperation. Bobby was a brave man, but he was not a team player, and that bore watching. So did Bo's blood pressure. He felt tension building in his veins and chugging even faster through his heart as he observed the couple's antics. Neither sat down, nor did they invite him to sit. They bickered about everything from what to fix Juan for his homecoming dinner, to which shirt Bobby should wear to pick him up. Their manic behavior set Bo's teeth on edge. Christ, they were talking like parents retrieving their kid from summer camp.

By the time Bo escorted Bobby to his truck, he was emotionally exhausted. "You remember the plan, right?" He coached. "I go first. You wait ten minutes, then follow."

"Yeah, I got it," Bobby said. "You wait for me at the ramp to Interstate 77, then I pass by like you ain't even there."

"You know the way to the Speedway, right Bobby?"

Bobby smiled. "When I was a young man, I could find that Speedway with a blindfold on my eyes."

He hoped Bobby's current sense of direction was equally sound. "Now remember, I have to stay out of sight, several cars back. If you get lost, I can't help you, Bobby."

Bobby nodded solemnly, but the color drained completely from his face and his eyes seemed uncertain. Bo knew he could grill the man until doom's day, hoping to avoid the one slip that could cost lives. And though Bobby was his senior, Bo felt almost paternal towards the trembling little man. "What happens when you get to the convenience store?" He asked more gently.

"I wait till he lights his cigarette, then I give him the money."

"That's right, now raise your arms. I have to check you for a weapon, Bobby."

His eyes widened as Bo patted him down, and then he automatically spread his legs. For some reason, it hurt to see that Bobby was no stranger to the drill.

"Told you I was clean." Bobby was also hurt, because Bo didn't trust him.

"Well, you better be clean. Juan's life is at stake, and we have to play by the book." Without further words, Bo climbed into his car and drove away. He did not look back.

Bobby's old Ford pickup merged onto I77 right on schedule, and he kept to the right lane, as agreed. Bo waited until a string of traffic flowed between them before pulling onto the Interstate. Trailing Bobby would be tricky. He couldn't follow too close, but he also couldn't allow Bobby to get into trouble. In spite of what Bo had implied, if anything did go wrong—flat tire, overheating, missed turn—he'd be watching Bobby's back and would fix the trouble, because absolutely nothing could get in the way of the rendezvous with the kidnappers.

He tapped the sentinel button above his rearview mirror, and the digital readout said 94 degrees. Hot as hell, and they were heading due south. So far, so good. Heat shimmered from the blacktop and sun glanced off the chrome of passing cars. The glare stung Bo's eyes and aggravated the headache that had plagued him all morning. Drinking that fourth cup of coffee had been a big mistake, because now it was sloshing around in his stomach like battery acid.

He imagined the scene at the stakeout, the details running through his brain in vivid Technicolor. He saw agents in place in the parking lots and the convenience store. He pictured scenarios where everything went wrong.

He couldn't help himself, because he'd seen too many perfect plans go sour. Today offered too many variables. This perfect summer day would bring every beer-guzzling yahoo out to the racetrack. The human mix complicated everything, and poor Bobby was a time bomb waiting to blow. Already he was behaving erratically, Bo noted as he peered up the highway and saw the Ford pickup passing a caravan of semi-trailers. What was Bobby doing? They had agreed to stay in the right lane and drive safely. With only twenty-some miles to their exit, they had the luxury of time.

Damn! A slow-moving car carrier pulled up beside Bo, blocking him from shifting into the passing lane. Up ahead, Bobby had picked up speed. If Bo hadn't know better, he'd have sworn Bobby was trying to lose him.

Bobby was carrying a dedicated cell phone, in case they needed to communicate, and Bo was poised to dial, ready to tell Bobby to cool it, when he took an opening into the passing lane and closed the distance between them. He figured Bobby was nervous and that his burst of speed was unintentional. Sure enough, ahead and around the bend, Bobby had eased right and was slowing down.

But then Bobby veered off the highway at the Mooresville exit. *Jesus Christ!* Bo cursed and panicked. He nearly rear-ended a small compact as he floored the gas and jerked into the exit lane. An angry chorus of horns blared as he nosed in between a boat trailer and a UPS truck on the ramp, and hardly noticed when the UPS driver saluted with his middle finger. Instead, Bo's mind weighed the possibilities. Was Bobby having car trouble? If there was a major problem, then time was no longer a luxury.

He jabbed his phone's speed dial, programmed directly to Bobby. It rang and rang, but Bobby wouldn't pick up. *What the hell?* Either Bobby had forgotten to turn on his phone, or he was choosing to ignore it. *Shit!* Bo craned his neck to see around the brown walls of the UPS truck and spotted the old pickup turning west on River Highway. If car trouble was the issue, then Bobby was headed in the wrong direction. All the repair shops were east, on the way into town.

Bo started to sweat. He could no longer fool himself—Bobby had his own agenda, and that agenda was a complete unknown. Bo hits another button on his phone, and in seconds Supervisory Special Agent Maxfield Grim was on the line. His boss, whom he had interrupted at the stakeout, listened in ominous silence as Bo explained. First Bo heard a heavy rasping sound as the Grim Reaper sucked oxygen into his smoke-damaged lungs, then the rough rattle of his voice:

"Damn. The preacher got to him."

Grim's words confirmed Bo's worst fears.

"But how?" Bo moaned. "We have that house wired up tight. No call gets through without us hearing it."

Max Grim sighed. "Maybe Bobby's got his own cell phone, one we don't know about. Point is, something's happened, Beaufort, now what the hell are you gonna do about it?"

The use of his full name startled Bo. Never before had Grim called him anything but *Agent Miller,* and this aberration alone scared the shit out of him. "I won't lose him, sir."

"Damn right you won't, but we better get you some backup ASAP. Say again, where are you…?"

Bo finally got a green light and made a right turn off the ramp, but Bobby had disappeared. "I'm moving west on River Highway, but I've lost visual contact…"

"Shit," Grim muttered. "That highway doesn't run but one direction, so Porter's not far ahead. Get moving, son, but keep a close watch to both sides of the road. It's a mess up there, a tangle of gas stations, marinas, and local taverns. Since Porter has the money with him, we have to assume the kidnapper's given him new instructions. If Bobby pulls off *anywhere,* he's going for the drop. Do you understand?"

Bo grunted in the affirmative. Again Grim's words confirmed the fear that now grasped his heart like a boa constrictor. He pictured the team in Concord, how Grim would be forced to abort the operation and send the men home.

The preacher's plan was brilliant. There wasn't an FBI agent with a hope in hell of reaching Bo in time. He was on his own. "What about backup, sir?"

Grim ground his teeth. "When you cross a big bridge across Lake Norman, you'll be straddling the line between Iredell and Catawba Counties. That means the Iredell police are behind you, and the Catawba Sheriff's dead ahead."

"Can you call them *both?*" Bo laughed nervously as he caught sight of Bobby's truck stopped at a light, with only a half dozen vehicles between them. "I see Bobby, sir. He's at a traffic light."

"Good. That light means you're at Perth Road, so I'll call in the coordinates. You won't hit another light until you reach a little country store at Terrell, then again at the Denver intersection of Highway 16."

Grim made this predicament sound like a vacation cruise, but Bo sensed he was in hostile territory. Exactly how long would it take these local authorities to come to his aid?

"Don't worry, son, we'll call in the troops. Stay on speaker, and for Christ sake Beaufort, don't be a hero." Grim cleared his throat. "Stick on Porter like a fly on shit, but don't make a move until help arrives."

Bo swallowed hard, and then muttered his compliance. In his wildest dreams, he'd never thought he'd miss the Grim Reaper, but when Max's voice crackled off the line, he felt an awful void where the old man had been.

Sunshine streamed across the highway, which was crowded with Saturday revelers. Cars towed expensive boats, and the atmosphere was festive. Bo kept Bobby's truck in sight, but his mind wandered. He noticed the lush green summer foliage lifting at the roadside and how brilliantly blue the lake was as he crossed one, then two bridges. Somehow he was numb, allowing the world around him to blur the horror of his own reality. He willed himself to think about Carla, the soft warmth of her lips when they'd kissed last night. And he watched the sailboats, their white wings floating like doves of peace.

How would it feel to drift free in the wind?

TWENTY- EIGHT

Much like a dream...

Bo looked around after he crossed the third bridge and noticed a subtle shift in the atmosphere. The change brought him sharply back to his senses. A Confederate flag was boldly stenciled across the tailgate of a pickup truck filled with three shirtless, sunburned country boys with nothing better to do than stare backwards at Bo. Was it his imagination, or had the truck slowed down when the driver spotted a black man in his rearview mirror?

This delay widened the gap between himself and Bobby, and even after the truck turned off down a dusty road, Bo's paranoia increased. It wasn't just the rednecks—the mood of the very landscape had changed. The resort traffic had thinned out. Instead of expensive, gated developments, he saw trailer camps and a makeshift Baptist church. Bo has crossed an invisible line from the New South into the Old South, which he feared beyond reason.

He addressed the speaker. "Are you with me, sir? Porter's still up ahead, but no sign of the local police." Bo hated the note of fear in his voice. As he waited for his boss, he vowed to put his old ghosts behind.

"Don't worry, we've got your back, Agent Miller," a stranger's voice answered. "Help's on the way, so hang in, sir."

It pained him that Grim himself had not responded, but then Bo had to laugh. The rookie at the other end had called him *sir,* when Bo felt utterly unworthy of such respect. Up ahead, the traffic light's green eye blinked to yellow, then red. At the same time, Bobby's brake lights came on as he stopped. Only two cars between them now. If Bobby knew Bo was on his tail, he didn't show it. Even at that distance, Bobby's somber profile was carved of white marble as he stared straight ahead.

When the light changed, Bobby passed through the intersection, then turned abruptly into a parking lot. Bo hit the brakes and turned in after him, keeping a discreet distance between them as he got his bearings. He saw an ABC store crowded with customers stocking up on booze for the weekend and a pair of gas pumps under a weather-worn Phillips 66 sign. Bobby pulled to the far side of the lot near the road, then turned off his engine, leaving room for cars to pass through for fuel. Bo counted six other cars and saw several people entering an old concrete block building set back from the pumps. Bobby made no move to leave his truck, but his head swiveled towards the door of the concrete building. What the hell was he up to?

Bo maneuvered to where he could surveil the scene without calling undue attention to himself, and then shut down his own engine. Heat built up inside his car, so he powered down the windows. Sweat pooled under his shirt, so he loosened his tie. He longed to shed his jacket, but it concealed the gun and shoulder holster hanging heavy on his ribs.

The concrete building had a narrow front with heavy iron bars on its one small window. A faded red awning mounted above a steel security door said Kit n' Pete's Sportsman's Store. Bo's heart raced with dread—the place was a gun shop. Images of White Supremacists crowded his mind. They waved their hoods and shouted epithets at Bo. He told himself to get a grip and focus on reality. He spoke into the speaker, relaying his situation and position.

"Good job, Miller…" another strange voice responded. "Sit tight. The Catawba sheriff's in the neighborhood."

Bo groaned. Okay, the good guys had a fix on his dilemma, but time was passing. Scanning the lot again, he saw one car with a lone occupant. The vehicle was a tan, late-model Ford Escort with a rental agency sticker on the back windshield. The driver was a large blond, much like the mystery man Diana Rittenhouse had seen at the Open House.

Adrenaline jolted through his body as he strained to see inside the car's dark interior. No sign of the plastic purse woman or the boy, but was it possible? Maybe little Juan was lying on the back seat? Bo had always had a second sense about these things. Was the prize less than ten yards away, yet hopelessly beyond reach?

As minutes passed, the blond man glanced at Bobby, then quickly looked away. But Bobby noticed the look and stared back from across the lot. The longer Bobby stared, the more agitated the man became. Bobby seemed like a bomb about to detonate in this explosive situation, so if this was really the ransom drop, what the hell was he waiting for?

Bo decided the blond guy wasn't working alone. Clearly everyone was waiting for some kind of signal, so likely the preacher was inside the Sportsman's Store. When he stepped outside, all hell could break loose, and Bo couldn't risk it.

"I'm going in..." he told whoever was listening.

"Negative, Miller!" Grim himself responded. "Take one step out of your car, and you're fucked!"

"Sorry, sir, too many bystanders. If our man's in there, someone's gonna get hurt."

Until a moment ago, he'd never heard his boss resort to obscenities, but as Bo disconnected, Grim's language would make a teamster blush.

Bo's legs were jelly as he crossed the concrete. He felt the blond guy's eyes follow him through the security door, and once

152

inside the dim space, he was assaulted by curious stares. His old goblins raised their ugly heads. He imagined the angry snarls of Ku Klux Klansmen superimposed on the faces of everyone in the store. He knew he was crazy. On the other hand, he'd bet a month's pay that black men seldom entered this place.

As his eyes adjusted, he saw the space was much bigger than it appeared from outside. It was laid out in a series of narrow, deep rooms. The first room was relatively innocent, devoted to fishing gear with a display of stuffed bass on the walls. The next passage was reserved for rack after rack of camouflage clothing and a bow and arrow display. Heads of slain deer adorned the hall. Their glassy eyes gazed down mournfully at the weapons of their destruction and the fashions worn by the well-dressed killer.

Next came the firing range, where for a fee, fathers could teach their sons how to shoot. These sons could whip up a good healthy blood lust—family values to pass down to the next generation.

Finally, Bo entered the gun sales room. It was almost as impressive as the firearms display at Quantico. The walls were lined with glass cases filled with rifles, carbines, and shotguns, while the cases below housed revolvers, semiautomatics, and enough ammunition for a third world army. Best of all, the featured assault weapons were currently available to the general public, thanks to Congress for allowing the ban to expire.

Bo took a deep breath, his mind reeling with the futility of it all. His eyes probed the room, seeking the face he had memorized from the bogus driver's license. He saw children much younger than the Columbine kids who'd shot up their school, some the same age as the first grade victims at Sandy Hook. Their little noses were pressed against the glass cases, hopeful that Santa would leave a shiny new gun under the tree.

Then, as Bo's gaze traveled up to adult level, he spotted the ponytail. The shock of seeing the preacher, just as he had visualized him in nightmares, caught him off guard. The man was smaller than he had imagined. He wore boots, jeans, and a black T-shirt depicting the agonized face of Christ on the cross. He was showing his Beretta Minx to the man behind the counter, asking to buy a magazine of cartridges.

For a split second, the preacher turned and they were face to face. Bo struggled to keep his expression neutral, but when the preacher registered surprise, then anger, then unconcealed hatred, Bo had to turn away. The man's eyes glowed like the burning coals of hell. Was it racial prejudice, or had Bo been made? With as much cool as he could muster, he turned and casually left the store. If a confrontation was inevitable, it would be less harmful if it occurred outside.

The sun blinded him—much like a dream. Heat shimmered in slow motion just above the pavement. Colors were so intense they hurt his eyes—bright blue metal case for the local paper, orange case for the Charlotte Observer. Outside the barred window, a white ice chest hummed like crickets on a hot night.

Bo casually dropped two quarters into the orange case and lifted out a newspaper. As he leaned against the wall and pretended to read, he saw the preacher coming out. The Beretta was still in his hand. He shoved in the magazine.

Then three things happened at once: The blond man stepped from the Escort and pulled a gun from under his jacket. Across the parking lot, Bobby spotted the gun and climbed from his truck, holding the red gym bag. Finally, the preacher lit up a cigarette.

That was the signal! Bo could hardly breathe. The preacher had flicked his lighter with one hand, while balancing his weapon and cigarette in the other. He grinned and winked at Bo, then turned his back, cupping his hands to shield the flame from the wind. Bo reached under his jacket for his Glock, but the preacher spun to face him, his gun pointed at Bo's chest.

Bo viewed the barrel point blank and the words *Jesus Loves You* on the front of the preacher's shirt. He heard the explosion and felt the bullet pass through his hand before it entered his heart.

TWENTY-NINE

The distant wail of sirens...

Bobby's eardrums shattered with the explosion as Bo jolted backwards, then lay lifeless on the concrete. Bobby dropped the red bag, and Bo's blood gushed in a river towards his shoes. At the same time, the blond man rushed at Bobby, his weapon drawn.

Adrenaline flooded Bobby's veins as he dove behind the door of his truck. Lying prone on the seat, he lifted Jed's shotgun from its hiding place in the boot, then rolled outside, using the door for cover.

The blond man pointed his gun, but hesitated a moment to reach down and grab the red bag. In that split second, Bobby aimed the old Winchester and fired. The blast sent the blond reeling across the lot, but then Bobby heard another explosion. A searing, red-hot pain burned his shoulder and his head cracked against concrete.

Every fiber of his being screamed at him to get up and run, but Bobby couldn't move. Gravel scraped his cheek, and his arm was twisted all wrong under him. Through the haze of agony, he watched the man with the ponytail disappear around the building. He heard the distant wail of sirens before his world turned black.

THIRTY

The hush of death...

The elevator lurched upwards, leaving her stomach on the first floor. Diana clung to Matthew's arm as the numbered buttons blinked, then chimed, and the door sighed open, spilling them into the brightly lit hallway of the Critical Wing.

Muffled hospital sounds always filled her with dread. "You okay, Matthew?"

"I'd rather be fishing." He smiled half-heartedly and gave her hand a reassuring squeeze.

All they knew about yesterday's tragedy was gleaned from the evening news: *bungled ransom exchange...federal agent dead...two men injured.* Not much to go on. Only one week ago, at the Open House, unspeakable violence had entered her life and it wouldn't go away. She didn't know why it had knocked at her door, but she was sick of speculating. Though the violence was indirect, like an assault on her *neighbor's* house, she was dizzy with guilt and grief.

Matthew pulled her close as they hovered outside Bobby's door, but her attention strayed to two uniformed officers. They were guarding the Intensive Care unit at the far end of the hall. "The jerk who shot Bobby's in that room," Matthew informed her. "A nurse told me the buckshot tore him up pretty good. He's in a coma."

Diana couldn't muster any sympathy for Bobby's attacker, but she was amazed by Matthew's ability to elicit information from total strangers. She'd left his side for only a moment to visit the restroom, and he'd used the opportunity to charm privileged information from some nurse.

"I'd like to get a closer look at that fella," he continued darkly. "From his picture on the news, I feel like maybe I know him."

"How could you possibly know him? Besides, they won't let you see him." Matthew's tone frightened her, but in fact, the snapshot of the boyish, innocent-looking young man shown on TV had looked familiar to her, too. He resembled the blond she'd seen waiting in the car at the Open House.

"Ready?" Matthew asked gently.

In truth, she was terrified to enter Bobby's private room, afraid of what she might find. Nothing made sense anymore. Bo Miller was dead, and little Juan was still out there somewhere—alone, frightened, or worse. The image was so unbearable that everyone avoided speaking Juan's name. This avoidance scared her even more, like evading the word *cancer* when everyone knew the patient was terminal.

She swallowed hard as Matthew pulled her towards the room, but suddenly the door flew open and Juanita Cruz burst into the hall. She sobbed and cursed in Spanish as she elbowed past Diana, then thrashed free of Matthew's concerned grasp.

"God, what's wrong?" Naturally, Diana feared the worst. A bitter, antiseptic odor drifted into the hall, along with the hush of death. She tasted fear at the back of her throat as Matthew reached out to steady Juanita.

"Leave me the hell alone! Both of you!" Juanita broke loose and bolted for the elevator.

"We best take a look..." Matthew's voice was hoarse with emotion.

But she couldn't tear her eyes from Juanita, who pounded her fists against the elevator before staggering inside. "No, I'll follow Juanita. She shouldn't be alone right now."

Before he could stop her, she pulled away. Seconds later, she was jabbing the elevator button, her heart pounding somewhere outside her chest. As she waited, the floor indicator lights followed Juanita's progress to lobby level.

When Diana finally boarded, the blasted lift stopped at the next floor to admit chattering interns headed for the cafeteria. When they finally reached the lobby, she shoved them all aside just in time to spot Juanita's purple halter-top flashing through the glass exit doors. Instead of heading towards the parking lot, Juanita ran across the lawn, scrambled over a stone embankment, and then jogged into a naturalized area that fell away to a pond. Diana sprinted after her. These grounds were off-limits to visitors, but Juanita kept running towards the water. Did the fool woman intend to drown herself?

Diana's sandals snagged in the heavy ground cover. Heat hit her like a wall, yet she managed to gain enough ground to see Juanita's platform heel catch on the stony bank. She tumbled down the steep hill, barely latching onto a young willow that saved her from a swim.

"What on earth do you think you're doing?" Diana panted. Juanita was sprawled out on the ground. Her hands and knees were skinned. Mascara streamed down her cheeks as she lifted agonized eyes.

"It's all *my* fault!" She choked as Diana looked on in horror.

Matthew's eyes slowly adjusted to the dim light. The room was unnaturally cold and reeked of antiseptic. The lump in his throat swelled as he observed the inert figure on the bed. Bobby's entire torso was encased in a cast, his right arm strung up to a network of

159

pulleys. A weak ray of sunlight bled through glass, illuminating bubbles in an IV bottle, its tube inserted in the patient's left arm. Bobby's eyes were wide open and unflinching—staring lifelessly at the door.

"How are you feeling, buddy?" Matthew's words were barely a whisper.

Gradually, Bobby's eyes focused in recognition, and he waggled his fingers in a greeting. Matthew was so relieved to find his friend still alive, that he failed to sense another presence in the room. But as he stood in silence, smiling at Bobby, hairs began prickling on the back of his neck.

Matthew jolted when he saw the stranger. "Who the hell are you?"

The man's heavy neck and sagging face were silhouetted at the foot of the bed. An unlit cigarette dangled between his thick lips, and his pasty complexion was the color of death.

His smile exposed a row of small, tobacco-stained teeth. "I'm Grim, FBI. You are Troutman, correct?"

Matthew grunted, but did not offer his hand. He turned to Bobby. "Is this man giving you a hard time, pal? Say the word, and I'll boot him out."

The flicker of a grin played across Bobby's face, then quickly faded. "This FBI asshole pissed Juanita off real bad. Did you see her run out, Trout?"

"Yeah, Diana followed her."

The news seemed to relax Bobby. He lifted his index finger off the sheet and pointed at Grim. "He's replacing Beaufort. I reckon we're stuck with him."

Matthew frowned at Grim. The name sure suited the old geezer. He must be doing something right for the Bureau to keep him on at his age, but his bedside manner left something to be desired.

160

"I'm really sorry about Bo," Matthew offered with sincerity. "He seemed like a good man."

Grim cleared his throat. His baggy eyes were rimmed with red. "Bo was one of our best agents. It's a great loss for our department."

He sensed that Bo and Grim had been close, but Grim was too hard-nosed to admit it.

A sad, haunted look invaded Bobby's odd eyes. "I was just telling him how weird it was. Both the kidnappers were waving their guns and shooting up the place. I saw Bo go down, but I never saw him draw his weapon."

"Why not?" Grim asked gruffly.

Bobby licked his dry lips and closed his eyes. "I figure the psycho with the ponytail spotted him inside. Bo didn't fit in, know what I mean? He never had a chance. Ponytail come out of the store set on killing him. He just turned, took aim, and blew him away."

Matthew tried to concentrate, but Bobby's account was almost too painful to bear. Bobby couldn't remember what happened after he was shot, and Grim said the witnesses at the scene had all offered conflicting testimony. The blond man Bobby nailed had been driving a rental car, but no trace of Juan's fingerprints was found inside. The killer with the ponytail had escaped in a truck, but no one could verify the make, model, or even which direction he had taken.

"The bystanders were hysterical." Grim tugged at his ear. "Noise, confusion, and blood everywhere. Two of the witnesses require therapy, and the others have suffered amnesia." He pulled the unlit cigarette from his mouth and rolled it between his thumb and index finger. "At least we've now identified the kidnappers. Bobby's shooter, the kid down the hall in the ICU, is Darryl Clontz. The one we call *the preacher* is his uncle Floyd Clontz. Young Darryl had no criminal record until now, but Uncle Floyd has a history long as my arm."

161

"Will you release those names on television?" Matthew asked. "Someone's bound to know them."

Grim growled deep in his throat. "If I had my way, we'd leave the blasted reporters out of the loop, but it's too late now. The media is on this thing like turkey buzzards."

"Makes you FBI guys look like royal fuckups." Bobby smirked.

"That's not the point," Grim said. "Before we go plastering Floyd's face on the post office wall, remember, he promised to kill Juan if he sees any more publicity."

Matthew wandered to the window and gazed out at the grounds. He saw Diana and Juanita seated under a willow tree. As the silence in the room deepened, he dragged his eyes from the women and sat on the edge of Bobby's bed.

"Floyd Clontz was dishonorably discharged," Grim continued. "He sliced a fellow enlisted man in a knife fight, so the army booted him out. Then he started getting into scrapes with the law. That same year, the soldier Floyd cut was found murdered in his cot, his neck severed under the jaw."

"Jesus, Floyd tried to cut the guy's head off? That's what he said he'd do to Juan!" Bobby cried.

"They never proved Clontz was the murderer, but the authorities down at Lejeune have suspected it for years." Grim started to pace. "In the meantime, Floyd's been in and out of prison for everything from petty con games to armed robbery." He pinned Bobby with one angry, drooping eye. "He's a mean son of a bitch, Mr. Porter, but I promise you, every law enforcement agency in the Southeast is looking for the bastard. We know the Clontz family hails from West Virginia, so we have an APB out in the Wheeling area as well. Catching Beaufort's killer is our top priority."

Matthew took Bobby's hand, but couldn't meet his friend's worried eyes. Grim seemed hell bent on avenging Agent Miller, but in Matthew's opinion, Juan, not Bo, should be their top priority. He hoped the FBI wouldn't drop the ball. "What about the money? Can you trace it?"

A strange look came over Bobby's face, while Grim seemed embarrassed and looked away.

"The preacher didn't get the money. He ran like chicken shit and forgot to pick up the bag." Bobby sighed. "Agent Grim took it away for safe keeping, but to my way of thinking, that's *our* money, and they got no right to hold it. Juanita told him to give it back, then freaked when he said no. That's when she ran out. What do *you* think, Trout?"

THIRTY-ONE

A web of deceit...

"It's all my fault," Juanita repeated.

Oblivious to the rocks and mud, Diana scooted under the willow and sat down beside her. "But what about Bobby? Is he all right?" She wasn't sure she wanted to hear the answer. The atmosphere had been bleak outside Bobby's hospital room, so she still expected the worst.

"That old FBI man's a jerk!" Juanita choked back tears. "He's up there talking to Bobby right now, and he blames *me* for not telling Bo about *my* cell phone."

Diana's mind reeled as she tried to piece it all together. If Bobby was talking to the FBI, at least he was alive.

"Bo had already driven off, planning to follow Bobby..." Juanita continued. "Bobby was already on the highway heading towards the speedway, when the call came in on my cell. Bobby had my phone in his pocket, so he answered the kidnapper's call."

Diana knew the Porter's ground lines had been tapped, with agents listening in on all calls, so what was this about?

"I never told Bo about *my* phone because it's dedicated to my beauty salon customers," Juanita explained. "I keep it with me at all times, so people can reach me after hours to make appointments. It just seemed like a good idea for Bobby to carry it with him that day, so we could keep in touch. But that's how the kidnapper contacted Bobby. How the hell did he get my business number?"

Diana's brain raced ahead. Juanita's failure to tell the authorities about her private cell phone had been a tragic mistake. "Listen, Juanita, one of the kidnappers must have recognized you from the television appeal. Maybe he knew where you worked and got your number that way?"

Her eyes darted in panic. "Christ, if he knows where I work, what if he knows where I live?"

Diana knew agents had been stationed full time at the entrance to the Porter residence, yet the implications were terrifying. "I think you're safe at home," she said without conviction.

"Bo had also warned Bobby not to take a gun, but thank God, Bobby didn't listen. He hid his daddy's old Winchester away in the boot—otherwise Bobby would be dead, too."

Juanita lifted her eyes as a passing cloud crosses the sun. "Do you know what the kidnapper said to Bobby before he ran away? That bastard claimed he had Juan right there with him. By all that's holy, Diana, Bobby said he spoke these exact words:

And Abraham bound his son, and laid him on the altar, then took the knife to slay his son...

"He called our little Juan the *sacrificial lamb*. He said Juan's blood was on *our* hands if Bobby didn't do exactly what he said."

Clearly this kidnapper was insane. Diana watched in helpless silence as Juanita pulled into herself. She sensed the woman was still holding something back, but what could Diana do?

In the meantime, a group of Latino gardeners had assembled on the far side of the pond. At first Diana thought they'd come to chase them back to where they belonged, but then realized the men were staring at Juanita. No wonder! Juanita's enormous breasts were bulging from her laced halter, while her long legs dangled seductively from tight shorty jeans.

165

"Ignore them." Juanita snorted derisively. "I dress this way for Bobby, not for them." She dug into her purse and brought out a jeweled cigarette case and the infamous cell phone. She set the phone on a rock, tapped out a slim cigarillo, and lit up. "You don't smoke, do you, Diana?"

Juanita's tone implied that Diana was incapable of human vice. In fact, Diana had given up smoking several years ago, but she'd kill for a puff about then.

The Mexicans started catcalling. One boy made a rude gesture with a hose at the front of his trousers. In response, Juanita screamed obscenities in Spanish, surprising the men to silence. They retreated to the far side of the grounds when Juanita jabbed the middle finger of her right hand into the air.

"Fucking retards..." she muttered as she lifted the phone off the rock and stared at the instrument. "From now on those FBI clowns will be listening in on *my* calls, too."

That sounded like a prudent plan to Diana, but obviously Juanita did not approve. The cloud that had drifted over the sun darkened like an angry bruise, and a skim of rain drenched Interstate 77 in the distance.

"Don't you get it, Diana? The FBI should have been listening before. Now it's too late."

And whose fault was that? Diana watched as a personal storm filled Juanita's eyes and streamed down her face. Diana found a wad of Kleenex in her pocket and passed it to the woman.

"I haven't told Agent Grim, but that jackass he calls *the preacher* called again last night," Juanita suddenly confessed. "He called after the TV news, right after I got off the phone with Bobby in the hospital. When the creep introduced himself, I near shit my pants. He was drunk and mean, Diana. He called me a harlot and a whore—and worse. I can't tell you."

166

Diana was truly stunned. "The kidnapper called you last night?"

Juanita blew her nose. "He was loco, comprende? He said his nephew's blood was on Bobby's hands. He said we have to pay double now to wash our hands clean."

Diana crawled closer and wrapped her arms around the trembling woman. "He demanded more ransom?"

"One hundred thousand dollars, or Juan will die! The preacher said he'd carve Juan up on the altar of our sins, and he wants the money in one week, before the next Sabbath."

Diana's last hope drained away along with the gentle rain streaming down her skin. She knew for a fact that Matthew had already contributed his last penny to the cause. Her mother, after putting Diana through holy hell, had also given all she could afford. Diana had no funds left, while Juanita and Bobby were dead broke. "What did you tell the kidnapper, Juanita?"

"I said we'd get the money!" she wailed. "What else could I say? That's why I told Agent Grim I want the money back *now*. It's only half, but God willing, we'll get the rest somehow."

Diana wanted to believe in God's goodness, but just then a miracle seemed unlikely. "What does Bobby say about all this?"

"I didn't tell him. He's sick and hurting. It would kill him if he finds out."

She appreciated Juanita's instinct to protect her man, but this secret was far too deadly to keep. "You have to tell Agent Grim," she told her.

"No way! That man doesn't care about Juan. All the old fart wants is to get even for Bo's death."

Her heart ached for Juanita. She was carrying this burden alone, heading for a breakdown. "I'm sorry, but we have to tell him," she gently insisted.

Juanita's long fingernails bit into her arm. "If you say one word, I'll kill you, Diana. I swear I will. You can tell Trout, that's all, but if he opens his mouth…"

Tears filled Diana's eyes as she pried herself loose. She couldn't make a promise she wouldn't keep, and she refused to be caught up in a web of deceit.

Long hair clung in sodden black strands around Juanita's stricken face. She shoved the cell phone into her bag, stumbled up the hillside, and never looked back. Diana followed, but by the time she reached the parking lot, Juanita had escaped. The taillights of Bobby's old truck were two bloodshot eyes disappearing into the gloom.

Diana exhaled in defeat. She had tried to comfort Juanita, but instead, she'd made matters worse. Now the woman had fled, and nothing had been resolved. She stomped her sandals and ran fingers through her short hair. She was soaked, dirty, and totally exasperated as she stepped under the hospital awning and spotted a strange man lurking nearby.

He stood in the shelter of the awning, not ten feet away. He had thin, grizzled hair and the thick, hunched body of an aging bull. Something about the way his eyes moved restlessly under drooping lids, the way the collar of his rumpled rain coat tucked up around his jowls, convinced her that he was the FBI agent Juanita had described.

She looked around for Matthew, but he was nowhere in sight, so she boldly approached the pillar where the man leaned, chain-smoking.

"Hello, I'm Diana Rittenhouse." She extended a wet hand.

The man blinked in surprise as he shook her hand. "Max Grim," he answered curtly. "I've been upstairs with your friends."

She sensed a sudden, compelling connection. She appreciated his no-nonsense approach, the lack of preliminaries, and in spite of everything she'd just heard, she instinctively trusted the man. They stood in silence, appraising one another, until Grim dropped his cigarette and ground it under his heel.

"What can I do for you, ma'am?"

This was her opportunity to betray Juanita and reveal everything she knew about the kidnapper's phone call, but instead, she searched the man's face and saw his pain.

"I'm so sorry about Bo Miller," she told him. "I'd like to attend his funeral."

Again Grim blinked in surprise. "That's kind of you, Mrs. Rittenhouse. Believe me, I want to go, too, but I can't leave town just now."

They stood side by side, watching the rain until Max Grim continued.

"As soon as the Medical Examiner's done with his body, we'll follow Beaufort's instructions to the letter. He wanted to be cremated, his ashes scattered on Beaufort Inlet down on the coast. Half the department's already on the road. One gal, our Director of Public Relations, was so upset she up and quit on us...." Grim paused, surprised to have shared so much information with a total stranger.

"I am so sorry, Agent Grim. Is there anything I can do?"

He slowly shook his head, prepared to walk away. "Maybe there is one thing you can do, ma'am...." He tapped out another cigarette. "We have an ugly mess on our hands, and the worst is still ahead. Could you say a little prayer...for us *all*?"

He turned and left before she could respond. Disarmed, she'd failed to tell him Juanita's secret. Should she chase after him? The flame from Grim's lighter was quickly receding through the mist, yet she hesitated. She would not break Juanita's trust quite yet, not until she'd sought the advice of one other person, who was just then exiting the hospital.

"Matthew, over here!" From his defeated gate, she saw he was tired and worried, emotions he never revealed except in unguarded moments.

"Hey, Diana!" He smiled, his unguarded moment was over. "What happened to you? Bobby and I were waiting…"

"Hey, yourself!" She called back. "Do you have any money, Matthew?"

He approached, a puzzled look on his face. "Why? Do you need a loan?"

If he only knew! Unfortunately, he didn't have the kind of money she'd love to give Juanita. "I need food," she answered. "I'm starving."

Matthew looked her up and down, his gaze lingering on her soaking, mud-stained backside. "You expect me to take you out to dinner looking like that?" He chuckled.

She wrapped her arm around his waist. "No, but will you buy some takeout to share with Juanita? Let's follow her home. She's in trouble, and she needs our help."

THIRTY-TWO

Never trust a woman…

Floyd Clontz stared out at the rain. It came down heavy, beating on the trailer walls until he felt like a sardine laid out in a tin can. It streamed down the dirty windows as he peered at the steaming green forest. He couldn't see anything out there, not even the river.

As dark came on, he pulled down all the shades and turned off the lights, except for the kerosene lantern set on the floor near his chair. An eerie glow flickered through the small, cluttered space, and he started to sweat. It reminded him of his long nights in solitary, when he was penned up with no place to go.

He peeled off his shirt and unscrewed the cap from a fifth of Wild Turkey. The warm liquor burned his throat and eased the pain throbbing behind his left eye. Digging into a can of cold beans, he spat out the hunk of white pork that came up in his spoon. It was the flesh of an unclean animal.

This time the Lord had given him a rough row to hoe, and Floyd was like a sorry old hound holed up to lick his wounds. This hunting trailer had a well and septic, but only a trickle of rusty water flowed from the tap, and the toilet wouldn't flush. The place stank like a shithole, but Floyd reflected on how when Jesus came upon the blind beggar sitting by the roadside, Jesus gave him sight. Beggars couldn't be choosers, but the Lord had given Floyd the sight to find this place again, like he did once before, and for that blessing, he was grateful.

The trailer belonged to his good buddy, a former cellmate who'd given Floyd a key last time he needed to lay low. The camp was set way back from any road, on the Yadkin River, and it had been abandoned so long even his buddy likely couldn't find it. The rutted path leading back to the camp hadn't been traveled in years, and weeds covered the trailer's rusty walls like camouflage.

Far as Floyd knew, he had no neighbors, but it never hurt to be extra careful. No telling when a strayed fisherman might wade down the river, or a low-flying pleasure plane might spot his lights. So he had planned in advance and stocked the cupboards long before the fucked-up ransom drop.

Floyd had also taken precautions with his vehicles. He chuckled at his own cunning. In the past week, he'd bought, hid, or discarded so many clunkers he'd near lost track, and his license tag collection had come in real handy. He always paid cash for the cars, and the folks he bought from weren't likely to blab, nor were they particular about ownership titles.

Floyd had covered all the bases, so he blamed that asshole, Bobby Porter, the FBI man, and Floyd's screw-up nephew for everything that went wrong. The black man came out of nowhere, but Floyd had known he was a Fed the minute he entered the gun shop. Nothing left but to kill him. If Darryl hadn't panicked and drawn his gun, then Porter wouldn't have fetched his shotgun, and Floyd would be a rich man today. They were all a bunch of stupid, screwed, fuck-ups.

He took another long swallow of whiskey, then hurled the can of beans against the wall above the sink. In his mind's eye, he could still see the red bag of cash laying there in a pool of blood. If all those screaming people hadn't got in his way, Floyd could have grabbed the bag and run—to hell with Darryl.

His nephew got what he deserved, and Floyd hoped he was suffering for his mistake. He pictured Darryl all strung up to machines to pump his blood and do his breathing for him. Too bad they couldn't hook Darryl up to a machine to do his thinking for him. All brawn, no brain, his nephew was good for nothing but fetch n' carry. Floyd pictured a gang of cops guarding Darryl's hospital door. Under those circumstances, Floyd figured it would be best if the kid never woke up.

On the other hand, Darryl couldn't incriminate Floyd, because Floyd had never shared his plans with Darryl. Even if the poor slob regained consciousness, he didn't know about the secret hideaway or the spare car Floyd had hidden down the road for his getaway.

Floyd was sure the Feds had identified him by now. They'd left fingerprints all over that rental car. And even though the blood Floyd had spilled was only nigger blood, those guys would be hunting him down with an eye to his slaughter. Floyd wasn't scared. He'd come this far without a scratch, and now he stood to get twice as rich as before.

When he called Bobby Porter's Mexican whore, she'd been scared shitless, but she'd come up with all the right answers. She had raised the cash before, she could do it again. He congratulated himself with another deep drink and recalled the first time he'd seen Juanita.

Several years back, when he first moved to North Carolina, Juanita was new in town, too. She'd hung out with the illegals who came up from the Rio Grande and worked so cheap that decent white folk were losing their jobs. Floyd asked around back then and learned her name. He figured her for an easy lay and followed her to work. But then Porter came on the scene. After that, Juanita didn't come around to the bars no more, but Floyd never forgot her fine set of boobs.

Last night on the phone, he told her he didn't care how she got the money. He told her to go set her fat ass on a rich man's face, if that's what it took, or he'd cut her little boy's prick off. By the time Floyd was done with her, she was crying so bad it gave him a hard-on.

He groaned and staggered to his feet. He opened the trailer door and smelled the dead fish odor rising off the river. He unzipped his fly and peed into the rain. One thing he knew for sure—never trust a woman. He lifted his face to the downpour, and the warm water coursed down his neck and bare chest. He stepped back into the trailer, shut the door, and felt his way to the sagging cot that would serve as his bed these next few days. When he fell on his belly, his thoughts turned to Leona. He fantasized about the many ways he'd enjoy her before he killed her.

The stupid bitch had betrayed him. She'd meant to all along. She'd seemed so tired and confused as they moved from one motel to the next. She wasn't sleeping nor eating proper, so Floyd figured she was whupped. He was wrong.

When he and Darryl left to meet Porter, Floyd had wanted to lock Leona and the boy in the room, but Darryl said no. He kept saying, "What if there's a fire, or what if a storm comes up?" So like a fool, he'd finally given in to that nonsense and made Leona promise to stay put.

Then after the fuck-up, when Floyd returned empty-handed to the motel, Leona and the boy were long gone. So was the old blue station wagon. Floyd was so mad he near strangled the desk clerk who, as always, never saw nothing. Thing was, Floyd never figured Leona cared about the money, but he figured she cared about Darryl. Why hadn't the bitch waited for her husband?

Never trust a woman. Floyd listened to the steady throbbing of rain on the roof, then reached down and took hold of himself. As

174

his excitement grew, he recalled the last time he raped Leona, how he tied her to the bed and took her three times before Darryl came home.

The memory took him where he needed to go as his hand finished its work: *for a harlot is a deep pit, a narrow well, she lies in wait like a robber.* He prayed, and once his physical needs were met, he was at peace.

After all, by taking the boy, Leona had done him a favor. The boy was a sniveling, puking nuisance. When all was said and done, Floyd knew damn well where to find her and the boy. When Leona ran, she never ran but in one direction....home.

THIRTY-THREE

Some kind of miracle...

They found her sitting alone in the dark, drinking beer at a small table overlooking the back acres, where rain gusted across the valley and ruffled the surface of the gray lake.

"Hey, Juanita," Matthew called out cheerfully. "We brought dinner!"

Diana let him take charge. They had stopped at Lancaster's Barbeque on the way to Porter Farm and purchased enough meat, slaw, and hushpuppies to feed a volunteer fire department. Juanita seemed disconnected as Matthew cleared away her ashtray, wiped off the table, and created three place settings with paper napkins and plastic forks. He put out the food, rummaged through the refrigerator, where he found cold beers for Juanita and Diana, and then poured sweet tea for himself.

All the while, Juanita's eyes never left Diana's face. She looked tired and miserable, but above all, suspicion.

Once everyone was seated, Matthew said, "Well, ladies, do we say grace, or dig right in?"

"You *told* him, didn't you?" Juanita said.

Diana nodded. "Yes, you said I could confide in Matthew. Now we can talk about it."

"Eat first, talk later," Matthew commanded. "Not one more word until your plates are clean."

Juanita continued to scowl, but a heartbeat later, a chuckle bubbled up from her throat. "Damn you, Trout!" She tossed a packet of hot sauce at him. "You're a pain in the butt!"

"Yeah, but I feed you, right?"

Once again Matthew had worked his magic. The tension eased from the back of Diana's neck, and suddenly she was ravenous. His good humor was contagious. Even Juanita seemed infected as she gobbled hushpuppies like a starved animal, while Diana marveled at how Matthew made her feel calm and protected. In his own quiet way, he had that effect on everyone. Had they been alone, she would have reached out and touched him. She would have smoothed away his worry lines and burrowed into the strength of his arms.

Yet on the drive to Juanita's, they had argued. She'd told him she was impressed by Max Grim and wanted to tell the FBI about the new ransom demand immediately. But Matthew didn't trust Grim. In fact, he'd been inclined to take matters into his own hands. Maybe it was a male thing—two strong egos clashing, but Matthew also feared that Grim had lost interest in Juan.

She'd argued that the FBI was better equipped to handle this dangerous situation, and in the end, they had compromised. Juanita's landline was still tapped, she'd promised not to answer her cell phone, so Diana and Matthew figured the agents would overhear Floyd Clontz if he tried to contact her that evening. They had granted her a reprieve, but if Clontz did not call, then they'd tell the whole story to the authorities first thing in the morning.

"Juanita, you should at least tell Bobby about this latest demand," Matthew advised after they'd finished eating. "He has a right to know. Juan's not his flesh and blood, but Bobby loves him like a son."

Stained napkins lay in a crumpled heap on the table. The food was gone, and the last beer had been drained. Diana braced herself as

177

Juanita's eyes snapped. But instead of the anticipated explosion, Juanita stood up, walked to the counter, and started brewing coffee.

"Matthew's right," Diana said. "It's true Bobby is hurt and vulnerable, but he'll never forgive you if you don't share this with him now."

When Juanita turned to face them, coffee sloshed from the cups in her trembling hands and tears cascaded down her face. "You don't get it. Bobby's strong, but he's helpless in this situation. Don't you see? It's the *money*. Bobby's a fighter, but he can't fight this."

Diana hastened to help with the coffee. She placed the cups on the sofa table, then gently eased Juanita onto the couch. Following her lead, Matthew moved to the armchair.

It was always about money, she reflected bitterly. On their ride over, the subject of money had turned their argument into an emotional standoff. Diana had confessed that although she desperately wanted to ask Vivian for more cash, she'd be putting her mother's financial security at risk. Matthew admitted that after his first contribution to the ransom, his resources were all tapped out. They'd both felt angry and useless because of their financial impotence.

"Please don't tell Bobby," Juanita pleaded.

For once, even Matthew seemed at a loss. Diana sat beside Juanita and wrapped her in her arms, which made Juanita break down completely. She sobbed and buried her face in Diana's shoulder. Diana stroked her long black hair, cradling her like a baby, and murmured reassurances into her ear. Outside, thunder rumbled in the distance and lightning snapped above the dark lake.

Matthew sat in the shadows, sipping coffee and watching Juanita cry. Gradually the sobbing subsided and Juanita relaxed in Diana's arms. But then, sudden as a scream, the phone on the table rang. Everyone froze. Juanita clung harder to Diana as it continued to howl.

"It's the kidnapper!" Juanita shrieked.

Diana was terrified, but said, "What if it's Bobby?"

"It's not Bobby." Juanita struggled to flee, but Diana held her firmly.

Finally Matthew snatched the remote. He answered in a tense, husky voice, then listened intently, his eyebrows knit in concentration. Finally, he held the phone out to Juanita. "It's a woman. She wants to talk to you."

Juanita looked from one to the other, then reluctantly accepted it. Her eyes darted back and forth as she listened. Next she abruptly rose and carried the conversation to the privacy of her bedroom.

"*What woman?*" Diana demanded when Juanita was out of earshot. "Was it the country girl from the Open House?" Many times she'd prayed that the girl she saw stealing food really was involved, for in her heart, she believed that girl would never hurt a child.

Matthew shook his head. "Sounded more like an older woman."

When Juanita returned, she seemed stunned.

"Well?" Diana could hardly contain herself as Juanita sank to the couch.

Juanita blinked "That was Mrs. McCord, Juan's paternal grandmother…"

Diana remembered the name from that afternoon when they'd sat in this very room with Bo Miller. That day Juan's grandparents had called and rejected Juanita's plea for help. "What did she want?"

Again Juanita blinked. "The McCords saw the story on the national news. When the commentator described the shootout, suddenly it all got real for them."

"I don't understand…"

"Neither do I, Diana. When I talked to her before, she called me a whore. Today she was respectful to both me and my dead sister, Maria. She said that after all, Maria was Juan's mother, and she was his grandma…"

"But what did she want?" Diana pressed.

"She wants to help. The McCords are wiring twenty-five thousand dollars towards Juan's ransom."

A slow smile spread across Matthew's face. He rolled his eyes at the ceiling. "Someone up there's looking out for you, Juanita. It takes a miracle to turn folks around that way. The McCord's contribution sweetens the bad news, don't you agree? So let's call Bobby."

Juanita said, "But we still need twenty-five thousand more."

"Yeah, but we're three fourths of the way to the finish line. I'll wager Bobby can live with those odds."

As Juanita weighed Matthew's suggestion, Diana's heart rejoiced with the turn of events. In her experience, wolves never became lambs, and reconciliation, such as the McCord's sudden acceptance of Juan, was a miracle she could hardly believe. As she questioned her lack of faith, the phone rang again. Again the trio startled at the sound, but this time Juanita answered without hesitation.

Matthew and Diana had no trouble hearing the voice bellowing across the miles:

"Damn it, Ms. Cruz," Agent Grim barked. "I just played back the tape of your call from California. What's all this shit about a *new ransom*?"

THIRTY-FOUR

A snooping expedition…

On Monday morning Diana received five frantic phone calls, one right after another, and the first was from her mother. Viv always let the phone ring long enough to raise the dead, and this time she dragged Diana dripping from the shower. Like everyone else in America, Mama had seen the evening news and wondered whether the kidnappers had gotten away with her money. If not, would she get her contribution back?

"The FBI is holding your money in a safe place, Mama, but frankly, we're more concerned with getting Juan back," Diana told her.

"Where were you yesterday, Diana? I rang a hundred times, but you never answered."

Diana explained how she'd split her day between the hospital and Juanita's house, but her excuse cut no ice with Mama.

"You should mind your own business."

Next she covered the same ground with Liz, who was star-struck by all the national attention focused so close to home. After wringing every grisly detail from her, Liz said, "Don't forget our real estate class tomorrow night. You missed all of last week, Diana, and if you skip this week, you're screwed."

Professor Miles Lawton called with virtually the same admonition, and then added another warning to the list, "You've been ignoring the Sorvino listing, Diana. That pediatrician who showed an interest is back. He wants to see the house tomorrow afternoon. I expect you to go there, close the deal, and then attend my class afterwards. Is that a problem?"

She couldn't guarantee Miles a sale, but she had agreed to the showing and the class. She did not agree to a date afterwards, and if that was a problem, too bad.

Miles' smarmy advances had put her so on edge, that by the time poor Matthew called, she snapped at him.

"Sorry to bother you," Matthew gulped. "But Juanita has agreed to let me tell Bobby about the new ransom demand. I'm on my way to the hospital. Wanna tag along?"

She'd desperately wanted to go, but had to study or risk flunking her course. So she begged off, and that proved to be a mistake. Had she gone, she might have missed Juanita, caller number five. Juanita's tale was wild beyond belief, so it took several tries to sort it out.

"You say your friend actually *knows* the kidnappers?" Diana was astonished.

Juanita could hardly contain her excitement. "Yes! If Bobby and me hadn't moved away from the trailer park, the kidnappers would've been our neighbors!"

"They still live there?" Juanita's excitement was infectious.

"No, they moved out the day Juan disappeared. Don't you get it, Diana? We need to check it out right away."

As it turned out, Juanita's informant friend was the rental agent for the trailer park. She'd recognized the picture of Floyd Clontz on television.

Diana's pulse accelerated. "But if she called your phone, the FBI heard it all. Let them handle it."

"They didn't hear, because my friend met me at the salon and told me in person. The Feds don't know a damn thing, and you promised not to tell them, remember?"

Not true. Had Agent Grim not overheard Juanita's call with Grandmother McCord, Matthew and she had already decided to tell him about the newest ransom demand. But this trailer park lead wasn't part of that agreement, and it might be fun to investigate on their own.

"I'm calling from a pay phone, Diana. When I hang up, I'm driving over to the trailer park, Sylvan Acres, and I want you to meet me…"

So that's how Diana got roped into a snooping expedition.

Her GPS took her down an unfamiliar road. She almost missed the faded sign announcing Sylvan Acres, but negotiated a fast left onto a gravel pathway leading through a valley of trailers. They stretched into the distance, row upon row of steel elephants laid out to bake in the sun. Once upon a time, someone had planted a perennial garden near the gate, but except for a stand of sturdy yellow coreopsis, the attempt had gone to weed and seed.

Apparently the most recent occupants, those with newer doublewides, had been assigned lots near the entrance. But as she traveled deeper into the complex, ignoring curious stares from residents who knew she didn't belong, the character of the place changed. Many of the ancient, rusted trailers seemed to have put down roots in the red soil. Their tiny yards were littered with junk, and it was depressing to imagine the lives lived behind those drawn shades.

Diana heard Juanita before she saw her. She was laughing, smoking, and sharing a can of Coke with a skinny African American woman. Both were seated on the cinder block steps of a metal building labeled Rental Office. Juanita was in high spirits as she introduced her friend, and Diana suspected the unexpected donation from Juan's California grandparents, coupled with this new lead, had put the spark in her dark eyes.

"Ready for some private investigation, Diana?" Juanita twirled a key chain on one long, red-tipped finger.

Diana frowned at the rental agent. "Shouldn't you come with us?" In all her years as a real estate agent, she'd never given a key to a total stranger.

"No, y'all help yourselves. Those folks are long gone, and they're behind two months' rent. I'm of a mind to have their sorry old rig towed off the lot when you're done."

As she followed Juanita down a back alley, picking her way between garbage cans and ducking under clotheslines, her apprehension grew. What they were doing was wrong, and if this trailer turned out to be the preacher's lair, it should be impounded by the authorities, not towed off the lot. They had no business adding their fingerprints to the mix, yet she couldn't bring herself to voice an objection. Instead, she allowed Juanita to capture her arm and lead her to an old green trailer at the end of the row.

"Are you sure this is the Clontz trailer?" It wasn't what Diana had expected. It had a tiny garden with yellow daisies, purple phlox, and tall red cannas blooming in gaudy profusion. A kidnapper with a green thumb? Go figure.

Juanita gazed wistfully at the flowers. "Actually, this is where me and Bobby used to live. Bobby planted these."

She sensed a certain melancholy in her friend. "Yes, I can see Bobby's talent on full display in this garden."

Juanita laughed bitterly. "Looking back, our life wasn't half bad then. When Bobby inherited the house from his daddy, I thought our luck had changed for the better. But then we got stuck with Juan, and look what happened."

Diana understood. Juanita hadn't planned to fall in love with the boy. Just when she thought her life had improved, fate stabbed her in the back. "Do you want to go inside, for old time's sake?"

184

She shook her head. "We don't own it anymore. We gave it to Sylvan Acres, so they could rent it cheap to someone who couldn't afford something better."

Diana was moved by Juanita's generosity, but kept her thoughts to herself as they walked on. Better than most, Diana knew that one could never go home again.

Sun glinted off the silver walls of the Clontz's classic Airstream. Under different circumstances, she would have been charmed by this piece of campy Americana, but as it was, her skin crawled with goose bumps as Juanita twisted the key. "This is Breaking and Entering. Maybe we should stop right now?"

Juanita grinned, pushed the door inward, and the stench of something rotten escaped the closed space. "Yuck!" She fanned the air as she climbed into the cluttered interior. "It stinks like something died in here."

Diana sincerely hoped not as she followed her inside, and their eyes adjusted to the gloom. "Smells like spoiled milk—or eggs."

"You have a good nose, partner." Juanita forged ahead to where bowls of musty cereal grew mold on a filthy table, and an army of ants swarmed on eggshells abandoned in the sink. "Somebody left in a hurry. If that girl from the Open House lived here, she wasn't Mrs. Clean."

But as Diana continued to explore, she sensed that diametrically opposed personalities once inhabited the place. "The floors and windows are spotless," she observed.

"So what?" Juanita brushed flies off an open can of peanut butter, then dropped it into a soggy paper trash bag on the floor. The bag was already filled to brimming with coffee grounds and empty whiskey bottles. "These people were pigs!"

Diana peeked inside a tiny broom closet where cleaning supplies were neatly stacked beside a poster of a near-nude Brittany

185

Spears tacked inside the door. Someone had drawn obscene hearts on her nipples with a red magic marker.

"Gross!" Juanita peered over her shoulder.

What exactly were they looking for? Telephone numbers, address book? Diana figured she'd know it when she saw it. She watched Juanita sort through a cardboard box filled with old gospel records.

"These must belong to the preacher," she said. "It makes me feel dirty just touching them."

"I'll check the bedroom," Diana said.

"If I were you, I'd look behind the door first. I wouldn't want the magic marker freak catching *me* alone in that bedroom."

Diana laughed uneasily. Juanita was trying to inject a little comic relief to their mission, but she detected a glaze of desperation in her eyes, an emotion they shared. Time was not on their side, as Juan's situation became more precarious with every passing minute.

Her heart knotted like a fist as Diana moved into the cramped room, where everything was miniaturized to fit the small scale of the Airstream, making her feel excessively claustrophobic. She noticed that the lace curtains and chenille bedspread had been freshly laundered, but the air was close and musty. She suppressed an impulse to flee.

Half the room was distinctly masculine. She stepped on a pile of dirty socks, underwear, and a jockstrap as she leaned across the bed to crank open the window and let in some breeze. On the feminine side, she found a shelf filled with an antique doll collection. Each doll had been lovingly positioned in relationship to its neighbor. Some held hands, others had one arm propped around the next, and each tiny porcelain face was tilted to smile at the doll to her right.

This sad attempt at harmony broke her heart. She felt the presence of the girl from the Open House who had carried a plastic purse, limped, and stolen food. That girl had been little more than a child herself and would never hurt Juan.

Diana started bonding with the girl, feeling her sorrow and desperation as surely as she smelled her scent—old-fashioned talcum powder. Her excitement grew as she touched each doll, and then lifted a black and white photo off the shelf. The picture was mounted in a primitive wooden frame and was obviously prized by the girl. It depicted an older woman in a dark, crudely-sewn dress. Her hair was streaked with gray at the temples and drawn back into a severe bun, but her expression was kind and loving. Her gnarled hands rested on the shoulders of a tiny girl, maybe four years old. The child's dress was fashioned of fine lace, and yet she was barefooted.

The loving grandmother and child were surrounded by a natural wilderness, with mountains falling away into a hazy distance. Diana had not yet visited the Carolina Appalachians, but she knew instinctively that she'd found a photo of the mysterious country girl on her home turf.

She explored the frame for clues—name of a photographer, location, and date—but found nothing. She suppressed an impulse to hide the photo in her purse, so she could take it apart at home, but her conscience said *no,* so she replaced it on the shelf with the dolls.

"Any luck in there?" Juanita hollered.

"Still looking…" Diana called back.

Next she dropped to her knees and summoned the courage to reach under the bed. She fully expected a mousetrap to smash her extended fingers, but instead she touched an old shoebox. She slid it out and ran her hand over the yellow happy face stickers pasted all over the lid, and then she placed it on the bed to open it.

The scent of talcum powder was strong as she peeked inside, but the ugly, shriveled face staring back at her made her gasp in horror. What was this awful thing? She looked again, and saw that the

187

creature was only another doll. The little manikin was clad in Swiss lederhosen, with fat pink stuffed legs and red leather booties. Once it had been a baby doll, but time had transformed his face to a shrunken mass of black rind. She eventually realized the deformed head had been fashioned from a piece of fruit, likely an apple, and recalled how a long time ago, her own mother told her a story about these apple-headed dolls. Her blood raced with the discovery. Repulsive as it was, the country girl had clearly loved this thing.

"Let's go, Diana!" Juanita yelled. "There's nothing here, and this place gives me the creeps!"

Again Diana wrestled with her dark angels, but this time they won.

As Juanita and she stumbled from the Clontz trailer, locking the apparent futility of their search behind them, Juanita had tears in her eyes.

"What a waste. Did you find anything, Diana?"

"Nope, not a thing." The lie brought heat to her cheeks, and the stolen apple doll was a mighty weight hidden at the bottom of her purse. She had committed her first, truly felonious act.

THIRTY-FIVE

What about Johnny…?

As Diana steered into Yacht Club Lane, she blinked into the early afternoon sun and shook her head to clear the cobwebs. The last thing she wanted was to show the Sorvino home to clients she barely remembered, but she'd promised Miles, and a promise was a promise. Plus, she was still angry with the Sorvinos. In the nine days since Juan's abduction, they'd turned their backs, refusing to help in any way. She'd sooner deliver a swift kick to their privileged derrieres than help them sell their house.

Also, she'd been dogged by a strange sense of foreboding ever since she'd awakened that morning, with the horrible doll staring at her. Its beady currant eyes had seemed to focus in its shriveled-apple face and connect with her from across the room. It was propped up on her dresser, leaning against the mirror, seeming to say: *You've crossed the line, Diana. We're in this together, and there's no turning back.*"

Good lord, now she was listening to dolls? When she turned into the Sorvino's driveway, trying to organize her thoughts, she saw a Cornelius police car parked out front and recognized Andy Monroe, the baby-faced officer she'd met the night of Juan's abduction. He was leaning against his car, which looked exactly like her *Queen Vic*, and talking into a hand-held radio.

She parked behind the police vehicle and noticed the front door hanging wide open, an oversight Brenda Sorvino would never commit. Something seemed terribly wrong, although Officer Monroe was smiling and beckoning her to come. When she entered the house, Brenda tackled her, pulled her off balance, and then into a frantic embrace.

"Thank God you're here, Diana!" Brenda's honey-colored hair was in massive disarray, her perfect makeup streaked with tears. "It's *Johnny*! They've kidnapped my Johnny!"

Every brain cell in Diana's head closed down. The words made no sense. As Brenda dragged her deeper into the house, her fingernails biting into her arm, Diana found it impossible to process the unthinkable. At the same time, a man walked briskly towards her, extending his hand. His dark, restless eyes darted bird-like in his sharp, clean-shaven face.

"Remember me, Mrs. Rittenhouse? I'm Chief Jay Keener. We recently spent the night together." He teased.

Not funny. One of the most painful nights of her life had included the grilling at Keener's station house. "Johnny's been kidnapped?" she gasped.

He passed one arm around her waist, the other around Brenda's, leading them both into the kitchen. "The boy *is* missing, but I suspect he's out for a joy ride on his new bike. I'm guessing we'll find him somewhere in the neighborhood."

Diana wasn't convinced. If this was so routine, then why was Keener here?

"I called the police the minute I realized he was gone," Brenda wailed. "Johnny was driving me crazy because I'd kept him cooped up inside all week. When he promised to ride only in our driveway, I let him go out. God, what have I done?"

In spite of her obvious distress, Diana's heart turned to stone. Everyone knew the kidnapper's original intent had been to snatch Johnny, so how could she let him out of her sight?

Keener had them sit at the kitchen table. "Johnny's only been missing an hour. No cause for alarm," he said.

"Then why are *you* here?" Diana demanded.

He smiled reassuringly. "Under the circumstance, it's a valid precaution, but let's not jump to conclusions."

"Easy for *him* to say," Brenda moaned. "But you don't know the whole story, Diana. Once they identified the man who killed that poor FBI agent, they realized the whole plot was a hate crime aimed at my husband."

Diana could hardly catch her breath as she looked from one to the other.

"Not sure I'd call it a *hate crime...*" Keener frowned "But Floyd Clontz was likely bearing a major grudge. Seems he applied for a loan to buy a logging truck, and John Sorvino turned him down flat."

The missing pieces of the puzzle were falling into place, and a terrifying picture was emerging. Capturing Juan hadn't produced a high enough ransom, so Johnny was still the desired prize. The prospect of a big payoff, coupled with sweet revenge, had compelled Clontz to strike again.

"Don't you get it, Diana?" Brenda sobbed. "That monster will kill both boys and never blink an eye!"

The sailboat clock on the wall ticked out the rhythm of despair.

Finally, Keener cleared his throat. "Point is, Clontz might be a psychopath, and he's cunning as a fox, but he's bound to make mistakes. Even if the worst were true, and it's too soon to know that, we're on top of it. Agent Grim told me they've demanded a second, larger ransom for Juan. When Clontz gives new instructions for that drop-off, we'll nail the bastard."

Famous last words. They sure as hell hadn't "nailed the bastard" last time. Plus, in spite of Juan's grandparents' generous contribution to the ransom pot, they were still short. "We still need another twenty-five thousand dollars," she muttered, casting a bitter look at Brenda.

"We've called Johnny's father," Keener continued. "He'll be here any minute. In the meantime, I suggest we all calm down."

Diana was fed up. She left the table and stared out the kitchen window. The sun was still shining and the sky was heartlessly blue, in cruel contrast to the darkness in her heart. She also saw an expensive car pull into the driveway and recognized its occupants— the skinny pediatrician and his fat wife from the Open House. Her clients had come to see the house! God help them all! No way could she proceed with that charade.

She offered a sick smile. "Your buyers are here, Brenda. Shall I send them away?"

"Fuck yes! Get rid of them!"

She met them at the front door, told a cock n' bull story about the owners being ill and contagious, and then sent them away, grumbling and confused. As soon as they left, she stuck her head back into the kitchen.

"Sorry folks, I can't breathe in here. I'm going for a walk…"

With that, she escaped through the back door.

THIRTY-SIX

Will they forget me, too…?

Johnny Sorvino was suffocating in the cramped space, and he couldn't get comfortable. He was lying on his side with his knees tucked up under his chin. His legs ached. The ropes and metal beneath him on the hard floor bit into his ribs, but he couldn't stretch out. And it was so very dark.

The place stank of rubber and gasoline, and the fumes made him sick to his stomach. He pictured how his mama would be calling him for lunch and wondered if she'd made peanut butter sandwiches or pizza pockets. He wished he had his glow-in-the-dark dinosaur watch, so at least he'd know how long he'd been in this scary place.

Tears streamed down his face and sweat soaked his T-shirt. Twisting, he managed to pull off the shirt and wad it under his head like a pillow, and burying his face in the moist fabric helped stifle his sobbing. One thing he knew for sure—he shouldn't call attention to himself. He was the boy who deserved to be here, not Juan. All along they'd wanted him, not Juan, so Johnny was the one who should die.

His parents thought he didn't know what had happened. They'd sent him to his room when the TV news came on, but he'd put on his earphones and watched his own set. He saw Juan's Aunt Nita and the man called Bobby asking everyone to help save their boy. And he heard his dad tell the policeman that he would not help.

They'd be sorry now. Mama and Daddy would cry, but it would be too late, and they'd never see him again. Not ever!

On TV they'd shown a picture of Juan holding his fish, the one he caught the day when they went out with Mr. Trout. The rocking motion under him now, the part making him sick, was like being on that boat. Johnny squeezed his eyes shut and tried to bring the good times back.

The day they all went fishing, they enjoyed sun and swimming and the awesome storm, but already Juan's face was getting harder to remember. It was so much like his own, that Johnny couldn't tell them apart. Juan was his blood brother. Again he saw the knife flash and heard Juan chanting the secret oath. They had shared their blood like Indian warriors, and that meant *true until death.*

But where was Juan? Did he feel the same pain and fear? Mama and Daddy didn't talk about him anymore, like he was already dead. *Will they forget me, too?* He wondered.

Johnny held his breath when he heard footsteps right outside his black prison. They came closer, then stopped, as every muscle in his body froze in terror. At first he saw only a crack of light, then a blaze of sunshine blinded him when the tarpaulin ceiling rolled away.

"Who's in there?" A woman's face loomed above him. He couldn't see her features because of the sun, but her pale hair was like an angel's halo. "My God, is that you, Johnny?" she said.

His legs were so cramped that Miss Diana had to lift him out of the sailboat. He clung to her shoulders. "How'd you find me?"

She carried him to the bushes near the pier, where the handlebars of his bike reflected a tiny glint of light.

"I guess I didn't hide it so good," he muttered.

They sat together in the cool grass while Johnny took deep breaths and his heart slowed down to normal. He was glad she didn't talk. His mom would have freaked by then. Plus, his mom would never sit on the ground in a new suit, or step off the dock in high heels, like Miss Diana just did.

194

People came out of the Club and started strolling towards their boats. Still she said nothing, just kept watching and smiling at him with those big blue eyes. Soon she got up and found his wadded shirt in the bottom of the hull. Then she buckled up the tarp where he'd pulled it loose, like he'd never even been there. Johnny figured he could've hidden there forever, if only he could've snapped those buttons from the inside.

"Your mother's worried about you," Miss Diana said. "Are you ready to go home now?"

He nodded, then pulled his bike out of the bushes. Miss Diana spread his wet T-shirt across the basket. He started to mount, but then changed his mind. She couldn't keep up if he rode, so they walked side by side. She took long strides for a lady. They'd be home soon at this rate, so Johnny figured he'd better ask her now.

"You promised you'd find Juan, Miss Diana. Don't you remember?"

She stopped and put her cool hand on the back of his neck, gave him a little squeeze. "You ran away because of Juan?"

"Nobody cares!" he cried. "You've already forgotten him!"

"No we haven't…" She leaned close and Johnny noticed she smelled like flowers. "I think about Juan every minute of the day, just like you."

"But you promised!"

"Yes, I did."

Johnny searched her face. She hadn't made another promise, but he trusted her all the same. As they rounded the corner, he saw a police car in his driveway, and even worse, his daddy's silver BMW was parked there, too. "They're gonna kill me!" he wailed, grabbing onto Miss Diana's hand.

"Would you blame them?" She sounded stern, but she was smiling. "Maybe they won't be too upset if you tell them you just wanted to go sailing."

She wasn't going to tell on him! He dropped his bike and flew through the front door, hitting an immoveable object—his mom—before he'd even gotten into the hall. She hugged him so tight he couldn't breathe, and covered him with big slobbery kisses.

Then Daddy came running from the kitchen, followed by the policeman who was there the night Juan disappeared. Daddy looked funny and pale and mad as a grizzly bear. He tried to escape, but Daddy grabbed him. He smacked his bottom three times, so hard Johnny cried all over again. But Daddy was crying, too. He lifted him up and squeezed so tight, Johnny thought his ribs would crack.

No one asked him any questions. Instead, they hugged and patted him like he was a baby. Miss Diana stood in the doorway like she was going to leave.

"*She* found me," Johnny pointed at her. "I was gonna go sailing, but then I decided to come home."

"I'm so glad you did, son." Daddy lowered him to the floor and walked to Miss Diana. "And we are *very* grateful to Diana."

Everyone was acting real weird. The policeman stood back watching with his arms crossed, while Daddy went to his desk and took out his checkbook.

"Diana, I don't know how to say this…" Daddy's voice was gruff and strange. "But I've been wrong about a lot of things lately…" He glanced at Johnny, and then looked back at Miss Diana. He took out a pen. "Brenda told me you folks still need some money to help Juan. How much?"

Johnny's heart broke with pride.

THIRTY-SEVEN

Between parents and children…

"It's none of your business, Diana," Mama said through a mouthful of cheeseburger. "You should be tending to your own life. Why aren't you at that real estate class?"

Diana sighed. Mama knew perfectly well why she wasn't in class. An hour ago Mama had left an urgent message saying she'd suffered a severe low blood sugar, an emergency that would land her in the hospital. But when Diana arrived at Shady Oaks in a panic, Mama was sitting in her room eating junk food. Apparently the episode was yet another bid for attention.

"You worry about that Mexican child day and night," Mama scolded. "Too bad you never worried so hard about your own children."

In fact, after the scare at the Sorvinos that afternoon, Diana's maternal need had been so powerful that she'd rushed home and tried to call both Robbie and Amanda. In both cases, she got an answering machine, proof that her children had lives of their own.

"And I suppose you think you're some sort of a hero just because you found that Sorvino boy?" Mama was relentless. "But really, Diana, you know those policemen would have found him eventually. It was just a matter of time…"

Diana tuned out, refusing to let Viv's criticism dampen her joy. First Juan's grandparents had come up with part of the cash, then John Sorvino had supplied the rest. Both were generous bids for redemption. Redemption was a strong word, but it seemed to apply.

197

Unfortunately, finding Johnny had not earned Diana any absolution. Her only hope was to keep her promise to Johnny and help save Juan.

"Those people should've given money in the first place, like *I* did," Mama continued. "Now, with God's help, they'll rescue that boy."

Diana prayed Mama was right, but also believed God needed the help of human hands. At the same time, she watched with growing tenderness as Mama licked her lips and closed her eyes from the simple ecstasy of food well-enjoyed. Vivian was a terror, but she was Diana's terror, and she loved her mama dearly. If this mess had taught her anything, it had renewed her faith in the fragile, yet abiding bond between parents and children.

"Mama, I have something to show you…"

At the last minute, she'd decided to bring the apple doll to Shady Oaks. She'd tell Mama the whole story, then endure the inevitable lecture about how *stealing was a sin*. But in the end, Viv's curiosity got the better of her. Diana propped the doll on the dresser, in Mama's direct field of vision.

A bar of golden sunlight leaked through the Venetian blinds and fell on its grotesque little face. The room was so silent she feared her mother had fallen asleep, as she often did after a big meal. But instead, Mama's eyes looked magnified behind her thick glasses as she stared at the little creature.

"May I touch it?" Her veined hand trembled as she reached out from her chair.

Wordlessly, Diana handed her the doll. She took it gently and held it near her eyes, as though a very close look would reveal all its secrets. She sniffed it, then fingered its leather breeches and straw hat. "This doll is mine," she said.

"No, Mama, it came from the trailer, like I told you."

"Yes, but it belongs to *me*."

Mama had finally lost it. Diana reached out to take the doll, but Viv slapped her hand away.

"Let me hold it! I don't mean it's *literally* mine, but it's identical to the one your daddy bought me on our honeymoon."

This was news to Diana. She remembered that her parents had honeymooned in the North Carolina mountains. It had been the first and only time her father, a gentle Quaker from Pennsylvania, had ever seen the state.

"Where did Daddy buy it?"

Mama stroked the doll lovingly. "My mother, your Nana, always promised to buy me one when I was a little girl. We went to Boone each year on summer vacation, but Mama never bought me that doll."

"So the doll came from Boone?

"Aren't you listening, child? Of course this doll came from Boone, and the only person in all the world who made them was a girl from Switzerland, not much older than me at the time. We called her The Apple Lady."

Diana's blood pumped with excitement. Everything fit. Hadn't the photograph of the mysterious country girl been taken in the mountains? Her mouth filled with a hundred unanswered questions, but Mama had fallen asleep with the gnarled head of the apple doll tucked under her chin. The sight made Diana ache with love, and she decided two things: First, this particular doll would live with her mother from then on, and second, Diana would get herself to Boone. She'd never been to the mountains, didn't know how to get there, but she was determined to get there soon.

THIRTY-EIGHT

Apple dolls and wooden reindeer...

Matthew was nervous as a schoolboy as he stood outside Diana's condominium. He rang the bell and wondered why she'd summoned him for breakfast at such short notice. But he wasn't complaining. His body ached to see her, and his mind was hungry for her conversation. It seemed he'd arrived too early, though, because Diana answered the door wearing a white terrycloth nightgown, her hair wrapped in a towel.

"Oh, Matthew, come on in!" She seemed surprised.

"You said eight o'clock, right?"

"I should have said nine." Yet she took his arm and pulled him into the hall.

"Hey, Motherfucker!" her blasted bird hollered from the bedroom.

Fortunately, he was used to Perry, Diana's foul-mouthed parrot, but the unlikely relationship between the pet and his mistress never ceased to amaze him. Theirs was not a match made in Heaven.

"Get lost, asshole!" Perry's strident squawking followed them through the living room.

As they entered the kitchen, he noticed that Diana had set the patio table for breakfast. She'd arranged a little bundle of pink daisies in a glass bottle. He knew she'd picked them from the makeshift garden she'd planted in a barrel. The gesture filled him with tenderness.

"Coffee smells good," he ventured.

"I should get dressed." She smiled. "Just how hungry are you, Matthew?"

He liked the way her breasts moved inside her thin robe. The intense hunger he felt had nothing to do with food. "I can wait…" He helped himself to the coffee. "But don't change on my account. You look mighty fine in that getup."

She blushed and tightened the cinch on her robe. "I'll feel more comfortable in clothes, so will you excuse me?"

When she left, he took his coffee out to the patio and sat alone, sipping and staring out at the blue lake. Diana's coffee wasn't half bad, but her view of the Main Channel was downright outstanding. He'd like the scene better without the towering tiers of condominiums marching along the shore like a battalion of concrete soldiers, but what could he do about that? He hated progress and the developers who spoiled the land and the lake. He could understand why Diana had felt compelled to preserve a little bit of nature, if only in a barrel garden.

When she returned, wearing a dress and carrying a tray of food, the sight of her took his breath away. He climbed to his feet and helped with the tray. "How come you're all dressed up?"

"Why not?" She giggled. "You look pretty sharp yourself, Matthew."

The turntable compliment caught him off guard, as did the shy formality that seemed to have crept between them. He wondered, not for the first time, if she'd had an ulterior motive for inviting him to breakfast. He'd seldom seen her in a dress, especially one like this, that revealed her shoulders and the gentle curve of her bosom.

And he realized she'd seldom seen him in anything but jeans and old flannel shirts. Was that why she was staring? That morning he'd ironed a new pair of slacks and unwound a fresh cotton dress shirt from its laundry cardboard. Both items, along with his polished loafers, had been hidden away at the back of his closet for a special occasion.

They ate in companionable silence. Diana's cooking, like her coffee, was mighty fine, and soon his new slacks felt tight at the waist. Over a third cup of coffee, she told him about her adventure at the Sylvan Acres trailer park. He wanted to scold her for putting herself in danger, but by the time she described the apple doll, he was hooked.

"So you think this mystery woman is hiding in Boone?" he asked.

"Seems like a possibility."

This revelation was too coincidental not to be true. It seemed Diana had been reading his mind, which brought him to the surprise he'd been saving for just the right moment. He walked into the living room, where he'd seen last night's Mooresville Tribune lying in Diana's easy chair, and then he carried the newspaper back to the patio. "Take a look at this…" He spread the paper open on the table.

She followed his finger down the column to an article about a truck the police had pulled from a gully near the dump. "So what?" She tried to make sense of the black and white photo of the truck hanging from the wrecker.

"Read the name on the truck," Matthew prompted. "It says Clontz Lumber, right? It belonged to the kidnappers. The police have already figured that out, but they can't understand why the bad guys ditched it, or why they found little pieces of handmade furniture and broken reindeer sculpture scattered everywhere…"

Diana looked blank. "Reindeer sculpture?"

"Yep, and I happen to be the proud owner of two such sculptures myself. I was planning to give one to you and one to Juanita for Christmas, but they won't be much of a surprise now."

"What on earth are you talking about, Matthew?"

He took a long swallow of coffee, savoring the suspense. Ever since he saw the picture of Darryl Clontz on the evening news, some elusive memory had nagged him like a toothache, but he couldn't pin it down…until now."

"I *know* the kidnappers, Diana. That article jogged my memory."

Her mouth hung open as she stared at him.

"I never knew Darryl's name until now, but he used to come into my store to buy sodas and tobacco. He always flirted with the college girl working the counter, but it seemed harmless. His wife was a pathetic little thing named Leona. She's the one who sold me the reindeer."

"My God, Matthew, do you know where they live?"

"All I know is what Leona told me, that Darryl made the reindeer with his own hands, and they used to sell real well along the roadside back home."

"In *Boone*!" She completed his sentence.

Matthew nodded. It was then, or never, so he screwed up his courage: "I think we should check it out, Diana. Maybe we should go to Boone together?"

THIRTY-NINE

A chance at happiness…

Diana was nervous as a schoolgirl as Matthew's truck sped towards the mountains. Yesterday morning at breakfast, she'd expected resistance when she asked him to take her to Boone. As it turned out, she need not have worried. She'd never had to use her wiles, or charms, or whatever means necessary to convince him. Instead, he'd come to the desired conclusion on his own. Even better, he thought the trip was all *his* idea.

But now she was concerned about the accommodations waiting at the end of their journey. At such short notice, they weren't able to reserve two motel rooms, but Matthew had come up with an alternate solution.

"We can still go," he said. "My cousin owns a little piece of ground up at Blowing Rock, only a few miles from Boone. He has a small tag-along camper set up there, with water and an electric hookup."

The idea of camping concerned her, but Matthew pressed on.

"He's offered to let me use it. We could use the site as our base of operations, then fan out looking for Leona and Juan."

"How many beds in this trailer?" She'd asked, sounding like a prissy old maid. From Matthew's expression, she'd guessed there was only one.

"Hey, we're adults," he'd answered. "We'll work it out…"

She knew they'd work *something* out, but she was still conflicted as to what she wanted that *something* to be. To make matters worse, Matthew had been acting strange all morning. Did he feel guilty because they'd left town in absolute secrecy? They'd decided not to tell Agent Grim their theory, because what did they really know, anyway?

"If we mention apple dolls and wooden reindeer, he'll laugh in our faces," Matthew had said.

But she'd been the one who decided not to tell Bobby and Juanita: "We don't want to raise false hopes," she'd said.

So maybe they both felt guilty as they drove through the beautiful countryside? Yet she suspected Matthew's somber mood had more to do with the stop they'd made at a pawnshop on the way out of town. He was worrying about a ring.

She held it up to the light, and the diamond glittered in its ornate silver setting. An old-fashioned design of intertwined ivy leaves held the stone in place. She experienced a twinge of melancholy as she pressed the ring between the cushiony pink lips of its little velvet case and snapped the lid shut. She tucked the case inside a brown paper bag and locked it in the glove compartment.

"I hope we did the right thing," she said wistfully.

"What else could we do? That ring's been in the Porter family for generations. When it came right down to it, *I* couldn't be the one to sell it down the river."

Diana agreed, but she also knew that Bobby had specifically instructed him to sell the heirloom for whatever money it would bring. Bobby intended to use the proceeds to help pay folks back for their contributions to the ransom. He'd actually sat up in his hospital bed, begging Matthew to do this favor for him.

"Was he really planning to give the ring to Juanita?" she asked.

"Absolutely. He intended to pop the question on the Fourth of July, at the Grand Opening of Porter Park."

This romantic notion filled her with a bittersweet, unnamed longing. Bobby had put his own happiness on hold in order to help Juan, and Diana hoped that delay would be temporary. Clearly Bobby had made an emotional commitment to Juanita. Would Diana someday commit to a new love in her life?

Matthew tore his eyes away from the foothills rolling endlessly on either side of Highway 40 and studied her. "Bobby will have my hide for this. He'll be furious I didn't sell the ring." He reached across the seat and took her hand. "Call me a sentimental fool, but someday he'll thank me for it."

Diana listened to the rumble of her suitcase, tied down with bungee cords in the bed of the truck, and questioned her motives for taking this trip with Matthew. An irrepressible excitement had been building inside her ever since they hit the road, and she couldn't even remember the last time she'd embarked on such an adventure. All her life she'd heard about the mysterious, majestic Appalachian Mountains, but she'd never seen them. So in spite of the dark purpose of this mission, the tensions of the past few days started falling away like a musty old coat.

Plus, she was finally taking positive action in the search for Juan, and this alone lifted her spirits. Or maybe she'd actually decided to trust again, feel again, and take a chance at happiness. She glanced shyly at Matthew and squeezed his hand.

While Matthew carried their bags into the trailer, she sat at the very edge of a ravine and gazed across to a range of mountains sleeping on the horizon. In her entire life, she'd never seen anything more beautiful. The close peaks were verdant green with the texture of pines and hardwoods, while the receding slopes gradually faded into a haze of blue mist. Her senses tingled with the sight, smell and feel of it. Even the ocean she loved so dearly couldn't compete with this rugged wilderness that propelled her backwards through the centuries, challenging some primal part inside every land creature.

Their campsite was situated on the crest of a *bald*, an area that rejected the growth of tall trees in favor of brush and other low-lying vegetation. It made for a stupendous view, helping her understand why Matthew always grumbled about civilization encroaching on the wilderness.

"When pioneers fist came, the forests were virginal, not second growth like this," he had complained while they traveled. "Back then, a man could see from these hilltops clean to Tennessee, but pollution has changed all that…"

"A penny for your thoughts?" Matthew had sneaked up from behind, gripping steaming mugs of coffee in his hands.

Since there was no way she could adequately convey her emotional response to these hills, *virginal* or not, she opened her arms wide to encompass the entire panoramic sweep in her embrace. "I love it!"

He cleared his throat "Yeah, I feel the same each time I come, but will you do me a favor, Diana? I'd rest a might easier if you'd scoot back from the edge." He lowered himself onto a boulder a good twelve feet back from the drop and refused to bring her coffee closer.

"Why Matthew! Are you acrophobic?"

"Let's just say I'm scared of heights."

She giggled as she scooted backwards to Matthew's perch and sampled her drink. The rich aroma and strong caffeine jolted her senses. "You make a mean cuppa coffee."

"Yes, ma'am." He grinned. "Then tonight I'll take you into town for some real country cooking."

They sipped in silence and admired the view until he shifted his long legs and watched her from the corner of his eyes. "Been meaning to ask you, Diana, how are your real estate classes coming?

I know you missed the last couple of weeks, so can you afford to take this trip with me?"

She dragged herself back to reality and answered truthfully. "I quit."

"Quit school?" He blinked in surprise.

"I was too far behind to catch up, so I'll repeat the class next term."

She omitted telling him about Miles Lawton's amorous advances. That day Johnny went missing and she'd banished her buyer clients from the Sorvino house, Miles had been furious, but that hadn't stopped him from making suggestive remarks. So she'd told Miles to take a hike.

"But what about Liz?" Matthew still seemed stunned by her admission. "I know how much you two wanted your broker's licenses, and then you were going into business together, right?"

She nodded unhappily. "That's still the plan, but it will be delayed six months. I phoned Liz right before we left and told her my decision. She did not take it well."

"I can imagine…" A slow smile spread across his face. "Did you tell Liz you were running off to the mountains with me?"

Her cheeks burned. No way would she tell him about the unbearable teasing and innuendo she'd endured once Liz learned about the trip. The juicy fact of her plans with Matthew had so distracted Liz, that she nearly forgot her disappointment over the real estate venture.

"Was Liz scandalized?" he asked.

She refused to satisfy Matthew's curiosity, but said, "She wondered if Miles Lawton, our teacher, was available. She wants to date him." Naturally, Diana had handed Miles over to Liz with her blessings.

"What did she say about *us*?" Matthew refused to be side-tracked.

Ignoring the question, Diana said, "I felt guilty about leaving Liz in the lurch, so I gave her the Sorvino listing."

He frowned. "Sorry to hear it, Diana. I know you need the money, and that Sorvino deal would've fetched a big commission. Maybe you should've thought twice before giving it up?"

"Honestly, Matthew, you sound exactly like my mother!"

He flung the dregs of his coffee out over the cliff. "God, I hope not."

FORTY

A toad's eye in a snakeskin bag...

The little town of Boone was bustling for a Wednesday night. Appalachian State University dominated the village, its modern buildings sprouting like concrete mushrooms in the surrounding hills, but since it was late June, very few students remained on campus for the summer session.

"So who are all these people?" Diana wondered as they drove down the quaint main street lined with shops and trendy boutiques.

"Tourists," Matthew grumbled. "Next month will be even worse when they flock to the Summer Music Festival."

The festival sounded like fun to her, but she knew Matthew hated crowds. In fact, ever since they'd entered the village, he'd been grumpier than usual. "Where should we eat?" she asked neutrally.

"You decide. It's my treat."

She was the stranger in town, so how was she supposed to choose? Yet she sensed he wasn't in the mood for indecision. "I saw a charming little white frame restaurant on the way in—The Daniel Boone Inn. Let's go there."

He spun around in the driver's seat, an odd look on his face. "Why'd you want to eat in that place? It's nothing but a tourist trap. We'll wait in line for hours."

"I'm not in a hurry, are you?"

Moments later, they parked in the Daniel Boone Inn's lot, then walked through lovely perennial gardens into a homey, wood-paneled foyer. They were told they'd have less than a five-minute wait.

"Guess we missed the dinner rush," Matthew muttered.

They stood in uncomfortable silence while she studied the décor including framed photos of old-timey Boone and a glass cases filled with antique tools, guns, and other frontier memorabilia. She dug into her wallet, fished out a penny, and pressed it into Matthew's hand.

"Okay, now here's a penny for *your* thoughts. What's the problem, Matthew?"

He exhaled loudly. For a fleeting moment, panic flickered across his eyes, but then his features relaxed into a smile. "Sorry, Diana. I used to come here with my wife, Lynn. This was her favorite restaurant. We ate here the month she died, and I need to put those ghosts behind me."

Her heart constricted with shame. Of all places, why had she chosen this one? She folded his fingers around the penny. "Can I help you drive those ghosts away, Matthew?"

He took a deep breath and shifted to his other foot. "Tell you the truth…" He smiled. "I know two ways to get rid of a ghost—either you put salt on the fire and carry the left hind foot of a graveyard rabbit, or you put a toad's eye in a snakeskin bag and tote that around. Mountain folks always knew best, and these two remedies came straight from these hills."

Diana stared. "Do you know a formula for good luck?"

"Yes, ma'am. I do. On New Year's Day you eat black-eyed peas, or maybe you'll find a cricket on your hearth. But seeing as it's the middle of summer, we'll have to conjure some good luck on our own."

He approached an ancient machine that looked like a jukebox. He placed the penny she had given him into a slot, added a pocketful of his own coins, and then the machine lit up and passed her penny through an embossing wringer. When it emerged, the penny had been flattened into an elongated oval bearing the image of a frontiersman holding a rifle and the words *Dan'l Boone Inn.*

He handed her the souvenir. "Hang onto this, Diana. It'll bring you good luck, and if *I'm* lucky, it'll always remind you of me."

Once they were seated, the waitress loaded their table with platters of fried chicken, country-fried steak, mashed potatoes, corn, fried okra, beans, and a basket of hot rolls.

"Don't be shy, Diana," Matthew urged. "The more you eat, the faster they'll bring on the refills."

She groaned in anticipation and filled her plate to brimming. She'd never been guilty of lady-like modesty when it came to food. But by the second round, they both slowed down and she tried a little conversation.

"Did Daniel Boone sleep here, or something?" Back in Pennsylvania, every old inn claimed that George Washington had laid down his weary head on their very pillows."

Matthew laughed. "No way. I reckon Daniel's bed was a blanket of leaves when he came to these mountains to hunt and fish, and he did not carve *D. Boone kilt a bar* on every tree, either. Matter of fact, he was a well-educated, land-rich Quaker from up your way, Diana."

"So he wasn't like Ben Franklin, then?" She winked. "When they claim *Ben Franklin slept here*, there must be a grain of truth in it, because the man fathered seventy-some illegitimate children."

"No kidding?" He offered a sly, suggestive grin.

And she wished she'd never opened that particular can of worms. During her brief survey of the Jayco trailer they were destined to share, she'd noticed the vehicle had only one big double bed.

"Want some dessert?" His eyes never left her face.

"Maybe some coffee?" She looked away as a telltale heat crept up her neck and night filled the picture window near their table. Most

212

of the other guests had departed, so she was grateful when an elderly woman approached, ending the intimate moment.

"I recognize that old gal," he whispered as she drew near. "She's been working here long as I can remember. Let's invite her to join us...."

Before Diana could object, he asked the woman to sit with them. In the meantime, Diana prayed the waitress wouldn't stir up painful memories by recalling the bygone visits of Matthew and his wife.

Instead, the woman poured fresh coffee and set out a cup for herself. She sat nearby on a free chair. "Feels good to take a load off." She sighed. "What can I do you for?"

"Maybe you can help us, Lucy." Matthew read the woman's nametag. "I know you've been around these parts for a long time, so I'm hoping you can help us locate a young gal used to live in the mountains."

"I was born and raised here." Lucy beamed. "What's this gal look like?" she asked Diana.

Stunned by Matthew's ability to strike up a folksy rapport with a total stranger, Diana stuttered her response. "The girl's name is Leona Clontz. She's in her early twenties with long blond hair, and she walks with a limp."

Lucy's brow knotted in a frown as she chewed her lower lip. "The name Clontz don't ring a bell, but I 'member a pretty little thing called Leona." The waitress's pale eyes drifted backwards in time as she absently stirred her coffee. "In fact, the girl used to work here. She was the last of the Birdsongs. Of course, that was a good six or seven years ago, and that child was only a teenager. Plus, she didn't walk with a limp."

"What's a *birdsong*?" Diana was intrigued.

213

"The Birdsongs have lived in the hills out towards Blowing Rock forever. They have Cherokee blood on the granddaddy's side, but it was Mother Mattie who held that family together."

"What about Leona?" Matthew asked.

"If it's the same gal, she's the last of 'em. Leona's mama, Mattie's daughter, died giving birth to Leona, and Leona's daddy got himself killed running a truck off the mountain. Like always, it was Mattie pulled herself together and raised the child."

"Then you actually know Leona?" Diana was amazed.

"We worked the same shift. Leona was real quiet and shy, but I reckon it was hard for her working alongside the college kids. Ordinarily the boss wouldn't hire a mountain girl, but he thought the world of Mother Mattie, so he did it as a favor.

"It ended up bad when the poor little thing got herself pregnant by some hillbilly out of West Virginia. The boy came to Appalachian State on a basketball scholarship. Once Leona began to show, the boss figured he'd made a mistake and fired her."

Diana's mind raced ahead. Everything in Lucy's story fit the profile of the mysterious country girl. "Where do the Birdsongs live?"

"Couldn't tell you." The elderly waitress shrugged. "Those Birdsongs don't want to be found, if you know what I mean. Once upon a time, Mattie's husband was a bootlegger. Family tradition, don't you know?" Lucy turned to Matthew. "But I recall Flake Brown always gave Mattie a ride when she came into Boone to sell her eggs and whatnot. Maybe he can show you how to find their house. Flake lives out somewhere on Route 321."

"Thanks, Lucy, you've been a great help." Matthew smiled. "Can I buy you a slice of pie?"

The old woman's laugh echoed through the empty dining room. "Lord no, sir. Do I look like I need another piece of pie?" She patted her round tummy, then turned a curious eye in Diana's direction. "I recall seeing your husband here before, ma'am, but I can't say I recognize you."

Diana longed to crawl under the table, because the old waitress had recognized Matthew, after all. No doubt she figured Diana was a home-wrecker having a fling with a married man. She was so flustered, she dipped her spoon into Matthew's cup at the exact same moment he started to stir his coffee. Both Lucy and Matthew froze at Diana's action. They stared at the cup, then at one another. Lucy began to giggle, while Matthew flushed red.

"Well, *now* I see how things are." Lucy winked. "So I'll leave you two lovebirds alone to get on with it."

"What was that all about?" Diana demanded once Lucy made an abrupt exit.

"It's another one of our folk beliefs…" Matthew averted his eyes. "When two people put spoons into a cup at the same time, it means that someday they'll get married."

FORTY-ONE

Blind man's bluff...

Floyd kicked the metal door open with the toe of his boot. Four days cooped up in the shitty trailer was worse than solitary confinement. In prison he had no choice, but now he was supposed to be a free man. A tune kept running through his head: *Freedom's just another word for nothin' left to lose,* and he didn't have a hell of a lot to lose—unless Juanita really came up with a pot worth one hundred thousand at the end of his rainbow. Then he'd have plenty to live for.

He stumbled down the broken steps and peed into the ragged bushes. The trailer's plumbing broke two days ago, so he'd been washing up in the stinking river ever since. At first he boiled the river water to make his instant coffee, but later he'd come to blame the water for the headache that would not go away.

His buddy, the one who owned this trailer, always bragged how Daniel Boone once made his home a few miles upstream on the Yadkin, where he lived off berries and wild game. Well, Floyd was no fucking pioneer. He'd already eaten all the canned goods, leaving a gnawing hole where his stomach used to be.

He fetched a rock and heaved it at the crows squawking their heads off in the river oak.

Behold the fowls of the air, they don't sow, neither do they reap,

Yet the Heavenly Father feeds them. Are ye not much better than they?

Damn straight! Floyd was a religious man, but he couldn't wait forever for the Lord to divvy up five loaves and two fishes.

Bloody bitches! Lately the image of Leona, the one who'd betrayed him, had begun to blend with the face of Juanita, the harlot holding back what was rightfully his. This shifting vision, a two-headed female monster, sharpened his hatred and made him strong, but the wretched isolation was definitely playing games with his sanity. It was high time to move on.

He knelt at the river, fetched a pail of water, and then stomped back to the trailer to stand in front of the mirror. He figured the good sharp razor would help him get reborn as a new man, so that even his own mama, God rest her soul, wouldn't know him. Neither would that snot-nosed kid up the road at the convenience store, the one with the pay phone.

He had given Juanita until Sunday to get the money. By now she should have an answer, and Floyd needed to know. A trickle of blood dribbled down his bald scalp, but Floyd felt nothing. All he knew for certain was that another night there was not an option.

Juanita shuffled barefoot across the living room floor and shoved the front door open with her toes. She glared into the humid night and lit up a Cigarillo. At that same moment, she saw the flash of another lighter, much like an echo of her own, from across the dark lawn. Next she heard the soft laughter of an FBI agent, who was smoking near the gate.

She inhaled. His laughter mocked her. She was lonesome, bored, a prisoner in her own house. The guards dogged her every move, even delivered her groceries right to the kitchen door. Then once each day, an armed escort drove her in an unmarked car for a quick trip to the hospital.

Bobby was tired of being a prisoner, too. They had no control, like their whole future hung on the fate of one little boy they both love too damned much.

She exhaled. The smoke drifted up to the treetops, where her mockingbird sang to the night. Juanita used to love the mama mockingbird. Bobby had taught her how to recognize all the bird's different songs, but she wondered, did the mockingbird have a song she could call her own? All spring she'd watched the creature building her nest, and then the mama taught her little ones how to fly and to imitate all their feathered friends. But could she teach them how to find their own voice?

Juanita decided she had lost her own voice somewhere along the way. She'd once been an easy-going gal, but now helpless anger gnawed a hole in her gut, and then filled that hole with violent nightmares of revenge.

Bobby claimed he was coming home Saturday, even if he had to murder every doctor to get there, but Saturday would be too late. As life went on, with more landscape workers arriving each day like clockwork, pretending Porter Park would open on schedule the Fourth of July, only Juanita knew the truth:

The sky was falling.

For the first time since she came to the States as a tiny child, she now felt alone in a foreign land. Everyone had deserted her, even Diana. All morning she'd tried to call her friend, but an answering machine informed her that Diana was on vacation. *Vacation*! She'd tried to phone Matthew all afternoon, but he too was missing in action. Even the employees at his store didn't have a clue where Matthew had gone.

She licked her fingers and pinched out the smoking filter. She smelled burning flesh and watched a tiny blister puff up, but felt nothing. Where were your friends when you needed them? She spit into the night, then backed into the house, closing the door behind her.

A crazy idea was writhing in her brain like a poisonous snake, and she wished she could try it out on someone. She couldn't tell Bobby, because he'd freak. The stupid FBI would never allow it, so Juanita was on her own. She was alone in the house with one hundred thousand dollars in ransom money, armed with nothing but this wild notion about how she might force the kidnapper to release her little Juan.

Then, when the phone rang, it scared her so bad she stubbed her toe on the coffee table and skinned her knee breaking the fall.

"Fuck!" she screamed into the receiver, intent on giving someone a piece of her mind.

"Fuck you, bitch!" a low male voice answered.

He was the demon from her nightmare. She was paralyzed by terror, yet longed to pick up a knife and cut the preacher's throat, like in her dream. Instead, she remained comatose as a dummy while he poured filth into her ear.

Eventually, he calmed down. "You guys from the FBI—I know you're listening in. In case you're interested, I'm calling to ask the bitch if she's got my money."

Juanita was chilled by the monster's total disrespect for the law. At the same time, all the frustrations of the past week rose like bile to the back of her throat. "I have your money, asshole!"

"Now ain't that good news." Floyd chuckled. "Seeing as how you've been a good girl, we should get together real soon."

"How is Juan?" she demanded.

"Little pisser's hanging in."

Suddenly she found her voice. "Why should I believe you? You don't get one penny until I know my boy's alive and well."

Silence, then laughter. "Oh, woman of little faith, I don't see you holding no cards."

"I have the *money*, but you don't get shit until I see proof."

More silence, and then a raspy whisper. "Don't be rude, Juanita. I could send you one of Juan's little brown fingers, but they're so tiny don't hardly seem worth the postage. We discussed other options, don't you remember?"

Dizzy with horror, she recalled how this maniac had threatened to send Juan's head in a box. She imagined the child's lifeless eyes accusing her of murder, yet she held back her tears. If her plan was going to work, she must show no fear. "Put Juan on the phone right now."

"My dear Juanita, you've been watching too many movies." The preacher's voice was dry ice. "The little pisser's taking his nap."

She sensed hesitation in his response. "Okay, take a digital photo of Juan waving his left hand and send it email. Get a pencil and write down my address..."

"I don't have no fucking computer, are you crazy?"

"Then send me a photo overnight FedEx. Call again when you know I've got it. Then, once I hear Juan on the phone, you have one hour to meet me in person."

"I don't have no fucking camera, bitch!"

"Then get your sorry ass to a drugstore and buy one. I have the money in my hand, and you sure as hell better have Juan in *your* hand when we meet, or the deal's off."

The preacher was breathing hard. She could almost smell his scared animal stink, but his voice remained neutral. "My answer is *no, ma'am*. I'll see the boy dead before I meet those conditions."

She held back her tears. If she weakened now, all was lost. "Then go on and kill him, asshole! I'll keep the money myself." She looked down at her clenched fist, where her fingernails were drawing blood. Seconds seemed to expand to hours as she prayed to Almighty God: *don't let him hang up.*

A third party on the line, coughed and cleared his throat.

"I know you're listening, you FBI shits!" the kidnapper roared. "So I'm telling this bitch she's got a deal, but she'll have to give me time to get the camera. Then, if I so much as smell you guys anywhere near our meeting, you can collect what's left of the boy in a body bag."

When the line went dead, Juanita's stomach lurched and she sank to the floor. She vomited on the carpet and almost choked when the phone rang again.

"That was an Academy Award performance, Ms. Cruz." Agent Grim's voice was the gruff rasp of a very tired old man. "You got guts, I'll give you that, but you're playing hard ball with Juan's life. Now the preacher's running scared, and that makes him desperate."

"At least I proved Juan's alive," she gasped. "Now *you* go find him!"

"We know Floyd Clontz never returned to West Virginia." Grim sighed. "But his nephew, Darryl, has regained consciousness. The kid can't talk yet, but he has indicated he wants to cooperate…"

Juanita felt drained and disgusted as she hung up on the man. In her experience, the only help she was likely to get would come from herself, or maybe, if she was very lucky, from God. Or maybe Bobby would come home Saturday, but it would be too late…

And where the hell were Diana and Matthew?

FORTY-TWO

The guardians of lost children...

Mattie decided her house didn't smell like itself. Layered on top of the usual odors—last winter's greasy wood smoke in the fireplace and ripe tomatoes on the windowsill—were the sweet and sour smells of powder and sweat. Mattie realized she was too familiar with her personal old-woman odor to notice that anymore, so she figured the new aromas came from Leona and the boy. Even as a child, Leona had favored flowery body powders, but Mattie had no experience with little boys. Sure enough, her granddaughter and the strange child who arrived with her, wore filthy clothes and both were ripe for a bath.

Seemed like Mattie's eyesight had faded while her other senses had gotten sharper. Nowadays she smelled the rain before the thunderclaps boomed over the mountains, and she heard the rooster before he crowed. But in spite of these talents, the sudden arrival of Leona and the boy had caught her unawares.

It was not Mattie's habit to sleep more than an hour or two each night, but while she slept her dreams took on the texture of reality. That particular night, five days ago, she dreamed she was a young woman of childbearing age, and little Leona was taking her first steps in the meadow out near the bootleg still.

Wild daisies tickled Mattie's bare knees as she sat with her legs spread open in the tall grass. She tossed a flower and Leona toddled off to fetch it, with sun vibrating around her baby blond hair

222

like an angel's halo. Leona found the flower, then fell laughing into Mattie's skirt.

This dream went on and on, the tossing and retrieving, until the sound of tires crunching on gravel penetrated her consciousness. Still groggy, Mattie figured it was her long-dead husband driving up the country lane with the revenue officers hot on his tail, but when she opened her eyes to the black of night, she saw headlights flashing on the wall. Disoriented, she couldn't find her way back through time, nor could she go for her gun before a strange car stopped outside the screen door.

Leona and the ghost of a boy were standing at the foot of her bed before her mind finally caught up with the truth of things.

"Hey, Mother Mattie," Leona whispered from behind scared eyes. "I'm real sorry busting in like this, but I got myself into some trouble. This here is Bird. You reckon we can stay awhile?"

So last Saturday night they came to Mattie out of a dream. Love did funny things, so at first Mattie just held her little girl, rocking and crying with Leona against her breast, and thanking the Lord for delivering back the long lost great grandson who never got born. In those long hours before dawn, she allowed herself to believe the boy really was the one killed by lightning so many years ago, but when the sun came up, she saw a rusty blue station wagon listing sideways in the yard and the strange, druggy-eyed kid staggering through the house like a lost soul.

She sat Leona down with a strong pot of coffee. "We need to talk, honey. Want to tell me what happened?"

As daylight lifted beyond the yellowed lace at the kitchen window, Leona spun a tale that chilled Mattie's blood to ice water, then got it to boiling like the pot on the stove. Mattie had no radio or television, so she had no way to measure the truth of Leona's bizarre yarn of kidnapping and murder, but she did know Leona. She saw the sickly pallor of her granddaughter's skin and the dark pockets of sleepless nights under her dead eyes.

She saw how her girl kept glancing nervously over her shoulder, like the Devil himself was sneaking into the barnyard. And since Floyd Clontz was involved, Leona's fears were warranted.

"You best hide that car in the barn," she told the girl. "If Floyd is coming, he'll spot it in the drive and there'll be hell to pay."

The boy slept while Leona hid the station wagon. In the meantime, Mattie visited the hen house to kill them a chicken. It gave her no pleasure to lose one of her laying hens, because nowadays the egg money and what little she fetched for fresh vegetables kept her alive. Flake came around once a week, of a Friday, and took her into town, where she sold to the diner and one local market. But now, with two extra mouths to feed, Mattie had no choice. Vegetable soup did her just fine, but a growing boy needed meat.

She gently lifted old Betty out of the coop and stroked her feathers. Betty had been with her a long time, but her production was down. Mattie's heart ached as she slipped her hand up the bird's long neck, so she made herself think about Floyd. Again hatred bubbled like water in the pot on the stove, the pot waiting for Betty. Mattie gripped hard under the head and spun the chicken around in a violent twist, breaking its neck. She wrestled the twitching creature onto the chopping block and lifted the ax. After that, time was a sorrowful blur.

She calculated she hasn't seen her granddaughter in a good five years, not since Leona came limping home, broken from her miscarriage. She brought her young husband, Darryl, with her. It took Mattie months to warm to the big man who'd caused her girl so much hurt, but in time she came to like his slow, kind-hearted ways. She saw he loved Leona and did what he could to provide. He sat for hours along the roadside selling furniture and carving little critters of his own design. Mattie had urged folks to buy from Darryl, but some, like Flake, never gave Darryl the time of day.

Mattie whacked off Betty's head and feet as she recalled how the community was just coming to accept Darryl when Floyd showed up. She drained the blood from the bird.

When Floyd convinced Darryl to up and leave with him, they took Leona along for the ride. It had all happened sudden-like, about the same time the Boone convenience store was robbed by a man who looked a lot like Floyd. Luckily, the townsfolk thought too much of Mattie to take up the chase, five long years ago.

"Bird ain't hungry," Leona said once Betty was boiled and served up in a stew. "He needs his sleep."

Mattie wiped her knotted hands on her apron and turned all her pent up anger on the girl. "All that sleeping ain't natural. What have you done to that boy? Filled him with drugs?"

After a spell of weeping, Leona produced a box of pink and white pills. "Floyd made me give him these. They don't hurt him, they just make him sleepy."

Mattie snatched the little box, soaked it under the faucet, then shoved it in the trash. "Well Floyd ain't here now, is he?"

After that, life turned more normal. By Tuesday, the boy was up and eating like a regular kid, but Leona was sleeping like the dead. Mattie was too excited to eat or sleep. She drifted in a haze of happiness as the small family relaxed in her care. She made them both strip and bathe. She gave Leona one of her housedresses to wear and dressed Bird in a blouse and pair of shorts from Leona's childhood. Once the two were clean and clothed proper, Mattie ordered Leona to climb up on Gee, one of their two white mules, and then Mattie hoisted Bird up behind her.

"Take the young'un out to the woods. Show him the secret place and the Indian caves," Mattie said. "That'll put the roses back in his little cheeks."

When Bird returned home that night, flushed with fresh air and full of mountain legends, he ran out to tell Mattie, who was tending to the new puppies in the barn.

His eyes widened when he saw the ugly little creatures nursing on Lassie's tits. "Are those *dogs*?"

Mattie giggled. "I guess they're part dog. Usually Lassie mates with Flake's old beagle, but not this time. Near as I can figure, she met up with one of them little wolves the government let loose in these hills."

"Wolves?" Bird yipped. "Awesome!"

"Now I can't say for certain," Mattie amended. "I call my dog Lassie, but that don't make her a collie."

He considered that, biting his lip, then lowered himself into the hay, a safe distance from the pups. "Well, if their daddy's a wolf, then they are wolves."

Mattie didn't argue. She watched in silence as the child inched closer to pick up a piece of straw and tickle the puppies' bellies. Soon he found a wad of string and fashioned a toy by tying little bits of twig and hay to the end of the string. He tossed the string toy at the pups, which started playing like kittens as one by one they slid off Lassie's nipples.

"You have a way with animals." Mattie smiled.

The child grinned through astonishingly white teeth and fixed her with his magnetic blue eyes. "Leona says your name is Birdsong. That's an Indian name, right?"

"Cherokee. It was Leona's name too, before she got married."

"Yeah, she married that creep, Darryl!" The boy frowned. "If her name's Birdsong, is that why she calls me Bird?"

226

Mattie had no idea why Leona called the child Bird, but his theory sounded reasonable. "Did Darryl hurt you, boy?"

The grin faded from Bird's face. "Not so much."

"What about the other man, Mr. Floyd?" she demanded.

His eyes flashed with fear, and then filled with tears. He crawled away from Mattie and the pups.

"He can't hurt you anymore, Bird."

"My name's not *Bird,* it's *Juan*!" The child spat into the straw. "If anyone calls me Bird again, I'll kill them!"

Mattie was shocked and saddened. Violence didn't come natural to this boy—it came from too much close association with Floyd, like ticks off a dog. "Trust me, Juan. No one can hurt you long as you're with me and Leona."

"I'm not scared!" The boy thrust out his jaw. "Because everyone's looking for me—Aunt Nita, Bobby, and my Indian brother."

"Leona didn't tell me you have a brother."

"Well, I do."

Mattie was captivated as Juan described a *blood brother* pact he'd made with a boy named Johnny, but he would not repeat their secret oath.

"You're an Indian, Mother Mattie. You should know all about that stuff."

Mattie racked her brain. "I never heard tell about blood brothers, but that don't mean it ain't so. I can tell you about the Yunwi Tsunsdi, though."

"The what?" Juan inched closer.

"Before the White Man came, the Cherokees told about a tribe of little people who used to hide away from the light of day. They were always playing dirty tricks on the Indians..." She paused to watch Juan's eyes light up. "Anyway, the little Yunwi people did one good thing—they were the guardians of lost children. When they saw a child was lost, they stood in the shadows at the edge of the woods to guide the child's spirit towards the village while they called their parents' name."

"Lost children like me?"

"Yes, Juan, exactly like you."

By late Wednesday, Mattie lost patience with Leona, because once the girl got her fill of sleep, she'd taken to crawling around like an old river turtle, afraid to pull its head out of its shell.

"You might could help me with the chores, Leona." Mattie's bones ached from the roots of her long white hair to her gnarled toes. "Go tend the garden, then fetch us some eggs!" she barked.

"I can't go out, Mother Mattie. What if Floyd's hiding in the shadows?"

"And take the boy with you. He's busting a gusset cooped up all day."

"If Floyd sees Bird, he'll grab him for sure!"

Mattie tromped across the room and snatched Leona's chin. "Listen to me, young lady. Like as not, Floyd's half way across the country by now, high tailin' it from the law like a gun shy hound."

Leona's eyes pleaded, but Mattie kept hold. "And the boy's name is *Juan,* you hear? Don't be calling him *Bird* no more."

Leona pulled loose and started to cry. Ever since she came home, she'd been moaning about her poor Darryl on his hospital deathbed, but Mattie sensed that Juan's safety was at the root of Leona's problems.

"It's time to give that boy back, Leona. No two ways about it. So far you ain't done no wrong you can't make right. No one knows you're here, not even that old busybody, Flake Brown. It ain't too late to drive into Boone, drop Juan at the police station, and take the medicine you got coming."

"But I love him, Mother Mattie."

"Sure you do, honey, but he don't belong to you." Her throat ached from the words, because she knew Leona's pain was real. "You don't need me tellin' you what's right, but you ain't got much more time. Come Friday, Flake will be knocking on the door to take me to town. What'll you say then?"

After their heart-to-heart, Leona's tears continued through the night, and Juan was so upset, he left Leona's room to curl like a baby at the foot of Mattie's bed. By Thursday morning, the plan of action was decided.

"Okay, I'll take him back," Leona said. "But I can't turn him in wearing my stupid old clothes and looking like a little girl."

Mattie walked silently to the sink and opened the metal doors. Down amongst the pipes she found the plastic waste can full of paper trash. She lifted out the liner and poured her life savings onto the kitchen table. "Now you got money, girl. Take Juan into town and get him some new clothes. Treat him to a nice lunch and buy him a little present to remember you by."

"But I'm scared, Mother Mattie." Leona sniffled. "What will the police do to me?"

The old familiar pain shot up Mattie's arm as she beheld her grandchild. She made herself a picture memory to last a good long time. "Can't say what they'll do. I hope they'll bear in mind how you've been protecting young Juan and how you done right in the end. Whatever happens, come straight home to me when they turn you loose, you hear?"

Leona nodded, but refused to look Mattie in the eye. She left to fetch Juan, then made him lie down flat on the back seat of the station wagon.

As Mattie leaned through the car window to kiss Leona's cheek, she considered the possibilities. With all that money, Leona could run far, taking the boy with her. Else she might drop Juan off at the police station, and then head out for parts unknown. After all, what did an old woman like Mattie have to offer? She knew Leona loved her, but what if this was the end?

She'd suffered too many betrayals in her long life to endure one more. The pain in her chest grew more intense as the blue station wagon careened down the mountain, leaving a rolling hubcap behind in the dust, taking Mattie's heart with it.

FORTY-THREE

Inside out...

Diana stood at a miniature stove frying the bacon and eggs Matthew bought on the way home from the Inn last night, and she gazed out the trailer window as the sun lifted through the morning mist above purple mountains in the distance.

Every muscle in her body ached in unaccustomed ways, and the heat from the stove was minor compared to the burning sensation radiating through every part of her like liquid fire. At the same time, she was filled to brimming with a long-forgotten contentment. No, not even that. How could she forget what she'd never had before? Loving Matthew was new and bright as the sunrise.

"Smells mighty good..." He poked his dripping face through the curtain of the closet-sized shower. "Wow, this means you've cooked breakfast for me two days in a row."

Seemed impossible. Had it been only yesterday they ate together, watching the lake from Diana's patio, and then decided to take this trip? Since then, her life had suffered a sea change, causing her to swim up from hidden depths to drown in Matthew's arms.

He stepped from the shower clad only in a towel knotted loosely above his slim hips. The towel hugged the private parts of his anatomy she'd come to know quite well. His powerful shoulders, flat belly, and long muscular legs were the physique of a young man hardened to maturity, while the gentle and generous technique he'd

231

shared with her spoke of a seasoned love unparalleled in her experience or imagination.

Now he approached from behind, wrapped his wet arms around her, and pulled her close. Once again she ached for everything he'd given her through the night. When he kissed the back of her neck, then moved his mouth to caress the soft hollow at the base of her throat, she returned that kiss and broke loose from her moorings, adrift in an unchartered sea of her own desire.

Only when a spray of hot grease spattered on her arm, did she breathlessly pull away. "Hey, I'll burn the bacon..."

He backed off and searched her eyes. "Thank you for last night, Diana." His voice was hoarse with emotion.

Her eyes thanked him back, and she knew he'd likely not speak of this again. In spite of their intimacy, they were both a little shell-shocked by this new state of affairs.

"Put some clothes on, will you?" She snapped a dishrag at his very fetching backside and sent him grinning like a schoolboy in the direction of the bedroom.

She hummed a tuneless melody as she set silverware at the tiny Formica table for two. Making love had been her idea, since Matthew would never have made a move without a clear signal from her. And she had no regrets, although every brain cell still functioning said maybe she should have a few. Those old synapses were grooved for self-defense, and she'd been avoiding the danger of relationships for so long that every function required reprogramming before she could completely trust anyone. What if the closeness ended when this trip was over? She took a deep breath and forced herself to live in this moment, to accept this interlude of great joy and peace.

When Matthew wandered out, bashful in soft faded jeans and an old plaid shirt turned inside- out, he was, if possible, more attractive than ever as he padded barefoot across the floor with an old-fashioned phone book tucked under his arm.

"Flake Brown's not listed." He frowned.

Diana laughed. "If you're talking about Miss Mattie's neighbor, I'm sure his name is *Blake*, not *Flake*. Your friend Lucy the waitress must have got it wrong."

"Don't count on it. Problem is, I see no Browns listed at all. Let's go into town and ask folks. Someone's bound to know him."

She wrapped her arm around his waist and eyed the phone book. "My dear Matthew, you didn't expect to find him that easily, did you?"

"Why not? Mama used to say it takes a smart man to try the simple way first."

She chuckled. "Yeah, but did your mama teach you to put a shirt on right?"

He glanced down sheepishly. "Whoops, I see what you mean, but this situation requires your help…"

A mischievous glint ignited his eyes, as Diana waited for the punch line.

"Remember how we were talking about folk wisdom? Well, if you put a shirt on inside-out, it's good luck. But unless you get *someone else* to turn it right-side-out for you, your luck will change for the worse…"

FORTY-FOUR

A cloud passed over the sun...

Leona pulled into the alley behind Mast General Store and parked between two delivery vans tall enough to hide the old station wagon. Her heart raced a mile a minute, and she couldn't stop looking over her shoulder, but so far... so good.

She'd never done something this important on her own, so she was extra proud when she found the secret road off the mountain. No one had used that trail since her granddaddy Birdsong hauled corn mash, but Leona had spotted it right off when she arrived with Bird last Saturday night. Thanks to her quick thinking, no one, not even that nosey Flake, had seen her coming, or going.

"Can I sit up now?" Bird whined from the back seat.

"Sure, honey. Tie your shoestrings and get ready. We're goin' shopping."

"For real?" Bird's head looked funny when he lifted it up in the light. Black roots sprouted at his scalp under the blond fuzz, and his eyes were wary and frightened. He looked like one of those punk kids on TV, but at least he didn't have no earrings pierced in strange places.

Like Leona, Bird had been on the run so long, he was half scared to step out of the car. "Where are we?" he demanded.

"We're in Boone, child, the town where I grew up."

"I thought you lived in the mountains?"

"Yes, but I came to school here sometimes."

The boy snorted in disbelief. Fact was, Mother Mattie had given up hauling Leona into town for an education before she reached high school. It was just too much of a hassle, and back then nobody cared, not even the truant officer.

"I'm supposed to start third grade this year." Bird grabbed hold of her hand as they sneaked in the backdoor of the store. "Bobby and Aunt Nita say it's a brand new school, and I'll be the best student."

"I 'spect you will be, honey." Her throat hurt as Bird's eyes asked an unspoken question. Ever since he'd perked up from those pills, the child had been a handful. He'd never stopped asking when he was going home, but she'd never answered. Of late his fear had turned to anger, and once he'd punched her real hard when she wouldn't talk.

"Why'd you bring me here?" Bird stalled at the edge of the sales floor. "Are you gonna let me go?"

Leona crouched down and tucked in his shirt. Her heart was breaking. "I'm fixing to buy you some new clothes, and then we'll get some ice cream. Okay?"

He stomped hard. "I'll run away…!"

An elderly man browsing through camping equipment overheard Bird's outburst and scowled at Leona.

"Be quiet, Juan," she whispered into his ear. "Else someone will take you away from me. Then what'll you do?"

Her words startled him silent. She'd never before called him by his real name.

"What's gonna happen, Leona?"

How should she know? A dozen times on the way into town, she'd almost turned off in a complete different direction, but where would she go? Darryl was gone, she had no friends, and Mother Mattie's money wouldn't last forever.

She pulled Bird close and hugged him real tight. "Don't worry, honey, everything will be just fine, I promise. Now be a good boy, and I'll buy you a special present, so you'll remember me."

Bird's eyes lit up like they did that day when she took him out to see the Indian caves. He broke loose and scampered across the oiled wood floor to an antique glass display case. "I want one of those, Leona!" Nose pressed to the glass, Bird pointed to a fancy red pocketknife with a little white cross on its casing. "It's a Swiss army knife. My daddy gave me one just like it, but Aunt Nita took it away."

Leona was tempted, but she couldn't give such a dangerous thing to a child. "Pick something else, Juan."

"No, I want the knife!" he screamed.

Again curious faces swiveled in their direction, until she wanted to shrink up and disappear. "Ain't there nothing else you can think of?"

A crooked smile crept across Bird's face. "Yeah, but it's not in this stupid store…" He pulled her close. "Give me one of those wolf puppies out in the barn."

Her chest tightened. She already knew Bird wanted a puppy more than anything in the whole wide world. "Sorry, but we ain't going back to the barn, honey. Not ever."

His eyes popped with surprise, but before he came up with more questions, she dragged him across the room to a rack of children's T-shirts. "My Lord, look at these!" Her voice jiggled as she ran the hangers back and forth. "Do you want one with Dan'l Boone, or this one with the Indian Chief?"

Bird shrugged. "The Indian's okay…"

She yanked the shirt off its hanger, and then chose a pair of green hunting shorts that looked to be Bird's size. She hauled him into the dressing room.

"Go on, try 'em on…" The painful lump in her throat swelled as she watched Bird change. She had dressed him in the original clothes he'd worn when they snatched him, so he stank to high heaven. She counted the ribs on his skinny little chest and made a memory of their last moments together.

The fitting room seemed to close in as an image came clear in her head: Once they got to the police station, she'd send Bird in alone, and then she'd take off. She'd never let them lock her in a cage.

"Can I wear these now?" Bird's face beamed at his reflection in the mirror.

"Don't see why not. In the meantime, I'll throw away your filthy old clothes…"

"No!" The child snatched his rags and clung like a baby to a teddy bear.

If she'd had doubts before, she then fully understood that the boy desperately wanted to go home to what he'd lost. These nasty old clothes were his only lifelines to the past, and he'd never let go. She couldn't hold him in her world any longer.

She counted out cash for the clothes, and then led the boy to the adjacent showroom, where a sign said *Mast's Famous Sodas, Sweets, and Sundries.* From her own childhood, she knew this was a magical place, where old-timey wooden barrels overflowed with every candy known to man. Shelves of cookies and tins of exotic confections lined the walls, while an old-timey soda fountain glittered all along the back.

"Cool!" Even Bird couldn't deny the allure. "Can I have some candy?"

"Choose whatever you want." She handed him a white paper bag. He could mix his own selections, then they'd weigh and pay later.

He stood on tiptoe to peek into the barrels, and then ran from one to the next in wild indecision. The room smelled of chocolate and coffee, but the odors didn't sit well on Leona's stomach.

She figured she'd tell Bird about the police station once they got settled at the fountain, and then turn him in directly after they'd finish their sodas. If she hesitated, she'd never do it at all, and the Good Lord knew that any old excuse would get her running in the wrong direction at that point.

She wondered if all the people milling around the room, tourists mostly, took her for Bird's mama. The idea calmed her some, even though it was just pretend. She noticed how the sunshine from the big glass doors opening to the sidewalk played across Bird's handsome little features, and her heart near to burst with maternal pride.

But then a cloud passed over the sun, and a strange look came over Bird's face. His big eyes froze in terror as they fixed on the front door. It was like someone ran a hot poker through his stiff little body. His fingers opened and he dropped his bag. All the candy rolled across the floor, as Bird slipped down to hide behind the nearest barrel.

Leona's gut seized up as she looked towards the door, to where a bald man, maybe some jerk from a motorcycle gang, leaned on the doorjamb talking to some other guy.

"What's got into you, boy?" She lowered down on her knees next to Bird and began scooping up the candy. He latched onto her arm with fingers cold as popsicles. His nails dug into her skin so bad she near cried out in pain. "What's wrong with you, child?"

A little trickle of pee ran out the leg of Bird's new shorts and pooled on the floor. The boy's mouth opened and closed, but at first no sound came out.

"It's *him*!" he chirped at last.

Leona lifted her eyes to just above the rim of the barrel and looked again. She saw the same two men. The bald one was trying to buy a dirt bike off the other. The one who owned the bike mentioned a price, and then the bald one hooted loud and mean. That laugh sliced through her groin like cold steel, and when the stranger turned his face towards the room, his eyes glowed like coals above the tiny scar across his mouth. She bit down hard on her tongue, drawing blood, anything to keep from screaming out Floyd's name.

At the same time, Bird crawled backwards on his hands and knees, then got up and ran towards the back door. She did the same, nearly slipping on the hard candies melting in Bird's urine.

No time to worry about her dignity or the curious, gaping eyes. Instead, she saw only Bird, with tears streaming down his face. He held his crotch as he made a beeline for the old station wagon. By the time she caught up, he was curled up in his old position in the back seat, but this time his knees were drawn up under his chin, like a baby in the womb.

Near as she could tell, Floyd hadn't seen them and nobody was following. She crawled behind the steering wheel and locked all the doors. If she drove through the back alleys to the police station, she figured Floyd wouldn't spot her when she put Bird out.

"Don't cry, honey," she pleaded. "I promised you it's gonna be all right, and it will." She drove slowly as she passed Bird's old shorts to the back. At least they were dry. "Put 'em on, and you're good as new."

He made a low, keening sound, like a hurt animal. If memory served, the station house was located in the next block. Leona's heart knocked inside her ribs as she looked both ways, then turned onto Main Street.

"You best get ready now," she called over her shoulder. "The police station's up ahead. When we get there, I'll open the door, and you'll walk inside all by yourself, like a big boy."

"No!" Bird's teeth chattered. "I won't go in without you."

Leona's heart stopped beating altogether. She couldn't carry a hysterical child through the station house without attracting attention. She could almost feel the cold bite of the handcuffs and hear iron bars closing behind her back. She saw the light fading from her life.

Yet she parked in the city lot behind a squad car, and faced the boy. He was clinging to the seat for dear life. "I know you're scared, Juan, but no one will hurt you here. The policemen will see you get home safe."

"I won't go!" The child choked on his tears. "Take me back to the farm. I want to stay with the wolf puppies!"

She lifted her eyes to Heaven and blinked back tears. Floyd had scared the child so bad he couldn't think straight, but she'd already warned the Lord not to tempt her, because any old excuse would send her running down the wrong road. So if this wasn't a sign from the Almighty, she'd never seen one. She'd never done much right, but then she'd never done anything so wrong that He'd ask her to spend the rest of her natural life in jail…had she?

"Don't cry…" She stroked Bird's fuzzy head. "I won't put you out, child."

She quickly shifted into reverse and headed back towards Highway 321. This time she'd avoid the main road and follow the old, untraveled lanes recalled from her youth. She knew Floyd would come for her and Bird, but at least she wouldn't meet him on the highway.

Fear pumped through her veins, causing her hands to tremble on the wheel. With Floyd nipping at their heels, she couldn't stay in her grandmother's cabin without putting the old woman in danger.

But for now, they were going home, *her* home. Mother Mattie would know what to do.

FORTY-FIVE

Salt of the earth with a shotgun...

The sun was high above the mountains by the time Diana and Matthew left the trailer. They'd never gotten around to eating the breakfast she'd prepared. Instead, they'd abandoned themselves to horseplay when she tried to turn Matthew's shirt right-side-out. One thing led to another, and they'd barely made it to the bedroom, where they spent several blissful hours losing all sight of purpose.

Guilt didn't set in until they wandered into the Boone Drug Company for a very late lunch. "Where do we start?" The image of Juan loomed heavily on her conscience.

Matthew guided her to a booth across from an old-fashioned lunch counter. "We start by eating. Right now we're running on a wing and a prayer."

He was right. She was existing on emotional steam, but hunger rumbled somewhere in that sweet pit that used to be her stomach. "Look at this place. Do you ever feel like a dinosaur, Matthew?"

She told him about the old Woolworth's in West Chester, Pennsylvania, where as a child, she'd eaten at a counter much like this one. "They tore the Woolworth's down in 1994, but the Warner Movie House went under the wrecking ball long before that."

"They call that progress?" He ordered homemade chicken salad. "Soon those memories will be long gone."

She recalled the lipsticks, costume jewelry, and craft kits that once sparked her imagination at the old dime store. This place offered all those plus a complete pharmacy, hardware department, and art supplies upstairs.

"I think I'll try the hot lunch bar," she said.

Matthew frowned at the stainless steel tubs filled with roast beef, mashed potatoes, gravy, steamed vegetables, and even hot apple dumplings. "You may want to rethink that, Diana. That food's been sitting since the lunch hour, it's past its prime."

"Who isn't?" She winked. Real diner food was one her secret vices, so she wasn't about to pass up the opportunity.

They ate in distracted silence, each occupied with private thoughts. She knew he was also desperately worried about Juan. That, coupled with a certain shyness with one another, made for a quiet lunch. Finally, Matthew shoved his uneaten food aside.

"I'll ask around about Flake," he said. "It's a small town. Flake has to shop somewhere."

She had noticed the stores lining Boone's Main Street—used bookstores, college boutiques, and local art galleries. They didn't seem likely haunts for farmer Brown. Suddenly her apple dumpling lost its appeal.

"I need to buy a few things at the pharmacy," she told him. "Maybe the druggist knows something?"

Matthew left the tip and paid. "I'll wait for you out front. I saw some old-timers warming the benches along the sidewalk. Likely one of them is willing to jaw a spell."

When she emerged from the store, a big cloud passed over the sun, chilling her with an odd sense of foreboding. She spotted Matthew in earnest conversation with an ancient bearded gentleman hunched over a cane. By the time he joined her, his face was flushed with victory.

"I found him, Diana. I know the way to Flake Brown's."

243

By the time they located Mr. Brown's remote little brick rancher, set far back from the highway, it was late afternoon and a storm was brewing. They saw an elderly man on a red tractor driving fast, hoping to finish mowing his yard before the rain started. They parked the truck, and then walked through a grove of graceful oaks.

At the same time, the tractor buzzed around the corner of the barn at full-tilt, heading straight at them. For a moment, she feared the man intended to run them down, but he shifted into neutral and coasted to a stop just short of Matthew's boots. He scowled from beneath the bill of his straw hat, and did not turn off the engine.

"Hey, Mr. Brown..." Matthew shouted above the din. "How you doin' today, sir?"

The old geezer's suspicion was as thick as the humidity as he cut the engine. "Ain't buying nothing."

"Good, 'cause I ain't selling nothing," Matthew countered. "We came to ask after your neighbor, Miz Mattie Birdsong."

Mr. Brown climbed stiffly off his John Deere, but ignored Matthew's extended hand. "Mother Mattie ain't buying nothing neither."

"Then you *do* know Miss Mattie?" Diana butted in.

"Maybe I do, maybe I don't." Flake scowled at her with a look to melt steel. He addressed his attention to Matthew only. "What do you want with her, anyways?"

Diana opened her mouth to speak, but thought better of it. She had experienced this phenomenon before, this male notion that women, like good little children, should be seen, not heard. So she shut up and let Matthew do his thing. Already he had gotten beyond Mattie and was asking about Leona.

Flake sneered. "That little gal ain't lived up to Mattie's for years. She wasn't nothing but trouble from day one, a real heartache

244

to her grandma. Leona run off in disgrace, don't you know? Girl got herself pregnant. Good riddance, I say."

Diana suppressed an urge to kick Flake in his self-righteous shins. Both Lucy last night, and now this joker, assumed that Leona had delivered her baby out of wedlock, but Diana knew from Agent Grim that Leona had been legally married, whatever else her sins.

"Sure you haven't seen Leona lately?" Matthew pressed. "It's very important that we get in touch with her."

"I might be getting on in years, but my eyesight's good as ever. If that girl came sneaking around, I'd have seen her."

"I understand, sir," Matthew said. "But do you think we could talk to Miz Birdsong herself?"

Flake's rheumy eyes narrowed as he sized Matthew up. "I 'spect it couldn't hurt nothing, long as you don't go and upset her. But them roads up to her place will shake your truck apart like a tin can, and what with this storm comin', you won't see the turns till you drive off the edge."

Matthew's neck colored. "My truck has four-wheel drive. I'll take my chances."

"Suit yourself." Flake cackled. "Come closer, fella, and I'll draw you a little map…"

The boys huddled together as Flake scribbled on a matchbook. In the meantime, Diana reeled with anger and impatience. When they finally left, Flake shouted at their backs.

"One more thing, folks, be sure to *halloo the house* before you go barging in."

"Come again?" Matthew called.

"Like I told you before, you don't want to surprise Mother Mattie. Old gal has a trigger temper and the shotgun to back it up. If you spook her, she's like as not to blow your brains out!"

"Thanks for the tip." Matthew turned his back on the man and rolled his eyes. "The old coot's a charmer, isn't he? You still want to go?"

Diana considered. Depending who told it, Mattie Birdsong was a cross between Mother Theresa and Ma Barker, or salt of the earth with a shotgun. Who on earth were these mountain people? It seemed like some of these folks were living in a previous century. Matthew had explained that a few of them had indeed been isolated from modern society for decades and remained quite primitive in their outlook. So not for the first time, she wondered what she was getting into.

At the same time, in the past few minutes, an odd premonition had gathered in her subconscious like the thunderheads forming in the sky. She sensed the presence of Juan, saw his face in the clouds and heard his voice in the whistling wind.

"What are we waiting for?" she said.

FORTY-SIX

This dark natural cathedral…

"This can't be right." Matthew pulled off the highway and stared at a rutted cow path weaving through an overgrown field.

Diana studied Flake's scrawl on the matchbook cover. "Must be right. There's the dead willow he described."

They eased onto the path, the shocks of Matthew's truck squealing in protest as they bumped towards the sky over brutal rocks and fallen branches. Finally, the open fields ended at the edge of a heavy scrub forest.

"Who on earth would choose to live up here in the middle of nowhere?" Her stomach lurched with each bump.

"Some folks prefer the company of nature to living cheek by jowl with their own kind. There have been times in my life when I've felt pretty much the same."

She glanced at him, wondering how long it would be before he tired of her close companionship. In the past twenty-four hours, they had lived and breathed as one, sharing their minds and bodies like a single organism. For two confirmed loners, this intimate time together had been an interlude she couldn't have imagined one short week ago.

Matthew reached across the seat and squeezed her hand. At the same time, he watched the needle on the thermostat climb dangerously high on the gauge. "Hope she won't boil over," he muttered as he downshifted.

Soon they were shrouded in fog. Inching forward at a crawl, they entered a dense forest where weak shafts of gray light penetrated the heavy green canopy above their heads. Again she sensed the presence of Juan and offered up a prayer in that dark, natural cathedral.

Matthew turned off the air conditioning and asked her to roll down the windows. She smelled heavy moss on fallen logs and rain hanging in the air.

"Look up ahead…" He nodded towards a sudden brilliant light stabbing through a tunnel in the forest.

As they drove into a haze of sunlight, he braked abruptly at the very edge of a mountain. Through the shimmering mist, they saw the deadly drop. "That was way too close for comfort," he growled. "Hope we can navigate these darn curves without breaking our necks…"

The sun receded as suddenly as it had appeared, leaving them both shaken and lost in the fog.

"Why don't I walk out ahead?" she offered, although her legs trembled at the prospect. "You can drive slow and follow me, then I'll yell if we come to another precipice. Hate to say it, but according to Flake's map, this *is* the road to Mattie's."

Matthew frowned. "Okay, but *you* drive, *I'll* walk."

She sniffed the air and detected a distinct electrical odor, like the truck was overheating. "If it's all the same to you, Matthew, I'd feel safer walking than driving."

They made the bargain, then she climbed gingerly from the passenger seat. The trek was slow going. Her legs ached, and once the truck stalled and rolled backwards. By the time they reached the top of the rise, she'd lost all sense of time.

But then she saw it and pounded hard on the truck's hood to get Matthew's attention. "There it is! Mattie's house is straight ahead!"

The old Ford lurched and sputtered when he cut the ignition a good distance from the crooked little structure. Through the fog, she saw that the weathered wood walls and tin roof hadn't been painted in years.

"We call that a *dog trot cabin*." Matthew joined her. "The rooms are laid out in a single row, so it's a straight shot clean through. That way, the old hound can chase a rabbit up the stoop, through the house, and out the back door without breaking stride."

She was more worried about the small, intent figure moving quietly from the house and into the shadows on the front porch. The old woman had a shotgun cradled in her arms like a baby. "You won't have to *halloo the house,* Matthew," she whispered. "Mattie already knows we're here."

He guided her gently behind him, shielding her with his body, and then started calling and waving as they approached the shack.

"You two best turn around and go back where you come from!" Mattie hollered as she brought the gun around and pointed it in their direction.

"Take it easy, Miz Birdsong." Matthew held out both hands. "We've come a long way. Can you spare us one minute of your time?"

"I don't know you, Mister." She stepped off the porch and aimed at Matthew's boots.

Diana searched the woman's face, but Mattie's eyes were hidden under the bill of a red baseball cap.

"I'm a friend of Leona's…" Diana stepped clear of Matthew's protection. "She's in trouble, ma'am, and we want to help her." She ducked away when Matthew tried to pull her back behind his wing.

She willed her feet to move towards the woman. "Please, Mattie, won't you talk to me?"

"You're lying, Missy. Leona don't have no friends!" She swung the gun towards Diana. "Even if she did, I ain't seen Leona in years."

Diana's stomach did flip-flops. The last time someone pointed a gun at her, she'd landed in the hospital with a bullet through her shoulder. "Okay, we won't talk about Leona, but help us find the boy," she pleaded through dry lips. "I know you don't want to harm him."

Ignoring Matthew's angry calls, she approached the woman and sensed the gradual lowering of the shotgun, as Mattie seemed to sink into herself. Diana smelled the acrid odor of the woman's fear and noticed the unhealthy gray pallor of her skin. "Are you ill, Miss Mattie?"

The gun clattered to the ground as Mattie wilted into her arms.

"It's my heart," she gasped. "Blamed thing's been skipping beats all day."

Suddenly Matthew was at her side. Together they helped the stricken woman into the dark house and made her sit down at the table.

"Where are your pills, ma'am?" Matthew was clearly alarmed.

Mattie dragged the baseball cap off her head. "Don't got no pills, but a glass of cold water would be welcome..." She waved Diana towards the sink.

As Diana held her finger under the tap, waiting for the water to run cold, she noticed the sink was full of dirty dishes. She saw three of everything—three cups, three glasses, and three sets of silverware. She couldn't speak for other women who lived alone, but Diana tended to rinse and use the same dishes again and again rather than bring clean ones out each time. If Mother Mattie lived alone, as she claimed, then this behavior was odd indeed.

"Thank you kindly, Miss." Mattie drank the water in slow, grateful sips. "Now I'm feeling like myself again."

Impulsively, Diana held her cool hand against the old woman's forehead. Mattie's skin was clammy, but color had returned to her cheeks. "Should we call a doctor?" she gently suggested.

"I don't hold with doctors, young lady. To my way of thinking, they'll make you sick before they'll make you well. This old heart of mine's been acting up long as I can remember, but it keeps on ticking. I wager it'll go on that way 'til someone up and breaks it."

"Who would break *your* heart, Miss Mattie?" Matthew lowered himself onto a chair right across from Mrs. Birdsong and looked her straight in the eye. "Would your daughter Leona do that? The way she stole that boy broke *my* heart."

The old woman stiffened and pulled away from Diana. She pounded a gnarled fist on the table. "I don't know you, young man. So far, I ain't heard the names of either one of you, yet here you are, sittin' at my table like invited guests."

Matthew apologized, then formally introduced himself and Diana. "Now, can I fetch you another glass of water, ma'am? We mean no harm to you and yours, but we do aim to find that boy."

"Already told you, I ain't seen Leona, and I don't know nothing about no boy. If you say otherwise, you're barkin' up the wrong tree." Mattie's parchment cheeks flamed. "'Less you want me to pick up that shotgun, you best leave my house."

Diana shot him a warning glance. This time his famous charm wasn't working. "Matthew, why don't you step outside while Mattie and I talk?"

251

Matthew was startled, but climbed respectfully to his feet. "I'm sorry, Miz Birdsong, didn't mean to offend you. You and Diana enjoy your chat, while I mosey out to the barn."

Fear flashed across the old woman's face, but she quickly recovered. "Mosey to the outhouse, for all I care. I got nothing to hide."

Left alone, the two women appraised one another, and Diana was struck by Mattie's beauty. Her handsome jaw and snapping dark eyes had softened with the years, and her wild mane of white hair retained only a few strands of raven black, but the power of her spirit transcended time. The memory of that face had been etched in Diana's brain. Mattie was the proud grandmother standing before a mountain range, her hands resting on little Leona's shoulders—the photo from the Clontz trailer.

"Please tell me about Leona..." she urged.

The ancient mantle clock chimed five, so Diana calculated they'd been talking for over an hour. Although Mattie seemed anxious to confide, Diana was no closer to the truth.

"You're not really Leona's friend, are you?" Mattie demanded.

"No, but I have met her. I visited her trailer and saw her doll collection."

"If you're not her friend...." Mattie's breathing became ragged and agitated. "I should've run you off this place whilst I still had my gun!"

"But I honestly want to help your granddaughter, Miss Mattie. Leona and the boy are staying here with you, aren't they?"

"No!" The woman's cheeks blanched white, while an angry blotch of red crawled up her throat.

Diana didn't want to cause a heart attack, but Mattie's resistance seemed to be weakening. "I saw the extra dishes in your sink, so I know you've been cooking for three."

"And what about that old station wagon out in the barn?" Matthew startled them both when he walked in from the shadows.

"That's *my* car!" Mattie insisted, her eyes brimming with tears.

"Beg pardon, ma'am, but that vehicle has an out-of-state license tag." He lowered himself into a chair. His hair was wet from the rain now clattering on the tin roof. "And by the looks of it, someone's been driving it hard. The engine's still warm."

Mattie lowered her face onto her arms. Sobbing racked her thin shoulders, and Diana pleaded with her eyes for Matthew to go easy.

"And what's this little gadget?" He pulled a piece of twine from his pocket, with odd bits of twig and straw attached. "Looks to be a homemade toy. I reckon Juan made it for those pups out in the barn."

Had Matthew lost his mind? Yet his words had an immediate effect on Miss Mattie, who lifted her red, haunted eyes. "You don't understand," she moaned. "It's too late…" She dragged the toy across the table and fondled it lovingly. "The boy's a sweet little thing, but they need to hide. *He*'s coming for them. *He*'ll be here any minute to kill us all!"

Her terror was infectious. Diana couldn't deny its stark reality. "You mean Floyd Clontz? He's coming here?"

Mattie's shrill keening wail said it all. "Please help me!" she begged.

FORTY-SEVEN

As the crow flies...

The rain stopped suddenly, as though a heavenly hand had drawn back the gray curtain to reveal a stage-set sky of shredded silver and gold. As the three wandered into the barnyard, the washed panorama of mountains and valleys sparkled like glass.

"The weather makes no promises..." Mattie picked up her shotgun to carry along. "But I 'spect it'll stay clear till nightfall."

Diana and Matthew followed her into a stall where an elderly white mule swished its tail. Mattie rested her hand on the animal's neck. "This here is *Haw*. Leona and the boy rode out on *Gee* long before the storm come."

Mattie had already told them how Leona had intended to hand Juan over to the Boone police, but then she'd spotted Floyd in town. Apparently, the girl had panicked and run home to Mattie, thinking the old woman could best protect them. In response, Mattie sent Leona and Juan into hiding, equipped with a two-day supply of water and canned goods, riding the other old mule. Mattie figured when Flake showed up on Friday, she'd hitch a ride into Boone, explain the situation to the police, and then ask for help.

"But where would Leona and Juan go?" Diana scanned the pasture and rocky ridge for signs of a bridle path, trying to get a handle on the whole bizarre turn of events. It was like a plot from a B movie about the Wild West.

"She was heading for high ground, up to the secret place where my husband made the whiskey," Mattie said.

"Where exactly is this still?" Matthew scratched his head and searched the horizon for some kind of road.

"The shack's hid real good, three miles, give or take, as the crow flies..." Mattie pointed her shotgun at the setting sun. "Which one of you city folks can ride?"

Diana eyed the mule skeptically. Sure, she'd won her share of blue ribbons at the Devon Horse Show, but Haw presented a new challenge. "I think I can handle him," she told Mattie.

Matthew scowled at the mule. "What about me? Even if this old fella could carry two, I don't get along with horses of any kind. We'll have to take the truck, Diana."

Mattie cackled. "You can't drive that sorry thing up the mountain, Mister. You might make it to the second ridge, but from then on you'd have to travel on the two feet God gave you."

"I'll ride the mule up there, Matthew," Diana volunteered. "Miss Mattie's not feeling well, so why don't you drive her into town?"

"You can't go alone, Diana." He stubbornly folded his arms across his chest. "I won't allow it."

"But what if Floyd comes looking for Leona and Juan? We can't leave Mattie to face him alone."

"Now that's just plain foolish!" The old woman stomped her foot. "I been takin' care of myself long before either of you was born. As for Floyd Clontz..." She hefted the shotgun. "See that feed bag over on the post? I'll show you how I deal with the likes of him..."

"Never mind, Miss Mattie." Matthew reached out and eased the gun's barrel down. "You convinced us, no demonstration is necessary."

"And Leona's a better shot than me," Mattie bragged. "She inherited her daddy's semiautomatic Enfield rifle, the one he carried in Nam. She took that gun with her, and she could shoot your balls off from one hundred yards distance." Mattie gave Matthew a frank appraisal. "What kind of weapon do you carry on your truck, Mister?"

He cleared his throat. "I don't own a gun, ma'am."

The old woman gaped at him in open disbelief, while Diana gave him a smile of encouragement. Maybe men from the Tar Heel State were supposed to come armed and dangerous, but she was proud that Matthew was an exception.

"Well, son, I don't hold it against you." Suddenly Mattie's face sagged and she looked old beyond her years. "The two of you are kind, helping me like this. The Lord must've sent you."

Diana hugged Mattie, yet feared that whatever assistance Matthew and she could offer would be too little, too late.

Mattie lifted her eyes to Diana. "My Leona never meant to do wrong. She loves that boy, and she'd never hurt him."

"We believe you, Miss Mattie," Matthew said. "But I can't allow Diana to ride into those mountains without me. We'll take the truck, and if it breaks down, we'll travel on foot, you hear? Now, can you give us directions…?"

Diana clung to the armrest as the Ford lurched upwards across the brutal terrain. In her opinion, attempting this journey on four tires was far more risky than trusting a mule's four steady hooves, but she knew not to argue with Matthew once he made up his mind. He was more stubborn than any mule on God's green earth.

"She's fixing to boil over," Matthew grumbled as low-lying branches clawed at the truck's fenders. "Would you say this is the first, or the second ridge?"

She had no idea. She only knew what Mattie had told them: "Drive into the sunset. Once you can't go no farther, leave the truck and keep headin' west. Follow the bluebird trail."

"Mattie's directions leave something to be desired," Matthew said. "If we don't make better time, we'll lose the light and get stranded on some boulder with just the bears to keep us company."

Or else they'd be looking up the wrong end of Leona's rifle. "I wish I had my cell phone," she said. "I'd welcome some contact with civilization about now."

"Who'd you call first—local police, Agent Grim, or the National Guard?"

Diana sighed as she pictured her phone locked safely in the camper trailer, along with her first- aid kit, including a bottle of aspirin, which could save Miss Mattie's life in case of a heart attack.

Be prepared. She'd flunked the first rule of scouting. As things stood, Liz was the only person who even knew where they had gone. Unfortunately, Liz believed they'd embarked on a romantic getaway, so if they disappeared for weeks, she'd be delighted. In other words, Liz wouldn't sound any alarms.

Under different circumstances, she'd have been awed by the dramatic sunset reflected on the windshield and enchanted by the prospect of spending a lost night in the mountains with Matthew. But they were trapped in a nightmare, so that even the lovemaking they'd shared last night now seemed like an almost-forgotten dream. "What's the plan, Matthew?"

He smiled from the corners of his eyes, but she sensed the tension around his mouth. "Very simple," he answered. "We'll find them, toss them in the bed of the truck and get the hell outta here."

She longed to believe him. They had discussed the pros and cons of driving back to Boone and putting the rescue into the hands of the police, but they'd also agree that time was running out for Leona and Juan. If Floyd was truly on their trail, could the two of them fight off the danger? Armed with only a rusty truck and a heartfelt prayer, how could they protect anyone?

Matthew downshifted. In order to proceed west, they climbed the next cliff at an extremely steep angle, exposing their rear to a sheer drop-off. Her stomach clenched with fear as the truck's back wheels spun for traction on the bald rock ledge.

"Jesus Christ!" Matthew swore.

She leaned forward in her seat, as if her body could somehow catapult them up and over the rise, but as the wheels kept spinning to gain one inch of progress, they kept slipping one foot backwards towards the deadly drop.

"I want you to ease yourself out of the truck, Diana." Matthew's face was a study in terror.

"No, I won't leave you!" She squeezed her eyes shut and fought off his efforts to reach across and open her door. He wanted her out of harm's way, but she feared her sudden exit from the vehicle would upset the balance, causing Matthew to plunge over the abyss.

"Do it now, Diana!" he begged as he lightly pumped the accelerator.

She prepared to die. Anguish burned through her heart as she clung to the dash and prayed for their salvation, but then suddenly, the tires dug in and propelled them up and over the rise. For one suspended moment, they were in flight, floating on air, but then the front wheels hit rock and sent them careening on a roller coaster ride down the cliff side.

"Hang on!" Matthew gripped the steering wheel as the truck listed sideways.

First she heard an explosion, like gunshot, as the right front tire blew out, then the scream of tearing metal directly under her seat. They were skidding downwards at lightning speed, sparks flying as the wheel hub ground on rock.

"Put your head down between your knees!" He shouted as they hurtled towards a pine forest.

This time she obeyed without question. When the impact came, her ribs compressed inward and she couldn't breathe.

Silence. When she regained consciousness, she was aware that the truck was canted at an odd angle, nose down. She heard an angry gang of crows squawking overhead and thought she was dreaming. But when she dragged her eyes open, she saw a man slumped in the driver's seat. "Matthew?"

A trickle of blood seeped from a nasty gash above his left eye, and then he began to speak. "That must have been the *second ridge* Miss Mattie warned us about, because from now on, all we got is our own two feet."

Suddenly, Diana understood the harsh reality and relived the crash. Obviously, Matthew's head had hit the steering wheel. Maybe he'd suffered a serious concussion? Every instinct told her to get them out and away from the truck. "Let me help you, Matthew…"

Oblivious to her aches and pains, she exited in a flash and half dragged Matthew to safety. Somehow they staggered across the field and settled onto a fallen log some distance from the wrecked Ford.

"What happened…?" At first Matthew seemed disoriented and couldn't place himself in time or space, but then his eyes focused. "I have a spare tire," he mumbled. "But from the sound of it, either the oil pan or the exhaust system got torn up."

His words were slow and jumbled, his face unnaturally pale. She pressed her fingers to his lips. "Don't talk, Matthew. You've been hurt, give me your handkerchief." She could count on this man for many things, including a pure white cotton hankie, which he carried at all times.

He fumbled at his pocket, so she reached in and fetched it for him. She wiped away the blood and saw that the wound was superficial, thank God. But at the same time, he had received a severe blow. As she folded the handkerchief on a diagonal and bound his gash, bandanna-style, she still worried about a concussion.

He grabbed her hand when she'd finished and held on tight. "Quit fussing, I'm all right. But what about you, Diana?"

She rolled her neck, squared her shoulders, stretched one leg, and then the other. Miraculously, all parts seemed in reasonable working order. "Good as new," she told him.

"You sure?" He wrapped his arm around her shoulder and pulled her close.

She nodded, rested her head against his chest and wondered, *what next?*

He kissed her softly on the lips, then stroked wisps of hair from her eyes, tucking them behind her ears. "Life with you is one hell of a ride, Diana."

"Oh yeah? Whose fault is that?" She kissed him back, then protested when he rose abruptly to his feet. "Where do you think you're going?"

"I need to inspect the damage." He walked unsteadily towards the truck, lay down on his back, and then scooted under the vehicle. "I was wrong. There's nothing serious broken under here, only a busted tailpipe. Will you hand me the tool kit? It's behind the seat."

"Absolutely not! Come out this minute, Matthew. I mean it!"

He took his sweet time, but when he finally rolled out, blood had seeped through his bandage. "Are you trying to kill yourself?" she asked. "We need to find Juan, but you won't be much help if you're dead."

"Okay, okay…" He spread his hands in a gesture of peace. "Now let's find us some bluebird houses."

The going was tough and light was fading fast. Matthew moved slowly, obviously in pain, but he was the best spotter of bluebird houses. They were primitive wooden structures nailed to available pines or abandoned fence posts. They were deliberately spaced one hundred yards apart, just as they should be.

"Leona can't be all bad if she set up this bluebird trail," Diana mused. "Mattie claims Darryl built the houses, but Leona placed and tended them."

Matthew grunted. "Nature and *human nature* are two different things. Just because Leona loves birds, doesn't mean she's not a murderous, cold-blooded kidnapper."

Mattie had cautioned them to keep a sharp eye out for the still house. It was built of weathered wood to blend in with the surrounding forest and located on a hill overlooking all the approaches, so the bootleggers could spot the revenue officers well in advance. Problem was, this territory was blanketed with forested rises, any one of which might conceal the shack and Leona's pointed rifle.

"Let's make some noise," Matthew advised. "We don't want Leona thinking we're sneaking up on her, otherwise she'll assume we're the bad guys."

"She won't shoot at us. She's not violent."

"Neither is a mama raccoon," Matthew countered. "But back her into a corner when she's protecting her young, and she'll tear your eyes out."

This said, they both started calling out Leona's name and waving their arms. Soon Diana spotted a glimmer of light beaming from a dark grove on the eastern rise. Just as quickly, the light disappeared.

"I saw something, Matthew." She pointed. "Right over there."

Still hollering and waving like a pair of fools, they approached the phantom light. Sure enough, the shack was almost invisible in a camouflage of mountain laurel and wild rhododendrons. They saw absolutely no sign of life.

"It's too quiet," Matthew whispered. "Go easy, Diana. I feel like someone's in there, but maybe it's not who we think…"

She refused to believe that Floyd had somehow beaten them to Leona and Juan, and yet her imagination ran wild. She fancied this stillness was the hush of death and that they were too late. She put that unspeakable thought aside and summoned all her courage.

"You wait here, Matthew. I'm going inside."

"No way!" He tried to tackle her, but she struggled loose and ran into the tall grass just as Leona emerged from the dark shack, her rifle aimed at Diana's heart.

"Don't shoot!" she screamed.

"Diana, keep your head down!" Matthew shouted. He had taken cover in the grass and was crawling towards her.

But she figured it was then, or never. "Don't shoot, Leona!" she shrieked at the top of her lungs. "Mother Mattie sent us. I'm a friend of Juan's!" She braced herself for the inevitable bullet searing through her flesh, and couldn't pull breath into her lungs as she waited for her final moment. But she heard only deadly silence and an odd, swishing noise, like a small animal, maybe a dog, rushing through the grass in her direction. Then suddenly, the weeds parted right at her feet.

When Diana looked down, she saw a pair of filthy sneakers, then short brown legs skinned at the knees. She saw a colorful T-shirt depicting an Indian warrior, and finally, a pair of enormous blue eyes gazing up at her. The child was peering from under an astonishing frizz of spiked blond hair, but she took a closer look.

"*Juan?* Dear God, is that really you?" She dropped to her knees, opened her arms, and the boy fell into her embrace.

In the meantime, as Matthew climbed cautiously to his feet, the woman standing on the crest of the hill began to sob. Tears racked her frail body as she carefully lowered her rifle to the ground.

FORTY-EIGHT

Deer in the headlights...

Diana was smothering the boy, yet couldn't let go. Lucky for Juan, he spotted Matthew and broke loose before she drowned him in sloppy kisses.

"Trout!" The child flung himself at Matthew, who nearly lost his balance.

"Hey, son!" Matthew caught him on the fly and gathered him into his arms. "You're a hard one to track down, boy. Has someone been teaching you some fancy Indian tricks?"

"No, Trout, those people stole me!" His eyes widened and the smile faded from his face.

"Yeah, I know. Did they hurt you?" He tilted up the child's chin while keeping a protective arm around the boy.

Juan didn't answer. Instead, he looked fearfully over his shoulder at Leona.

Diana followed his glance to where Leona stood at the crest of the clearing, both arms dangling limp at her sides. The wind whipped her long blond hair across her face, so that Diana couldn't read her eyes. She climbed to her feet and slowly approached the woman, one hand lifted in a gesture of peace.

"Remember me, Leona?" The girl stiffened, but did not run. "I was at the Open House the day you took Juan."

Leona brushed back her hair and stared. She seemed to make the connection, but then lost it, a look of pure panic on her face.

264

"That's okay, so much has happened…" Diana babbled reassuringly, hoping to win her trust. "We came to take Juan home. That's what you want, isn't it, Leona?"

Leona trembled like a trapped animal and glanced at her rifle lying in the grass.

"We just saw Mother Mattie. She told us what happened in town."

Leona's eyes flashed with fear as she scanned the dark horizon from where they came.

"Mattie's just fine," Diana said soothingly. "She's alone and looking out for herself."

Leona's mouth quivered. "You didn't see no *man* poking around her place?"

Matthew stepped up beside them, holding Juan's hand. "No sign of Floyd, Leona."

Floyd's name jolted the girl. Again she glanced at the rifle, just as Matthew bent over and grabbed it up. "I'll keep hold of this, ma'am. I don't think we'll be needing it from here on out."

Leona searched Matthew's face.

"I know you recognize me," he said. "I bought two wooden reindeer. We traded for lunch, remember?"

A shy grin snaked across her lips. "You're Mr. Troutman, the man who owns the store."

Matthew nodded.

"Trout and me went fishing together!" Juan piped up.

"That's right, son." Matthew winked. "And there's another big bass waiting for you out in Lake Norman. Don't know about you, but I'm mighty hungry for a fried fish dinner."

"I'm hungry for a Big Mac!" Juan shouted.

"Hush, child," Leona snapped. "They'll hear you shouting all the way back in Boone."

Juan's little face twisted in terror. He ran to Leona and buried himself in her skirt.

"Let's go inside the shack, where we're safe." Leona started dragging Juan up the hillside.

Matthew lifted his eyebrows at Diana as they followed. Had he noticed how Juan clung to his captor? She understood that victims often transferred their trust to their abductors, but Leona was no terrorist. To all appearances, Juan had not been abused. He was too skinny, his hairstyle left something to be desired, and he was definitely terrified of Floyd, but his spirit wasn't broken. In her heart, she believed Leona cared for the boy. In a pinch, she'd be an ally.

"Maybe one of us should stay outside and keep watch?" she whispered to Matthew.

"Or maybe we should all leave right now…" He looked to the forest, where the crimson sun had dropped below the tree line. "But I can't change a tire in the dark, and we'd never find our way off this mountain until daybreak."

In the end, they all squeezed inside the musty lean-to, a space no bigger than an enlarged closet. The place stank of mouse droppings and fermentation.

"It's the old corn mash gone sour." Leona nodded at a pile of rotting sacks lining the back wall.

"Leona's grandpa sold moonshine whiskey!" Juan proudly explained. "And this here's part of the old machine…" He waved a rusty, lethally sharp coil at them, brandishing it like a sword as Diana watched in dismay. The boy's education had certainly taken a bizarre turn, and the shard of metal was tetanus waiting to happen.

"Put the sword down, Juan," Matthew commanded. "Come over here and talk to me."

The child dropped the thing and flopped into Matthew's lap. He fingered Matthew's makeshift bandage. "You been fighting, Trout?"

"Nope. Diana and I tried to fly my old truck over a mountain. Instead we landed in a tree."

"Cool!"

Diana held her tongue, determined not to judge Juan's new fascination with violence. A little time at home with Bobby and Juanita, far away from the Clontz clan, would gentle his rough edges.

To her credit, Leona had brought clean blankets, a kerosene lamp, and a short supply of canned foods. But in spite of those perks, Diana couldn't breathe in the cramped space. "We could use some ventilation," she said as Leona barred the door with a heavy wooden brace.

The girl vigorously shook her head and kept her eye glued to the small, drilled-out peephole, their only source of air.

"What about fresh water?" Diana glanced nervously at Matthew, whose skin had blanched to a death-like pallor. He seemed unnaturally drowsy as he propped himself against the wall. Even in the dying light, she could see that he was desperately ill.

"Me and the boy drank all the water in our canteens, but we can dip all we need from the creek in the hollow," Leona said. "We can't go out till morning, though."

Matthew whispered something into Juan's ear, and the boy giggled.

"Trout has to pee!" he whooped. "Me too, Leona."

"Sorry, Mister Troutman," Leona said sheepishly. "I wasn't thinking clear about your needs. I reckon me and you can go down to the creek. I'll fetch us some water, whilst you tend to your business."

"What about me?" Juan wailed.

"You stay here and guard Diana." Matthew was firm. "We'll take turns, okay?" He eased Juan off his lap, and using the rifle like a cane, he limped to the door.

"Do you know how to use that gun, Trout?" Juan's eyes were round.

"Yes, I do, son." He winked at Diana. "Just 'cause I don't own one, don't mean I can't shoot one."

Matthew was definitely behaving strangely. Was he responding to her plea for water, did he really need to answer a call of nature, or was he just plain delirious? In spite of everything, she trusted his judgment and didn't try to stop them when Leona unbarred the door.

The girl found a heavy bucket and followed Matthew into the dusk. Halfway down the darkening hill, Matthew shifted the rifle to his right hand and waved at them. Was she mistaken, or had he also flashed a smile of encouragement?

"What about me, Miss Diana?" Juan, who'd been hanging inside the door watching the departure, hopped from foot to foot. "I really need to pee!"

"You'll have to wait."

"No!" The child grabbed his crotch and inched outside.

Before she could stop him, Juan bolted. He dashed away from the shack and headed for the high woods behind them.

"Get back here!" In her haste to catch him, she burst out the door and tripped in a stand of thistle, skinning her hands and knees. "Damn!" By the time she was up and running, Juan had disappeared. "Double damn!" She cursed to the night. Her own kids had led her on many a merry chase, and often she'd yearned to wring their little necks. Tonight she was in no mood for games.

"Juan?" She called to the black silhouette of forest, but saw nothing. Looking over her shoulder into the valley, she spotted the pale outline of Leona's dress and a tall figure that had to be Matthew. Both were oblivious to her plight.

She squeezed her eyes shut and listened, but heard only wind in faraway branches and a nightingale's plaintive song. Then, at some distance, she recognized the unmistakable rustle of hooves in grass. When she looked up, the moon cast an eerie glow on what surely must be a phantom.

A white mule lumbered down the hillside, led by its tiny master.

"Juan? Come here this instant!" She could barely contain her anger as the child drew near.

"This is Gee. Isn't he awesome?" Juan grinned from ear to ear. "I knew you'd want to meet him, Miss Diana."

The animal was identical to the mule she'd seen at Mattie's, only this fellow was considerably younger.

"Wanna pat him?" Juan dropped the reins to zip up his fly. "I can ride him real good."

Should she hug the boy, or spank his bottom raw? In the end, her great love of horseflesh won out and she stroked Gee's neck. "Do you ride him bareback?"

"Sure, except for this blanket." Juan adjusted a weird contraption across the mule's back. The ingenious blend of work harness and Indian blanket was rigged with rope stirrups that could actually accommodate a rider.

"I'm impressed."

"Leona keeps him hidden in the forest."

"Well, let's walk him back to the forest, then, before they see we're gone." At that moment, she noticed the boy's eyes were fixed on a far ridge behind her back. "What do you see, Juan?"

She turned towards the dark hill above, where Matthew and Leona had gone over the rise, where two bright lights now jogged in wild unison. That seemed strange, because Matthew and Leona weren't carrying flashlights. Suddenly Juan flung himself at her, pointing and gulping as he tried to speak. He clung to her legs as she tried to understand the problem.

"What's wrong?" As the lights came closer, descending towards the shack at high speed, she recognized the whine of a motorcycle engine.

"It's *him!*" Juan whimpered through chattering teeth.

She stifled the scream rising in her throat and clutched the child to her breast. Every instinct told her to run like hell. Then, the bouncing headlights illuminated the tiny clearing below just as an unsuspecting Leona walked over the rise.

The bike stopped immediately. Its twin beams blazed through an acid green patch of grass and lit up Leona's white face. She looked like the doomed deer in the headlights, frozen in fear before the moment of impact. When the shot rang out, Leona wilted in slow motion. The bucket filled with water tumbled crazily down the rocky slope.

Juan's fingers clawed at Diana's arms when a second barrage of rifle fire began. Diana realized that the man who'd shot Leona was Floyd Clontz. He revved up his dirt bike, and it zigzagged into the valley towards the shots, which were obviously being fired by Matthew.

She couldn't think or breathe. She was terrified for Matthew, but the only way to save Juan was to escape to the hills and avoid the valley. She gathered the frantic child into her arms and carried him. Every muscle in her body cried out in protest, but luckily, Juan was surprisingly light.

She broke his strangle hold on her neck and hoisted him up onto the mule. The animal was skittish from the gunshots and circled wildly as she clung to the reins. When she finally gained a foothold in the rope stirrup and mounted, Gee continued to spin and fight her. She pulled Juan into the cradle between her legs and leaned over him, all the while crooning and stroking the crazed mule. The explosive gunplay continued, but she tuned it out as tears blurred her eyes.

At last the beast wearied and stopped. Without one clue as to where he would lead them, she gave Gee his rein. Still cradling the sobbing child, she said a prayer to the dark heavens and swiftly tapped her heels on the creature's ribs.

FORTY-NINE

Like a hunted animal...

"Leona's dead, isn't she?" Juan's little body shivered against her.

"Of course not." In fact, she considered Leona's death a distinct possibility. They'd both seen her take the bullet, and then her seemingly lifeless body had fallen to the ground.

"What about Trout?"

"I'm sure he'll take good care of himself *and* Leona," she said with as much conviction as her aching heart could muster. If Matthew had survived the gunshots, why hadn't he called out to them, or attempted to follow?

"If Trout's okay, how come we're running?"

For an eight-year old, Juan was as incisive as a Supreme Court Justice. He was hyper from fear and juiced on nervous energy, but she wished he would calm down and fall asleep in her arms.

"This mule seems to know where he's going." She steered them onto a different subject.

"Yep, Gee knows everything about these hills. When Leona and me rode him up, he took us to the caves all by himself."

"What caves?"

The boy scooted back into her ribs and folded his sneakers across the mule's neck. "Indian caves. There are hundreds, maybe millions of caves where they could hide out forever."

She noticed a lack of feeling in her fingertips as she stroked the child's strange hair, but Juan seemed okay. He warmed to his subject and chattered on about the battles and exploits of great red warriors as they rode into the night. Matthew had warned her that Juan was prone to exaggerate, or outright lie, so she wondered if there really were caves where they could hide, at least until daybreak, to improve their odds.

Eventually, the boy's recitation slowed and his tales of Indian valor got all jumbled up with cowboy lore and cartoon heroes. Soon after that, he fell fast asleep. The silence was unnerving, and every limb in Diana's anatomy rebelled. So far, Gee had been sure-footed as he gingerly made his way to higher altitude through the dim moonlight. Once he had stumbled, but quickly righted himself, and next he had galloped down a ridge for no apparent reason but the sheer joy of not having to fight against gravity. Often he stopped to graze on what smelled like sweet clover, and then drank from a quick-running creek. From the sound of gurgling water, she believed the creek had paralleled their journey all along.

She couldn't gauge how far they had strayed from the bootleg still, but she didn't doubt that the old-time Cherokees could have hidden undetected in these hills. Many years ago Eric Rudolph, the abortion clinic bomber, had holed up here for years before the police caught him. Neither the cops nor the FBI could flush him out. That was a comforting thought if one was hiding, but a problem if one was lost.

As they traveled, she listened for the growl of a dirt bike in hot pursuit, but heard only the buzz of cicadas and Gee's rhythmic snorting. The night sounds conspired to lull her to sleep, to blessed forgetfulness, but she resisted.

When she was a child, a fever had almost claimed her life. She remembered the weightless drifting in and out of pain, the foggy disorientation that left her spiraling and unable to find herself. She felt that way now. Her legs, thighs, and bruised bottom were numb, while those parts supporting Juan had long since cramped beyond feeling. Worst of all, she had this dizzy sensation that at any moment they'd topple off the edge of a precipice to oblivion.

Through the misery, she gained a new understanding of blind faith. The mule, willing as he may have been, wasn't her ideal guide, one she'd have chosen to trust with her life, or that of an innocent child. But Gee was their savior all the same, so she gave her weary spirit over to his care.

And Juan slept on, even when they descended through a particularly nasty terrain where Gee balked, and then actually stumbled to his front knees. A dark roof of forest blocked the moonlight, which until then had provided a thin, silver ribbon to reality. After that, she was forced to make a decision.

She slid off the faithful creature, dragging a limp Juan behind her, then she dropped to her knees. For a stunned moment, no part of her body worked. A fiendish puppet master had cut all her strings, leaving every wooden limb useless. Yet somewhere a primal memory of how her parts once functioned allowed her to grope, push, and lift herself upright.

"What's happening?" Juan, half asleep, clung to her neck.

"Gee needs to rest," she whispered against his cheek. "Can you walk for a while?"

Fleetingly the boy opened his eyes and decided reality was worse than the scary dreams he'd left behind. A vigorous shake of his head and a wrestler's lock told her that Juan's answer was an emphatic *no*. Either she'd have to carry him, or enlist poor Gee for another round.

No contest. Once the beast had recovered his footing, she hoisted Juan aboard and prepared to walk. The lightened burden rejuvenated the animal, and he took off at a slow trot. Diana latched onto his tail, then pulled herself forward to his reins. "Slow down,

Gee!" She wasn't about to be dragged blind through that treacherous valley. Gee and she had to reach a compromise: he could lead, but she would set the pace.

Eventually, she lost all sense of time, and her abused feet lost all feeling. Luckily, Gee retained his sense of direction, and gradually their tempo slowed as moonlight, or maybe the first hint of dawn, seeped into a clearing where the mule came to a dead halt. The sudden loss of forward momentum nearly toppled her, but Gee refused to budge. In his mind, they had reached their destination.

Juan stirred and lifted his sleep-creased face from the blanket. He blinked and sniffed the subtle change of venue. Here the air was fresher, lacking the pungent, mossy smells of the forest. The roar of rushing water was strong and close.

"We're here!" Suddenly Juan was wide-awake. "I told you, Miss Diana. Gee brought us to the caves!"

She peered around the clearing where the first rays of morning hung in the fog like pale gray gauze. Trying not to dwell on the fact that she had walked all night, willing herself not to think at all, she strained to see signs of a cave.

"Over there…" Juan slid off the mule and ran full tilt to a bank of laurel growing on the face of a sheer cliff.

She dropped Gees reins, stroked the good creature, and didn't blame him when he shivered away from her touch in favor of a juicy stand of weeds. Once she was convinced the mule wasn't going anywhere, she hobbled towards Juan, who was beating at the laurel with a stick. Either the child had lost his mind, or his over-active imagination was playing tricks, for she saw absolutely no evidence of a fissure, let alone a cave, in the cliff wall.

"I found it!" His whoop echoed through the clearing and reverberated across the miles they'd just traveled.

Rushing to his side, she fell to her knees and clamped her hand across his mouth. She felt like a hunted animal. She waited until Juan's eyes reflected that same fear before slowly releasing her hand.

"Sorry, Miss Diana." He started scrambling ahead on all fours.

She followed in like fashion, but still saw no cave. Then suddenly Juan's head, chest, legs, and finally his little sneakers were swallowed up into a black void. She felt cold wet stone under her hands and an unexpected, chilly breeze on her face. Reaching ahead, she encountered nothing but empty space.

"C'mon, what are you waiting for?" Already Juan's voice was receding.

Images of slimy snakes and nests of bats aside, she took the plunge. Or rather, what was a plunge for the boy, proved to be a squeeze for her. Slithering on her belly, she worked her way forward on her elbows until, after a claustrophobic eternity, the tunnel opened up into a large black cavern.

"Where are you, Juan?"

"Over here…" His voice was close and off to the left.

Patting the moist moss cover that formed their slippery floor, she crawled towards the sound, certain that her next move would be an elevator drop to nothingness.

"Don't be scared," Juan said. "It's flat in here."

"How do you know?"

"I saw it in daylight."

Diana doubted it. Even at noon, this place would be as dark as any tomb, but then she felt a cold breeze on her cheeks and saw a pinprick of light in the vaulted ceiling.

"Honest, Miss Diana, this cave goes all the way through. It's like a bunch of rooms in a big castle."

She reached out and touched his warm flesh. "Since we're such good friends now, why don't you call me *Diana*, instead of *Miss*

Diana. Is that okay?" One second later, his little arms encircled her. He hugged and stroked her like she was a baby. Ashamed, she laughed out loud, and in an effort to reverse their roles, she rocked Juan against her breast.

He touched her face for tears, and found them. "We're safe now, Diana, just like the Indians."

God, how she wanted to believe him! She longed for release, the sweet healing peace of sleep. As her eyes adjusted to the gloom, her panic retreated and she maneuvered herself and Juan into a sheltering crevice that resembled a womb.

He curled into her body, a ball of warmth, and she told herself that Floyd would never find this cave. She needed to clear her head and regain her strength. Maybe it wouldn't hurt to sleep a little—just until morning?

FIFTY

A benign mountain morning...

She was drifting, floating face-up in a chilly sea under a starless sky—a pleasant sensation, but for the hard object pressing into her lower back and a heavy weight on her left shoulder. She felt a warm, rhythmic puffing on her neck, a tickling under her chin, and the smell of dirty scalp. In her dream, her little son, Robbie, had sneaked into their bed again, terrified to face another day of nursery school. His bony elbow jabbed her rib, and she groaned aloud at the pain in her spine.

A sharp flicker of light played across the inside of her eyelids, nagging her to wake up and face the day. But when she opened her eyes, the dark room was completely unfamiliar. Blinking away the grogginess, she shifted her numb limbs and cried out in panic to find a strange child asleep in her arms.

"What?" Juan yawned and stretched.

She saw a black, cavernous ceiling, with one penetrating ray of light illuminating the awakening boy. Then the truth hit home with terrifying force.

She stroked the child's head. "Did you sleep well, Juan?"

He rubbed his eyes. "What time is it?"

Was it early dawn, or high noon? Their shadowy pit warped reality, even the day of the week eluded her.

Juan rolled off her shoulder and crawled out of their stony nest. "I'm hungry," he said.

Her stomach clenched at the thought of food, and she desperately needed a bathroom. More pressing still was the need for action, a way to safety, and the sudden image of the white mule grazing outside their tenuous hiding place initiated a fresh panic attack. To friend or foe, the animal was like a beacon leading straight to their den.

"I'm going out to check on Gee," she said.

"Me too." Fully awake now, Juan's beautiful blue eyes reflected her anguish. In that strange, aquatic light, with the one bright beam dancing on his head, he looked like a tiny broken angel.

"I have a better idea…" she told him. "I'll be the Indian Scout, and you'll be the Brave."

"No, I'll be the Scout." He scrambled across the damp moss towards the exit.

She latched onto his ankle and squirmed after him, until they were lying side by side. "Listen, Juan. *I'm* the grownup and *you're* the little boy. It's my job to get help, understand? You must stay here where you're safe, where the bad man can't find you."

His eyes expanded. He knew the *bad man* was Floyd Clontz, so he crabbed backwards from the exit. "But I'm scared, Diana. I can't stay here alone."

"Sure you can. You told me how the brave Indians used to hide in here forever, and I know how brave you are."

The cave stank of damp and decay, and one portion of the rock floor glistened with an evil pool where the stream surfaced. She wouldn't wish this experience on a courageous adult, let alone a vulnerable child, but she had no choice.

"Think how proud Johnny will be," she continued. "Wait until you tell him how brave you were."

"You saw Johnny?" Juan perked up.

"Sure, I saw him right before we came to find you. He worries about you every day and can't wait until you come home."

"Am I going home soon?" he asked in a tiny voice.

"Absolutely. I promised Johnny, and I promise you—you *are* going home, Juan."

"No one's as brave as me." His chest puffed with pride.

"That's right, but you have to promise that you won't leave this cave, no matter what."

"I promise." He crossed his heart.

She gave him a quick hug and kiss, and then crawled into the narrow passage before her courage deserted her. Rubble tore at her elbows as she wormed along, trying to ignore the soft whimpering of the frightened boy she'd left behind.

How on earth had they navigated this torturous route last night? At least Floyd was highly unlikely to discover this cave, even by day. Unfortunately, her most dangerous moment lay directly ahead. If Floyd had spotted the mule, he'd be waiting right outside, ready to shoot the moment she flopped into the open.

She took a deep breath, lunged up through the hole, rolled down an incline full of laurel bushes, and then came to a full stop in an open meadow. For some time she lay still, braced for an attack. In those suspended seconds, all her senses were heightened. She felt the sunshine, so hot after the frigid subterranean cave. Her bare arms stung with scratches from the laurel bushes, the sky was blindingly blue, and the only sound was the steady thrum of crickets in the weeds around her body.

Nothing else. She was alone. She sat up and searched the meadow for Gee, but the mule was nowhere to be seen. Puzzled, she climbed stiffly to her feet and did an unsteady 360-degree turn to assess her position. Just as she'd thought, the entrance to the cave was fully concealed, but the clearing where she currently stood offered no cover from the rugged hills and forested copses surrounding it.

Quickly as her cramped legs would carry her, she sprinted towards the sound of a fast-running stream located in a stand of thick pines. She relieved herself, then headed towards the cascading waters. She drank deeply of the fresh cold liquid, then bathed her face and arms.

Only then did she allow the pent-up tears to flow. She longed to bring Juan out from his dark prison to enjoy the water and feel the warm sunshine. Had she been wrong to leave him behind? Should they seek their way back together, hand in hand?

But then she remembered the gunfire and how Leona fell. She ached for Matthew and refused to believe that he'd come to harm. No, she was right to leave Juan hidden. To bring him into the light of day and expose him to certain danger was foolish indeed.

Besides, she had no plan of action. Without Gee to guide her, how could she hope to retrace their steps? She was alone, unarmed, and lost—a terrible trio of disabilities. And the threat was real, not imagined. She felt evil lurking in the forest and heard it muttering in the sluggish breeze. It poisoned the benign mountain morning.

Plus, she had already lost too much time. The day was heating up fast, and by the angle of the sun, she judged it was almost noon. She shouldn't have fallen asleep, yet she was thankful to be clear-headed and able to think a whole new way—like a mule. Moving cautiously downstream, like the devil was on her tail, she followed the path of water, where the sweet clover bloomed.

FIFTY-ONE

Finish the job…

Floyd lifted his head off the rotten log, and the pain ricocheted like fireworks in his head. It was worse than a hangover from a weeklong binge, yet he hadn't drunk a single drop lately. Struggling upright in the leaves sent the pain shooting down through his neck and set his left shoulder on fire.

Damn it to hell! The treetops shifted in dizzy patterns up where the sun hurt his aching eyes. His right arm was numb and useless, and when he lifted his fingertips to explore the damage, he found his shirt soaked through with blood. A metallic stench filled his nostrils and made him retch like a puking baby.

Once the heaves eased up, he carefully lifted the shirt out and over his head and peeled it away from the wound. "Sweet Jesus…" he whimpered as little bits of scab and flesh stuck to the fabric.

He fingered the entrance and exit sites of the bullet and saw that the slug had gone clean through. At least it wasn't festering inside. He couldn't rightly remember how long he'd managed to ride the bike last night, nor did he know how far he'd come into the forest, but he thanked the good Lord for allowing him to pass out in the bushes by this creek, instead of out in the open like a sitting duck.

He lowered the rag of his shirt into the freezing stream and rinsed it out real good. When he pressed the cold water to his wound, it stung so bad, it brought tears to his eyes. So he fetched the flask of Wild Turkey from his knapsack, took a long swig to fortify himself, and then dribbled the rest on the wound. The pain almost made him pass out all over again. Tucking his head low between his knees, he waited for the agony to recede and tried to remember. What the fuck really happened last night at the still?

First off, he'd never planned on shooting Leona, at least not till he'd had his fun. During all the lonesome days in the stinking trailer, he'd dreamed how good it would feel have his way with her, until she begged him to stop. But last night something had snapped when he saw her limping along the ridge, hauling that stupid bucket of water. He saw her face shrink up in terror and smelled her fear, so he was obliged to strike her down on the spot, compelled by God's own vengeance.

Then the way she fell, her long white legs all twisted in the moonlight, gave him a hot rush like he was fucking Leona and that bitch Juanita, both at once. Those two women were the whores of Babylon, worse than Sodom and Gomorrah.

Giving themselves over to fornication, they are set forth for an example,

Suffering the vengeance of eternal fire.

No doubt about it, women were his curse. It didn't help Floyd's mood none that one hour before he'd spotted Leona, he'd seen her grandma Mattie at the Birdsong place. The old witch had started blasting away as soon as his tires raised dust in the drive. Without so much as a *howdy-do,* she'd begun scatter shooting, sparking shards off his bike. One bit of flying metal had bit into his leg below the knee. He'd roared out in pain, while Mattie, the old banshee, kept on screaming at him, gray hair flying around her head as she fixed to kill him.

Somehow he'd made it to the Birdsong's barn and drawn his weapon in case the crazy bitch decided to follow him. It was then he spotted the old blue station wagon, the one he'd bought for Leona back when they were staying at Johnson's Hideaway.

Dragging himself back to reality, Floyd staggered to his feet, dropped his jeans, and pissed in the creek. The cut under his knee had already scabbed over.

He'd been right all along about Leona running home to Grandma. Did she really think she'd escape that easy? After all, he'd once lived at the Birdsong farm for almost two weeks before Mattie kicked him out, but that was plenty long enough to learn the lay of the land. He knew, for instance, that Mattie owned two mules, and last night he'd seen only one. Plus, he knew that old Pappy Birdsong, the only family member with good sense and enterprise, once kept a whiskey still up in the hills. So it didn't take a genius to conclude that Leona and the boy had took off on the mule and were heading for the still. It took more than a pair of stupid bitches to put Floyd Clontz off the scent.

He zipped his fly and walked stiffly to where he'd dropped his dirt bike before he passed out. His injured shoulder throbbed with each step, to where he felt faint and likely to puke again, but the urge gradually subsided.

He carefully righted the machine, straddled the seat, and then kicked the starter. The Suzuki DRZ 400 had cost him his last car in trade, plus his life savings, but with a hundred grand reward at the end of the line, the bike was well worth it.

He hath multiplied your seed sown and increased the fruits of your righteousness.

As the engine vibrations circulated up from his loins to torture the bullet wound, Floyd again tried to piece together what had happened last night...

Right after Leona fell, the rifle shots come out of nowhere. At first he'd seen nothing in the dark valley, but then realized the shots had come from down at the creek. He figured the stupid little boy he was after didn't have the skill or the balls to fire a gun, so it stood to reason there was someone else.

Once he'd spotted the shack, which was well concealed at the crest of the hill, he'd guessed that Leona had hid the boy there. So driving a zigzag pattern, he'd climbed the steep slope and made it to the door. He'd still had hold of his Beretta when he dove into the dim space, all the while telling himself not to shoot the little pisser. But when he looked around, he saw the shack was empty.

Breathing hard, he'd put his weapon in a two-handed grip and eased out, his barrel pointed at the valley. Keeping his head low, he'd then picked up his bike and walked it clear.

Then he'd seen a man silhouetted on the ridge where Leona had fallen. The man was crouching over the body, but when he stood up, he spotted Floyd and swung his rifle in Floyd's direction. Even at the distance, the man looked to be big as a grizzly and twice as mean.

Floyd had mounted his bike and twisted the ignition. He'd braced his gun wrist on the right handlebar, kept to low gear, then commenced to circle around the man's ridge, all the while keeping sharp watch out for the kid. The tall man's rifle followed his progress, and once Floyd knew for certain the boy wasn't with him, he was forced to deal with that new complication.

They eyed one another for what seemed like an eternity. Floyd shifted to idle and tried to think. He still hadn't seen the white mule, so likely the boy had ridden off by himself. Catching a lone, scared little pisser wasn't a problem—but the man was.

He'd thought about how his brother Darryl was lying at death's door. Or, for all Floyd knew, Darryl had already passed on to his Maker. This man was to blame. He'd figured the stranger was fucking Leona before Darryl was even cold in his grave. The idea made him burn with righteous indignation. Any man who'd screw a widow, would like as not shoot Floyd in the back as he rode away.

So last night, Floyd had squeezed off a round, and then the asshole had dropped to his knees. Floyd was pretty sure he'd hit him, but before he could be sure, he'd felt an explosion in his shoulder. It spun him backwards off the bike and burned like the fires of Hades.

After that, his memories were hazy, but who the hell cared what happened last night? Today he was on the move, bumping along the rutted bank of a fast-running creek. Brambles clawed at his boots and raked his fenders as the noonday sun glared through the branches above his fevered head.

If the bastard who shot him wasn't dead, Floyd would go back and finish the job. He'd finish old Mattie Birdsong, too. But first he had to find the boy.

It seemed God Himself was leading Floyd by the hand, guiding him upstream to the high country. This Heavenly revelation caused him to focus hard ahead on a grove of river birch trees, where two long pale ears twitched in a camouflage of branches.

"Praise the Lord!" He had found the white mule.

FIFTY-TWO

Grownups don't get it…

Juan had never been so cold and hungry, and he had to pee real bad. He crawled back into the little stone cradle where Diana had held him and curled into a ball, keeping one eye on the single stab of sunlight that pierced like a Jedi beam into his darkness.

Little sparkles of fairy dust floated through the light, which he figured came from way upstairs in the castle. The light passed through all the rooms, like in Disneyland, and as long as he concentrated on Peter Pan and Tinkerbell, he might be safe from the snakes and bats clinging to the ceiling.

His parents took him to Disneyland when he was just a toddler. They'd pushed him all day in a stroller. He saw real cowboys and Indians and pirates and space ships, and then he threw up all the pink fluffy stuff he'd eaten off a stick.

In California, all the grownups called his parents *Mrs. Maria McCord* and *Mr. Randy McCord*, but Juan remembered them as *Mama* and *Daddy*. Mama was soft like Diana, but her hair was long and black like Aunt Nita's. Daddy's hair was yellow like Diana's and he smelled like vanilla.

Juan shivered and pulled his knees up under his chin, but he wasn't scared. Nobody but Juan had been to Disneyland—not Johnny, not Diana, not even Trout. Peter Pan's children had a dog named Nana, but she wasn't near as strong as the wolf puppies would be someday. Juan just knew Mother Mattie would give him one, and when he showed that pup to Johnny, he'd cry and want one, too. But Johnny couldn't have one. He could visit Juan's, though.

Diana said he couldn't leave the cave, but she didn't know about the snakes and bats and how he was about to wet his pants. He squeezed his eyes shut and listened. Maybe he'd hear Diana returning from the forest, or the clip-clop of Gee's hooves?

After all, *she promised.*

She'd him she was the grownup, and he was the little boy. She said Leona wasn't dead, but grownups didn't get it.

Like long ago, when Juan was in the back seat, strapped into a baby chair and the big truck came around the curve. The truck was all silver, red, and shiny in the sun. Mama and Daddy screamed when their car floated off the road and sailed into the sky, but after that, everything was dark.

Juan had waked up in a white room. Two old people were standing over him, and they said Mama and Daddy were in Heaven. His parents were dead, but the grownups didn't admit it. They didn't get it. Even when a fish floated up on the beach or the rabbit lay dead in the road, they always said "Heaven".

But Diana *promised.*

Juan listened hard and heard the scratching of tiny wings and a squeaky sound like mice. The bats! He saw a movie once where bats tangled in a little boy's hair and then clawed his eyes out. He had never promised to stay in *this* part of the cave. Scuttling across the gooey floor, he crawled up into the next cavern, where the beam was brighter. Just in time! Down below where he came from, the bats broke loose and screeched so loud it hurt his ears.

Hot pee trickled down his legs. *I'm not scared!* His fingernails dug into the crevice as he pulled himself up to the third tier, where a jagged hole opened to the sky. At the same time, sudden, blinding light stung his eyes and a loud, chugging sound, like Aunt Nita's electric eggbeater, echoed from above.

He'd seen a movie once where the giant bat of all times came down from space with glowing red eyes and pointy yellow teeth sharp as knives. It ate up all the creatures on earth before it drowned the crumbling cities in green bat goo.

Juan screamed as the beating moved to right above his head. He crawled under a craggy overhang as the black wings blocked out the sun.

FIFTY-THREE

Facing down the Devil...

Just as Diana spotted Gee, grazing and oblivious to all the trouble he'd caused, she heard an odd growling sound traveling up the creek bed. From her vantage point in the meadow several hundred yards below the cave, it was clear that Gee had heard it too. He pricked his ears and bolted from the copse of river birch trees.

Before she could process it all, a speeding dirt bike lurched from the forest and began herding the terrified mule. The rider was unsteady on his seat, listing to one side as he fired a round of bullets into the air, just for the hell of it, driving the beast to a crazed stampede.

She stifled a scream when she recognized Floyd Clontz. Neither the newspaper picture nor the eyewitness account from Bobby had prepared her for the sheer evil emanating from the man. She knew she was facing down the Devil.

Should she take cover, or run to get Juan? She was frozen, in a state of panic, while her senses were assaulted by yet another deafening sound as a surreal black helicopter lifted above the mountain housing Juan's cave. It hung in the air, beating its great wings, like it too was plagued by indecision.

It was a black silhouette. The sun behind the giant bird's wings stunned her vision as she read the bold initials *FBI* emblazoned on the chopper's body. Floyd saw it, too. His bike slowed, then stalled as he scanned the terrain, likely wondering if the chopper was going to land.

It was not. Although she was no expert, she believed the ground was not flat enough to accommodate a landing. Her heart raced as she followed Floyd's gaze to the hilltop, where a small boy had emerged. Sweet Jesus! Juan was out in the open, waving his arms like a maniac.

"No!" she screamed as adrenaline flooded her veins. "Go back, Juan!" Finally, her legs caught fire, and she started running towards the boy.

Unfortunately, her warning got lost in the roar of the helicopter's engine, as did the growl of Floyd's bike bounding up the steep mountainside. Juan didn't hear the bike coming. He was too busy trying to catch the pilot's attention. After Floyd snatched Juan from behind, he dragged the child across his lap as though Juan had no substance. He became a small, weightless bundle, flapping its arms and legs.

Diana sprinted full out, her lungs bursting as Floyd's bike careened drunkenly down the hillside. At the final steep incline, the machine toppled, sending man and boy into a headlong roll down the hill. They stopped against a stand of laurel bushes in the clearing.

"Run, Juan!" she yelled, opening her arms. "Come to me!"

The child tried, but Floyd grabbed hold of his leg. The man lumbered to his feet, dragged Juan against his body, and then he spotted Diana for the first time. He roared an obscenity, and then pressed a gun to Juan's head.

"Please let him go," she screamed. "Can't you see it's over?" She pointed at the helicopter hovering overhead, where an FBI sharpshooter was maneuvering a rifle into place for a clear shot.

"It ain't over yet, lady!" Floyd jammed his gun harder against Juan's skull. "Those assholes won't shoot so long as the boy's with me."

She was in agony. Then oddly, she noticed that Juan's beautiful blue eyes were riveted in horror on a spot somewhere over her left shoulder. She concentrated instead on Floyd, who was bleeding profusely. "You're hurt!" she shouted at him. "You need a doctor!"

The Devil's weird pale eyes glowed like white embers. He fixed her with a sick smile. "Deliver me…" his ugly lips intoned.

"Run, boy, run!" The rasping voice came loud and clear from behind Diana's back.

At the same time, Juan kicked Floyd hard in the groin. A flash of pain, then surprise, and finally fear ignited the Devil's eyes as the boy broke loose.

Everything happened at once, and yet Diana's reality seemed oddly suspended. She watched as Juan bolted through the weeds and Floyd lifted his gun to shoot. Then an explosion rocked the earth, and Floyd's snarling face shattered and scattered like the bloody bloom from a red rose. Petals of flesh and brain clung to the rocks as the headless man crumpled to the ground.

At first Diana didn't realize the screams were coming from her own throat, but when she choked on vomit, the screams stopped. Lifting her eyes to the helicopter, she saw that the sharpshooter had never fired a single shot. The flight crew was hanging out of the bird regarding the entire scene in stunned bewilderment.

Slowly, she turned and saw that Juan had made it to Haw, the elderly white mule. Mother Mattie sat astride, sheltering the boy from the horror behind him, cradling a smoking shotgun across her lap.

FIFTY-FOUR

War zone...

Matthew decided that Mother Mattie's barnyard looked like a war zone, with federal agents, local police, and emergency medics kicking up dust and trampling the innocent stands of wildflowers and verbena edging the yard. The din of revving engines, walkie-talkies, and static from a bullhorn drowned out the plaintive calls of the songbirds, while a television news van had just arrived with a crew of reporters and cameramen, all jockeying for position in a race for the big scoop. The atmosphere was charged with expectancy as everyone looked to the sky.

Including Matthew.

Seated on the metal steps of the ambulance, his aching head propped against the cool wall of the van, he, too, searched the clouds. Inside the emergency vehicle, Leona fought hard for her life, and she was winning, so they told him.

According to the young doctor who did the preliminary exam and hooked up the IV tubes, Floyd's bullet had lodged in Leona's abdominal area. The injury had likely ended her ability to bear children, but it would not end her life. In her delirium, the girl was said to have taken the news well: *The Lord already sent a bolt of lightning and made me barren, so I reckon it's His will.*

Leona's words made no sense, but neither did anything else about the past twenty-four hours. Time had taken on the texture of an absurdist nightmare in Matthew's jumbled mind, but each time they questioned him, the details became clearer. The only saving grace, if the authorities were to be believed, was that his beloved Diana and the boy were still alive and would join him soon.

"Let's have a look at your head, Mr. Troutman." The young nurse who had treated and bandaged his scalp hopped out of the ambulance. "We don't want any infections."

He gently slapped her fingers away from his face. "I'm fine, leave me alone." He was sick of everyone fussing over him. "Go tend to Leona. There's nothing wrong with me a fistful of aspirins won't cure."

"Miss Clontz is stabilized, sir. This ambulance is leaving now, taking her to the hospital in Boone."

He lurched to his feet. "Aren't you going with it?"

She glanced at a second ambulance parked in the shadows of the barn and made an ugly face. "I have to process the body they're bringing in—what's left of it."

As the young nurse trudged away, he tried to piece it all together. He'd heard bits of news about a shoot-out in the mountains, and he knew Floyd Clontz had been killed. Other than that, no one seemed to have the facts.

"Hey, you're Troutman, right?" A flashbulb exploded in his face, and a video camera started recording. "Leona Clontz, the kidnapper, is inside that ambulance, right? Step aside so we can have a word with her…"

All the worry, the pent-up fury, shook loose as Matthew shoved the reporter so hard he dropped his microphone. The kid's round cheeks turned pink as Matthew kicked the offensive mic through the dust.

"Who the hell are you, Leona's bodyguard?" the boy blustered.

Matthew fought off the urge to wring the reporter's neck. In truth, after caring for Leona against impossible odds, he felt a father's protective instincts.

"Go easy." A female cameraperson intervened. "Mr. Troutman's had a rough day. He's the one who rescued her."

Matthew mumbled a brusque apology, then escaped to the relative privacy of Mattie's porch, finding shade under the overhang. He settled wearily into an old rocking chair. As he looked out over the chaotic scene, he wondered what poor Mattie would make of it all, and as he thought about the old woman, he closed his eyes and allowed his mind to drift back through the confusing events of the night before…

Last night at the moonshine cabin, he'd been unable to completely stop Leona's bleeding, but the girl's pulse had been strong as he administered pressure to the wound. While the girl lay moaning in the cold grass, her breathing irregular, he was thankful that at least Floyd had stopped shooting. Matthew was pretty sure one of his bullets had hit the man, but clearly the shot wasn't fatal, because Floyd, like Diana and Juan, had disappeared into the night. Where the hell had they gone? He remembered saying a silent prayer for Leona, for Diana and Juan, and then offering a less charitable blessing for Floyd: *May he die on the trail!*

Matthew figured he couldn't take credit for saving Leona, because the guardian angel who'd came by moonlight was responsible. She had appeared over the ridge, a ghostly figure on a hobbling mule. The apparition had materialized at the moment of Matthew's deepest delirium. In those tortured seconds, as Mattie came over the rise, he'd never fully believed in her substance until she dismounted and laid her hand on his shoulder.

"Move aside, I'll tend to my own." She'd firmly pushed him away. "I saw the wreck of your truck down yonder. If you can get it up and running, I believe we can carry this child home."

Wordlessly, he had done Mattie's bidding. He'd been in no shape to question how the old woman intended to transport Leona to the truck, should he be lucky enough to get the tire changed. Nor did he point out that all their efforts would likely prove futile, since Leona was facing certain death. Instead, he'd realized that any constructive action was a blessing, and took inspiration from Mattie, who tore up her skirt to make bandages. The old woman rocked and sang and worked mountain magic on her stricken granddaughter. That ancient savior was not to be second-guessed.

Somehow, with the feeble moon as his guide, he'd found his way back to the disabled truck. With the help of a flashlight, tool kit, and divine intervention, he'd summoned the strength to put on the spare tire and coax the old Ford back to life.

"What took you so long?" Mattie had been an eerie sight in her bloody slip, with the night wind lifting her tangle of long white hair from under the red baseball cap. "Me and Leona's ready to go. Grab Haw's reins and follow me…"

Mattie had rigged a makeshift gurney from two long branches and a sling fashioned from the mule's blanket. "It's an old Cherokee trick." She grinned. "Help me weave these poles into Haw's harness, and we've got us a chariot fit for a queen."

Sure enough, the old woman's contraption worked. Together they'd lifted the limp Leona into the sling, and with Mattie leading, Matthew supporting, they'd slowly made their way down the mountain. By the time they'd settled the girl in the bed of the truck, the first rays of morning tinted the sky.

"Drive down the same way you come up," Mattie advised. "Only this time, head into the *rising* sun."

Matthew had hesitated.

"No, I ain't coming." Mattie had looked longingly at Leona. "Your lady and the boy are still up there, and they're wanting to come home, too."

Leona's wound had bled through the bandages, her face was as pale as the waning moon. He'd known it was killing Mattie to leave her granddaughter, just as it was more than he could bear to leave without Diana and Juan. "Look," he'd said. "I'll go up back to the hills, while you take the truck."

An odd, guttural laugh had escaped Mattie's throat. "Listen, Mister, you can't ride my mule, and I sure as hell can't drive your truck. So we'll do like I said the first time, and the rest ain't up to us."

FIFTY-FIVE

A prayer of Thanksgiving...

Matthew drifted back to reality as a shadow passed across his closed eyes,

"Are you asleep, Troutman?" a gruff voice asked. "The helicopter is on the way, but you'll hear it long before you see it."

He glanced at the sky, then turned his face towards the bulky figure blocking the sun. In his city clothes and rumpled coat, Agent Max Grim looked ridiculously out of place with the mountains at his back. If possible, his baggy jowls and jaundiced skin appeared even more unhealthy than usual in the raw light of day, and his eyes watered from the smoke drifting up from the cigarette dangling between his thick lips.

"You took your sweet time getting here," Matthew grumbled.

"Yeah? Well, *you* took one hell of a chance. Lucky we didn't have to carry you away in a body bag. I'm surprised Clontz didn't shoot you."

"He tried, but I ducked." Matthew still didn't trust the man.

Grim chuckled as he dropped his cigarette butt into Mattie's geraniums, grinding it out with the toe of his shoe. "I suppose I should thank you, Troutman. You saved my ass."

He was astonished by Grim's sudden show of humility. He was actually smiling through his small, pointy yellow teeth. "So, when did you catch on?" Matthew asked him.

Grim was embarrassed. He shoved the cigarette butt around with his shoe. "Darryl Clontz woke up in the hospital with a powerful need to save his soul. The boy figured his wife would go running home to Grandma, so he even drew us a map right to Miz Birdsong's door..." Grim paused to frown. "Trouble was, we didn't know that you and Diana were in the mix until you came barreling down from the hills with Leona in the back of your truck. The rookie agent at the scene was near scared to death. He figured you were Floyd carrying a dead body in the vehicle."

"I'm glad he didn't shoot first, ask questions later." Matthew recalled how gentle the young FBI agent had been.

"Our chopper was already airborne when you told the kid your story, Troutman. Thanks to you, we got to the scene on time. We weren't much help, though."

Matthew was eager to hear the details, but as he opened his mouth to ask, Leona's ambulance eased through the bystanders and picked up speed as it headed down the mountain. "What will happen to Leona?"

Grim's mouth sagged. "Well, her husband will do some serious prison time, but Leona's role in the kidnapping is more complex. I've been told she actually interceded to help Juan McCord. Depending on what you and Diana have to say, and if you're willing to testify on her behalf in court, they may go easy on her."

"We'll be more than willing." Matthew was beginning to like this man. "What about Mother Mattie? Did she really kill Floyd?"

Grim laughed so hard, he brought on a coughing fit. "That Mattie Birdsong is one for the books. When the chopper radioed what happened, none of us could believe it. Seems the old gal splattered the Preacher's brains all over the Appalachians. Did we arrest her and haul her down in handcuffs? Hell, no! She wanted to ride back on her ancient mule under her own steam, and I hope that someone gets around to giving her a medal."

Matthew smiled. For the first time, a great weight eased off his heart as he heard the far away drone of the helicopter. Max winked, lit another smoke, then walked away as the dark, mechanical bird appeared above the far horizon.

Matthew climbed unsteadily to his feet and shielded his eyes against the sun as the beat of wings got louder and the chopper circled above Mattie's farm. He started running, along with the others, as agents joined with police to hold back the pressing crowd. His heart thudded against his ribs, and a lump filled his throat as the great bird settled into the appointed ring. As it touched down, gale-force winds spun dust into his eyes, disguising the tears already gathered there.

The wings slowed, the heavy door opened, and two blue-suited sharpshooters jumped out first. A third agent handed a small bundle into their arms as Max Grim, ducking low, ran out to receive it.

Matthew looked on, his emotions in turmoil, as little Juan thrashed in Max's arm lock. The child was wild with excitement, his enormous blue eyes blinked as flashbulbs and video lights blinded him. At the same time, he searched the circle of faces for a friend, and spotted Matthew.

Matthew lowered to his haunches and opened his arms as Juan delivered a swift kick to Grim's shins and broke free. He jumped into Matthew's arms, man and boy colliding in an urgent embrace. Their tears mingled, and he felt the child's hands in his hair, tugging hard.

"Everything's okay, son," he murmured against Juan's ear, all the while keeping a sharp watch for the moment Diana would descend.

To their credit, Grim and his men kept the news hounds at bay while Matthew held Juan, but Matthew was troubled when the sharpshooters climbed back into the helicopter and slammed the door.

Then they took off, straight up into the clouds, heading west back into the mountains.

"Where's Diana?" Matthew asked the boy.

"Maybe she's coming back with Mother Mattie?"

The helicopter shrank to a tiny black dot, and then it was gone. For the next hour, with Juan nestled against his chest, he managed to fight off the reporters, but in the end, Grim repossessed the boy for questioning.

Exhausted, Matthew retreated to the periphery and watched the sky. When the big bird finally appeared again, his heart contracted with love and hope as it touched down. But as he drew near, the ambulance parked by the barn sparked to life and drove as close as possible to the chopper's door. The same two sharpshooters jumped out, but this time they retrieved a heavy black body bag, which they rapidly transferred to the ambulance.

The emergency vehicle took its time driving off the mountain—no flashing lights, no screaming siren, no hurry. Floyd Clontz was the only passenger. And when the helicopter crew took off again, their mission accomplished, they headed back to home base in Charlotte.

One by one the police cars exited the scene, leaving only Grim and a handful of agents to clean up the remaining details. Naturally, a few stragglers from the television news crews hung around, hoping for a last minute burst of excitement, but soon even they packed it in for the day.

But where was Diana? Withdrawn and worried, Matthew lowered his sights from the sky to the far horizon, where a violent red sunset burned the hills. At first he thought his eyes were playing tricks when the silhouettes of two mules materialized on the crest of the ridge. They approached in perfect unison, their ghostly white legs pumping in weary harmony.

This time Matthew offered up a prayer of Thanksgiving as the paths of the two riders split—Mattie headed towards Grim, Diana to his arms.

They met halfway. He caught her as she slid off her mount and into his embrace. He held her close, drinking in the scent and feel of her. He stroked her hair and rejoiced in the strong beating of her heart. Their kiss was deep with promise, and when they finally parted, neither could speak.

He folded his arm around her shoulder, and they made their way, Diana leading Gee, towards the small crowd in the barnyard, where Mattie was busy creating her own drama.

"This is *my* house and *my* yard..." She waved her shotgun at the small group of stragglers. "Get on home now, or I'll send the lot of you to Kingdom Come!"

Mattie looked the part of a crazed she-devil, half-naked in her bloody slip, her hair wild in the sunset. She put the fear of God into the hastily retreating bystanders, who scattered like buckshot.

Matthew and Diana knew the old gal was just having a bit of fun, but the young agent who cautiously relieved Mattie of her weapon, knew no such thing. Although she willingly relinquished the gun, the rookie scuttled off so fast he almost left his boots behind in the mud.

Chuckling, Mattie waved to Matthew and Diana. "Come over here, you two..."

When they were close enough, Mattie yanked them down and whispered into their ears.

"That sounds like a plan." Matthew grinned as Diana nodded in vigorous agreement.

Together, the three led the faithful mules to the barn. When Matthew and Diana emerged, leaving Mattie to care for her animals, Diana carried a wriggling bundle in her arms.

The remaining crowd parted as Diana knelt before Juan, who was half asleep in Grim's lap. "Hey there, buddy…" She kissed his dirty little cheek. "Wake up, Leona and Mother Mattie have sent you a present…"

Juan's eyes popped open when he recognized Diana, and no coaxing was needed as the mysterious bundle began to bark. The child sprang to his feet and grabbed the puppy.

"It's a wolf cub!" he howled in ecstasy. "Is he really mine?"

At the word *wolf,* even Grim's dour face registered shock and surprise, and the video cameras started rolling.

"Seems like maybe something good came out of this mess, after all," Matthew drawled.

"Yeah!" Juan yipped. "I got me a good dog!"

Epilogue…

The moment they turned into the familiar lane, gravel crunching under the four new tires on Matthew's truck, Diana was stricken by a powerful déjà vu, a bittersweet sense of loss. Yet so much had changed.

The country road was crowded with bumper-to-bumper traffic. Newly appointed park rangers in crisp brown uniforms were directing the cars to park in a remote field, where Fourth of July fireworks lit up the evening sky.

After a word with one of the rangers, Matthew was permitted to detour into the private path leading to the Porter's residence, where a sumptuous picnic dinner awaited them—a *thank you* celebration from Bobby and Juanita.

And they were late. Grim had detained them with last minute details concerning the preliminary hearing they had agreed to attend at the end of the month, to speak on Leona's behalf. But for tonight, they were determined to put all that aside and rejoice in the sheer wonder of being alive.

"You best behave yourself, Ursie." Matthew patted the giant Doberman wedged between them. She was slobbering on Diana's lap. "Juanita won't take kindly to you gobbling all her fried chicken."

Diana laughed. "That's right, Ursie, and you'll have a new little playmate to contend with. I suspect Juan's wolf puppy will give you a run for your money."

The Porter family was waiting on a grassy hillside overlooking the festivities. They had spread an enormous tablecloth on the lawn, and dinner was well under way. Ursie charged the group, baring her teeth in a ferocious smile, while her knot of a tail continued to wag a mile a minute. She stopped short when she saw the small boy rolling with a lively black puppy, which was also baring its teeth.

Ursie was worried until she realized the pup was only begging for a French fry. Ursie would beg, too, but only after she performed her famous stomach crawling grovel and engaged in some polite canine butt sniffing. Only then, would she accept a treat.

"It's about time!" Bobby hollered from the depths of a lawn chair. He was propped up like King Tut, a mummy with a cast officiating from his rustic throne.

"Don't get up on our account, pal," Matthew said as he and Diana approached hand-in-hand.

"Wasn't planning to." Bobby grinned. He seemed hale and hearty in spite of his affliction. "Can you believe all this…?" His good arm gestured, taking in the panorama, where crowds of excited citizens swarmed along the waterfront, enjoying the Grand Opening of Porter State Park. "I never thought they'd pull it off on schedule."

Neither had Diana. It was Tuesday evening, Independence Day, but only last Saturday, three short days ago, life had almost ended for three members of their little assembly. As she and Matthew hugged Juan, she felt grateful indeed.

"Check it out…" Juanita shyly extended her left hand, where the Porter heirloom engagement ring sparkled on her finger. "We're getting married as soon as Bobby can walk down the aisle." She cast a meaningful glance at Diana, and then Matthew.

"Congratulations!" they cheered in unison.

"I'm grateful you never sold that ring, Trout," Bobby blushed.

"Here they come!" Juan squealed as the Sorvino family appeared over the rise. "I knew they'd come!"

Brenda and John Sorvino looked relaxed in shorts and sandals, while Johnny exploded, running to Juan. The boys collided and tangled together on the lawn, amid wild wagging and barking from both dogs.

"This is *Wolf*, my new puppy," Juan bragged.

"He's not a *real* wolf," Johnny said.

"Yes he is!"

"Is not!"

Soon the two were tussling, tugging, and pulling at one another and the animals, all worries forgotten.

"Thanks for inviting us." Brenda smiled shyly as they all exchanged handshakes. Recent history had exposed the best and worst in each of them.

"Glad you could make it," Bobby spoke from his chair. "How's it goin', John?"

Sorvino patted his breast pocket. "I'm twenty-five thousand richer."

"My mother said the same thing," Diana told them.

The ransom money had been returned to everybody over the weekend, except the contribution from the McCord grandparents in California.

"They wanted us to keep it." Juanita lifted her eyes. "Can you believe it? They said we should invest the money towards Juan's college education."

"Yeah, and guess what else?" Juan interrupted as he and Johnny approached with the dogs at their heels. "My grandparents invited me to visit their ranch in San Jose next summer, when I'm on vacation from school."

"Is that the place with cowboys?" Johnny asked.

"Yep."

"Cool! Can I go too?"

"We'll see…" Juanita and Brenda said in unison.

"We sold the house." Brenda sheepishly informed Diana. "Your friend, Liz McCorkle, thinks you two should split the commission."

"I'm sure we'll work something out," Diana said as another familiar couple trudged up from the crowd to crash their private party.

"You may have to work it out sooner, than later," Matthew whispered. "Speak of the devil…"

Diana was truly astonished as Liz's red head bobbed into focus. On her arm, looking distinctly out of place in plaid shorts and city shoes, was Miles Lawton.

"Hey, girlfriend!" Liz winked. "I've been worried sick about you."

Suddenly Diana was in her friend's arms for a tearful, long overdue reunion. After introductions all around, Miles was impatient to escape with his flaming prize.

"It's not too late for you to rejoin the real estate class, Diana," he mumbled.

"No thanks. I'll pick it up in the fall, but for now I need a long vacation."

"Miles and I are planning a celebration vacation," Liz said. "If I pass the Broker's Exam."

As Liz and her current beau wandered back down to the party at lakeside, it occurred to Diana that compared to all that had happened, her career now seemed a relatively insignificant part of her life. Putting that strange thought aside, supper was consumed, jokes were told, and a good time was had by one and all.

While the pyro-technicians geared up for the Grand Finale, Matthew led Diana to a quiet haven behind Jed Porter's old barn. Moonlight filtered through the leaves of a lone sycamore tree, while a band played patriotic tunes in the distance.

"Do you really need a vacation?" he asked.

"Absolutely." She reached out and took his hand.

"Well, my cousin owns a tag-along camper near the beach at Wilmington…"

Diana had severe reservations. "Listen, Matthew, I've had my fill of mountains and nature treks through the woods. I want fine food, hot showers, and a soft bed."

"Wilmington's flat as a pancake—no mountains. No woods to speak of, either. I hear the city has some gourmet restaurants and a four-star hotel. I can't vouch for the beds…"

"Never mind." She blushed.

"Then you'll come with me?"

"You bet."

Kate Merrill is an art gallery owner and real estate broker with a lifelong passion for writing. She lives with her family on a lake in North Carolina. When she is not writing, working with the art community, or selling real estate, she enjoys swimming, boating, and allowing her two strong-headed Golden Retrievers to take her for a walk.

Diana Rittenhouse Mystery Series
A Lethal Listing
Blood Brothers
Crimes of Commission
Dooley is Dead
Buyer Beware
Amanda Rittenhouse Mystery Series

Murder at Metrolina
Homicide in Hatteras
Assault in Asheville
The Mayberry Murders

Mainstream Romance
Northern Lights (as Christie Cole)
Flames of Summer

www.katemerrillbooks.com
merrilljennings@aol.com

www.ingramcontent.com/pod-product-compliance
Lightning Source LLC
Chambersburg PA
CBHW062120170626
46813CB00002B/514